The Three Stones of Ebon

The Three Stones of Ebon

》◦《

by David and Keiko Mello

Illustrations by Keiko Mello

STRIVE
Publishing · Bookstore

ISBN-13: 978-1-948529-22-8
Library of Congress Control Number: 2023948385

Cover design by Paul Nylander | Illustrada
Interior design by Beth Wright, Wright for Writers LLC

Strive Publishing
Minneapolis, Minnesota
www.StrivePubAndCo.com

STRIVE
Publishing · Bookstore

Printed in the United States of America

To Charlie Russo
with love and admiration

STURGUS

Chapter 1

》∘《

"Okay, you scurvy dog, are you gonna tell me where the treasure is, or do I send you on a one-way trip to Davy Jones's locker?" Jack grinned devilishly. His tousled brown hair hung almost completely over his eyes as he held the cutlass at Timmy's throat.

Timmy lay on his back in the tall grass as Jack loomed over him. He knew he was out of options. His own cutlass lay mere inches out of his reach. Jack had beaten him once again, and Timmy knew it. His sky-blue eyes met those of his opponent. "You win. You win. It's over there," Timmy said.

Jack followed Timmy's gaze and there, under the slide, was a purple velvet bag, cinched at the top with a drawstring, which held the plastic jewels. Jack smiled as he rushed for the treasure and scooped it up. Holding the bag in the air victoriously on the unusually sunny Saturday afternoon, the eleven-year-old proclaimed, "The treasure is mine! I, Jack Russo, am the greatest pirate that ever lived!"

Timmy climbed to his feet and collected his own cutlass. He walked over and gave Jack's shoulder a light shove and laughed, "I still have one more win than you, though."

"We'll be tied soon enough." As Jack reached up to shove the side of his friend's head, Timmy ducked away, jabbing him instead with his cutlass.

Jack clutched his side and yelped. "Hey, no fair!"

Just then a voice broke across the grassy backyard of his home. "Jack! Time for supper. Timmy, it's time for you to go home."

Jack's mother stood tall in the frame of the back patio door. Her blonde hair was pulled back in a ponytail as she tended to do when she cooked. In one hand she held a wooden stirring spoon, and a big bowl of something in the other.

"Okay, Mrs. Russo," Timmy replied. Both boys followed her back into the kitchen, where Timmy grabbed his backpack and said, "Well, Jack. I'll see you tomorrow."

"Bye, Timmy, and don't forget to bring your action figures so we can play Save-the-Planet."

"Roger, Wilco," replied Timmy, and with that and a quick wave to the Russos, he was out the door and running down the street to his house three houses down.

"Go wash up, Jack," his mother called from the kitchen.

Jack turned to dash for the bathroom but ran straight into his father.

"Hey, hey, little buckaroo. Slow down! What do you think this is, the Indy 500?" Jack's father scooped him up and slung him over his shoulder.

"Dad!" Jack shouted with glee. "I'm Captain Jack Russo, pirate extraordinaire." Hanging upside down from his father's shoulder, Jack laughed and started poking him in the back. "You're the evil ogre and I'm bringing you down."

"Roar! Oh no, I'm being skewered by Captain Jack, and all I wanted to do was eat him." His father set Jack down and feigned death, falling to his knees, and then lying "dead" on the floor.

Jack sat on top of him and asked, "How was work, Dad?"

"Good," his father replied, opening an eye. "I worked at Mrs. Krauss's house today."

"Old Lady Krauss? The Crazy Lady?"

"Yes, but remember, *we* don't call her—or anyone—names like that," his father chided.

"Sorry, Dad," Jack said, ears reddening a bit. Inside, he was only a tiny bit sorry. All the neighborhood kids called Mrs. Krauss Old Lady Krauss, a.k.a. the Crazy Lady. Jack had invented the nicknames himself and was personally rather proud of how quickly they caught on. The other neighborhood kids thought it was pretty funny. Rumor had it that she boiled her husband in a cauldron and made soup of him.

Jack pressed his father. "So, is her house full of cobwebs? Does she sleep in a coffin? Does she have a flying broomstick?" He was eager to know the answers.

"That would be a no to all those things, Jack. Come on, what have we told you about making things up like that about people?" His father stood there, waiting. "Well, come on. What are our rules?"

Jack's face bunched up as he looked at the floor, bottom lip sticking out. "Don't start rumors," Jack mumbled.

"And—?"

Jack huffed, rolling off his dad's stomach. "And no name-calling."

"No name-calling. That's right, Jack," his father confirmed, climbing to his feet. "So, no more of that garbage, okay? I know it seems like just play, but rumors spread and can bring bad things about." He looked at his son, who sulked a bit. "Look," he continued, gentler this time. "I'll tell you what. I'll share more about my visit to Mrs. Krauss's place after supper, but first, you need to listen to your mother and go wash up."

Jack's gaze traveled up to meet the soft brown eyes of his father. "Okay, Dad." Jack said and did as his father instructed. While he washed up, he felt silently bruised over his father's scolding. He and his friends were just having some fun, he thought to himself. Right?

After supper Jack sat next to his father in the family den. The room was dominated by the presence of an enormous L-shaped couch that was so deep in cushiony goodness that one could easily sink in, but it felt like an amazing feat to get up without some difficulty. Plants overhung the backrest. A large, flat-screen TV sat in a custom inset that Jack's father, as a handyman, had installed in the wall himself.

Along the window ledge sat some of the many seashells that Jack's mom collected. She once told him that the reason they lived near Seattle was because it was by the water. She loved their trips to the coastline every summer to build sandcastles and to collect seashells. The collection, as a result, only grew and grew. Jack's cat, Lucky, a young, orange-and-white tabby cat, sat on the other side of Jack. Mom set out hot chocolate while Dad told Jack all about his experience in Mrs. Krauss's house.

"Yes," his dad said. "There were some cobwebs. No, I did not see any coffin, and yes, I saw a broomstick, but I don't think she used it for flying. I think she used it for sweeping. The most fascinating thing about Mrs. Krauss was all the stuff she had."

"Stuff?" Jack's eyes got bigger.

"Yes. She had all kinds of really old stuff all over the house. There was a black carousel horse right in the middle of the living room. There was an old-timey lamppost in the hallway. I saw dolls, old photographs, old paintings and knickknacks cluttering her home. She had so much stuff that you could barely see the walls."

"Wow." Jack's eyes widened. Old Lady Krauss's house was more fascinating than even he could have imagined. "What else?"

His father tilted his head thoughtfully, scratching his chin. "Let me see. Well, there were also nautical rope, antique clothes, swords, spyglasses, and statues. Some masks, too . . ."

Jack was still half-listening, but his imagination started to distract him. All of these things existed in her house. And all of it was probably old, like Mrs. Krauss herself. Come to think of it, Jack mused, the house itself looked older than any other house in the whole neighborhood. It was as if the house had been there long before there even was a neighborhood.

"Anyway," his father continued, "when I was done with my work, she gave me something to give to you."

"Me?" For the life of him, Jack couldn't understand why Mrs. Krauss would give him anything. He had never really seen her except from a distance or quickly on the rare occasions she came and went, much less spoken to her.

"Yes, you." Jack's father gave him that *I-know-something-you-don't* look that always led to a pleasant surprise. "Grab my work bag, will ya?"

Jack did as his father asked, running into his parents' bedroom and finding his father's black work bag sitting on the bed, full of work stuff. It was so heavy from all of the tools his father kept in it that Jack had to use both hands to lug the bag back to the family room where his father waited patiently for him.

"Thanks, son." Jack sat next to his father, watching as he opened the bag and pulled out a bunched-up towel. Setting the towel in Jack's lap, his father said, "Go ahead, open it."

Jack felt as if he were about to burst. It was like Christmas, or his birthday. Slowly, he unwrapped the towel, revealing—

"A vase?" Jack looked up at his parents, his face crumpled. "Why would I want a vase?"

His father chuckled loudly. "It's an urn, silly."

"Well, why would I want an *urn*?" Jack's eyebrows bunched up, his nose wrinkling. Why would someone he didn't even know give an eleven-year-old boy like him such a weird gift?

"Look closer," his father whispered.

The urn felt slightly heavy in Jack's hands. It appeared to be very old. It was mostly orange, except for some pictures on the sides of three different scenes. In the first picture, Jack saw a boy, roughly eleven years old like him, dressed as a pirate, sword fighting with a man who had long white hair. In the boy's hand—the one that was not holding a sword—was an unidentifiable object that emanated blue light. The fact that it was a pirate picture was enough to make Jack excited, but what amazed him more was the pirate boy's appearance.

"Hey," he said, "he kinda looks like me."

"Yeah." His dad studied the picture curiously. "I think so too, and look what's at his feet . . . an orange-and-white cat."

Jack's eyes widened. "Wow! Lucky."

"Let me see," said Jack's mother, who had joined them. She bent down so her head was level with theirs. "Well, will you look at that. He does look like you, and that cat looks just like our Lucky."

Jack turned the urn in his lap so they could look at the next picture. The next scene had the same boy in it. This time, he stood in a rowboat, holding a dwarfish branch in one hand and a small object that emanated red light in the other. The orange-and-white cat was at his feet, its fur raised as if it were ready to do battle. Jack's face lit up at what he saw. Breaching the water was a giant sea serpent, about to strike the boat. Jack's mouth hung open as he traced the outline of the sea serpent with his finger.

Jack whispered, "Cool."

Jack turned the urn again to the last picture. It was different from the first two. Here, the boy rode a winged horse, which flew through the thick, white clouds. Sitting in front of the boy was the cat, once again. But this time, on the horse behind the boy was a girl with fire-red hair, wielding what looked like a golden wand. The boy held onto the horse's mane with one hand, and in the other he held a small object that, this time, emanated purple light.

The urn was corked. Jack tried opening it but found that it wouldn't budge. "Can you open it?" Jack handed the urn to his father.

"I've already tried," his father replied. "It's stuck on there pretty good. I don't think there's anything inside, anyway."

Jack's shoulders sagged and he looked wistfully at the stubborn urn, wondering what kind of secrets and adventures it held. As the evening rolled on, Jack eventually set the urn down and went to play with his toys, but he kept finding himself going back to the urn. Was it just a coincidence that the boy in the pictures resembled him, and that the cat looked a lot like Lucky? Wouldn't it be great if a place *did* exist where serpents swam the seas and winged horses flew in the clouds?

Jack wondered about the Crazy Lady—or rather—Mrs. Krauss. He made the correction in his mind, remembering what his father told him. How great it would be if he could see the inside of her house? Though the way his dad described it, it was like she wasn't even from around here. She was so strange, staying in her house all the time, curtains drawn. She opened her door to accept package deliveries or groceries, but otherwise the house was always closed. Jack had almost thrown a rock at her door the other day, just to get her to open the door so he could see what she looked like better. So why would the Crazy Lady give him the urn? Was it because he looked like the boy in the pictures, or was it something more?

"Time for bed, Jack." His mother beamed at him. "Go brush your teeth and I'll come read you a bedtime story. Okay, little man?"

"Okay, Mom," Jack replied. He brought the urn into his bedroom and set it on the dresser. After Jack finished his bathroom duties, his mother read three chapters out of *Treasure Island* before kissing him on the cheek, wishing him wonderful dreams, opening his window a smidge to let air in, and closing the door to his bedroom.

That night, Jack had a tough time falling asleep. He kept thinking about the urn. The boy and the cat . . . *were* they Jack and Lucky? Surely it was more than just a coincidence. It took a while, but eventually Jack did fall asleep.

Sometime during the night, Jack was awakened by a faint noise.

Tap, tap, tap.

Lucky sat at the foot of the bed, ears standing alert, looking at the urn.

Tap, tap, tap.

The noise came from the urn. Jack sat up and remained motionless. His heart pounded. Was he hearing things? No, Lucky heard it, too.

Tap, tap, tap.

Jack could barely see the urn, highlighted by only the night-light that shone from the wall outlet.

Jack inched his way to the foot of the bed until he was side-by-side with Lucky. Both boy and cat were quiet and still, staring at the urn with the conviction that this was, indeed, more than just an urn. A mixture of fear and curiosity gripped Jack. On one hand, a feeling of panic and flight gripped him tightly, and he wanted to duck under the covers. On the other hand, Jack was an inquisitive boy and he had to know what was making that sound. He forced himself off the bed. First one foot, then another touched carpet tentatively, and Jack inched his way toward the urn, toward the *tapping*. As he approached the vessel, he remembered what his father had said about how the corked top was stuck shut. His arms trembled as he reached for the urn.

Tap, tap, tap.

Jack was a hair's length from touching it when he suddenly pulled back. He began to have second thoughts. Should he call for his parents? No. He could do this himself. He *was* eleven, after all. He calmed himself and ever so slowly reached for the urn, again.

Tap, tap, tap. Was it getting louder?

TAP, TAP, TAP. Yes, Jack decided, it was.

TAP, TAP, TAP!

He touched the urn, and just like that . . . the tapping stopped.

It was incredibly quiet in his room except for Jack's own heavy breathing. He stood frozen, with one hand on the urn. It felt warm to the touch. Slowly, ever so slowly, Jack picked up the urn and sat at the foot of the bed. Next to him, Lucky stretched forward and cautiously sniffed at the urn. Now, Jack found himself no longer feeling afraid. In fact, he felt unusually calm and collected. He turned the urn in his hands and admired the pictures of the boy and his cat again.

He ran his hands along the urn's clay construction and glazed finish that had mostly worn off and gripped the cork that sealed whatever was inside. *It's stuck on there pretty good*, his father had said. Yet, when Jack pulled on it now, the cork came free and opened right up. Jack was so surprised that he dropped the urn, which landed on the carpeted floor with a heavy thud.

Then the strangest thing happened. The urn began to shake, roll, and spin. Creaking, croaking, and rumbling. Green fog started streaming out of it like steam from a tea kettle. Jack grabbed Lucky and darted toward the bedroom door, but the fog overtook him before he could find the doorknob.

"Mom! Dad! Come quick!" Jack yelled, groping at empty space for the doorknob, but no one came.

The green fog became so thick that now Jack could not even see the floor beneath his feet, could not see Lucky in his arms.

Then, it was over. Just as quickly as it appeared, the fog dissipated. Jack stood motionless. Apprehension and confusion enveloped Jack and he wondered if maybe his eyes were deceiving him. What he was looking at just should not be. It was impossible.

Jack was not in his room anymore. He stood in a lush, green meadow, still in his pajamas and still holding Lucky.

Chapter 2

〉〉 ○ 〈〈

Jack stood motionless. A soft wind lightly brushed his hair. He shivered slightly, taking in his new view. Jack's mouth hung open as he looked all around him, because the sun was out when it had been nighttime just a moment ago. He stood in knee-high grass that swayed rhythmically in the breeze. Before him, the meadow sloped downward to reveal a bluish pond at the bottom of the hill. At the edge of the meadow, trees stood thick together, forming a natural fence around its border.

Jack tried to take everything in, because surely all of it had to be a dream, and any minute now, he was going to wake up. Behind him, overlooking the meadow, was a stone statue of a winged horse. Life-sized, Jack figured. The wings of the horse were outstretched and its front legs raised high in the air.

Lucky wriggled out of Jack's arms, dropped to the ground, and crept forth in this strange new place, sniffing the grass. Jack leaned against the statue with a sigh, then slowly slid to the ground. "Where are we, Lucky? What's happened?"

"I don't know, but I think that urn has brought us to a different place."

Jack stopped, turned his head slowly and eyed his cat. Impossible. Cats cannot speak. "Wha . . . what did you say?"

Lucky turned and looked at him. They silently stared at each other. Eventually, Lucky inched forward. "I . . . said . . ."

"Aaaahhh!!" Jack screamed.

"Aaaahhh!!" Lucky screamed.

Jack jumped to his feet. Lucky instinctively latched his claws around Jack's leg in a panic, hair standing on end, tail bristling, and ears flat against his head. Both continued to scream as Jack tried to shake Lucky off. Jack hopped in circles until finally he lost his balance and tumbled into the grass.

Lucky jumped away from the boy as he fell and landed silently next to him.

Again, both sat, staring at each other. "You . . . you can talk," Jack stammered between heavy breaths.

"So can you," said Lucky, a bit frazzled himself.

"But . . . I could always talk," replied Jack, trying to catch his breath.

"Maybe," Lucky growled, "but I could always understand what you and the Giants say most of the time. Gotta say, though, it's tough to get you people to understand my needs sometimes. I have to repeat myself a lot."

"Well, all I ever heard from *you* was '*meow*' this and '*meow*' that," Jack retorted, a little hurt by Lucky's comment. "I can't tell one meow from the other." They continued to study each other for a while longer until Lucky finally broke the stalemate and approached. He rubbed up against Jack's leg in a silent apology. Jack reached out and scratched Lucky behind the ear, and his feline friend purred.

"Well, what now?" asked Jack.

As if on cue, a mouse scurried out from behind one of the legs of the horse statue and approached them at a very mouse-like speed. When it was several feet from them, it stopped and stood on its hind legs. For a moment Jack wondered if the rodent was going to speak, too, but the thought was interrupted when Lucky also noticed the mouse.

"Yummy," Lucky declared. "Dinner is served, or breakfast, or lunch, or whatever time of day it is."

"Lucky, don't." Jack placed himself between Lucky and the mouse.

"Hey," said Lucky as the mouse sped into the tall grass and disappeared. "What did you do that for?"

"Lucky," Jack said, "I think he was about to say something."

"Don't be silly," Lucky scoffed, waving off Jack with a furry paw. "Mice can't talk."

While Lucky pouted over his lost meal, Jack contemplated what they should do next. A rush of questions hit him. Where were they? How was it daytime when it was just night a moment ago? Where was home from here, and how were they going to get from here to there?

He looked up again at the statue of the flying horse. It was a majestic-looking animal, full of confidence and nobility. It was made of black stone, with three indentations in the breast of the horse. Jack guessed that they were each twice the size of a quarter and about as deep. The statue reminded Jack of the picture on the urn, the one of the boy, girl, and cat riding the black horse in the clouds.

If Lucky can talk in this place, then maybe flying horses exist here as well. Jack raised an eyebrow at the thought. He was still pretty freaked out about their new and sudden change of surroundings, but he didn't want to scare his cat into latching onto his body again. Boy, did that hurt. He rolled up his pajama leg to inspect the dozen or so tiny punctures and scratches that Lucky's claws had left behind. A couple of them smarted a bit.

Lesson learned, Jack thought as he rolled his pants leg back down. *Don't scare Lucky like that again.*

"I'm thirsty." Lucky's voice broke into his thoughts.

Jack nodded and winced a bit at how his throat felt as dry and scratchy as sandpaper. "So am I. C'mon, let's go over to that pond." Jack rose and began walking down the hill toward the water, the grass tickling his ankles through his pajamas.

Lucky followed close behind, still sullen over his missed meal.

Arriving at the pond, Lucky was the first to drink. "Hey, not bad . . . better than the water I drink at home." He lapped at the water vigorously, clearly not minding that his muzzle got wet.

Jack knelt next to him and cupped his hands together. He scooped up water and said, "Mom told me never to drink water from a pond . . . Oh well, here goes." He tasted it. "Wow." He grinned. "This is better than bottled water, even."

After they'd had their fill, Jack and Lucky lazed at the edge of the pond for a bit. The sun felt soothing, and Jack found that any fear he still carried was now completely out of his system. He liked being in the meadow. This was a special place. Everything about it was special, from the winged-horse statue to the water in the pond. Jack couldn't describe the feeling, but it was a sensation that called to him. It was comforting, almost loving.

"Could there have been something in the water?" He squinted at the pond as if the answer would magically appear.

Jack stood up. "C'mon, Lucky, it's time to go."

"Where?" Lucky purred, half-asleep on his back as the sun warmed his belly.

"I don't know, but we are not going to find it if we don't look for it. I think that, until we learn more about this world, maybe we be nicer to the animals here and not mess anything up. Please."

"You know, what you say kinda makes sense," said Lucky. He scrambled to his feet and followed Jack toward the edge of the meadow by the line of trees. They entered the woods.

Jack and Lucky trudged through the woods for a while before coming across a dirt road. Then they traveled the dirt road until they happened upon a village. By that time, Jack's bare feet were terribly sore. The village was like no town Jack had ever seen. Most of the houses were a single story with straw thatched roofs. There were a couple of two-story buildings. One looked something like a general store. Jack could see various foods and clothing through the windows as they walked by. The roads of the village were simple dirt roads, and the only vehicles that Jack saw were several different types of wagons being pulled by a number of different types of animals. Some were pulled by oxen while others were pulled by horses, and llamas, too. Jack let out a "whoa" when he noticed two zebras hitched to a smaller wagon.

"Well, that's weird," said Jack as they entered the village.

"What's that?" Lucky looked around.

"I don't see any cars. Everyone is just . . . *walking*. There's a horse by that building. Why is everybody is dressed like in olden times?"

"Olden times?" asked Lucky. "You mean like the Victorian Period or the Mesozoic Era?"

Jack made a face, scowling a bit. "The Mesozoic Era was dinosaurs, silly. And anyway, how do you even know stuff like that?'

"Hey, I watch TV," Lucky declared.

Jack stopped walking, eyeing Lucky. "How? When do you watch TV?"

"When you are at school and the Giants are at work. I figured out how to use the remote."

"'The Giants,'" Jack repeated, momentarily confused. "Oh! You mean my parents. I guess, compared to you, they *are* giants." Then Jack fell silent, realizing for the first time how much he missed them and wished they were with him right then.

The village was as Jack had described it to Lucky. It had a flair of the medieval. People wore tunics made from rough fabric and uncomfortable-looking pants with rope used as belts. Only a few wore fancier clothing with puffy sleeves, lace, or embroidery. In fact, Jack would not have been surprised to see a knight in armor ride by on a great steed at any moment. The townsfolk seemed pleasant enough. Farmers leaned on pitchforks as they chatted, a blacksmith donned a heavy leather apron, and Jack and Lucky spotted a couple of hunters carrying a stag, fresh from a kill. What Jack also noticed was that many of the villagers were giving him odd stares.

"People are looking at us funny," he said cautiously as they walked along.

"Maybe it's because you're still in your pajamas," Lucky replied, padding along beside him. "Or maybe because you're a little boy wandering around without his parents. Ooh, I know. It's because you're in the company of a really cool cat!" Then Lucky froze, furrowed his brow, looking a little afraid. "Or maybe it's because they're hungry and want to dine on stewed cat." He dashed between Jack's legs, whiskers twitching. "Don't let them eat me, Jack."

"Don't be silly," Jack said. "Why would anybody want to eat a scrawny little cat like you?"

"Because. I'm probably really, really delicious."

"Don't worry. I won't let anyone eat you," Jack said with a smirk.

It was then that both boy and cat spotted a green wagon. It was quite sizable, made mostly of wood and canvas, with a colorful curtain covering the back entrance. The four horses that Jack assumed were normally hitched to the front stood off to its side, grazing from four separate buckets. Behind the wagon, a large tent loomed, made from various colorful canvases and draperies. It stood out compared to the rest of the village's buildings that appeared to be made of things like wood, mud, and straw. Some of the large sheets on the tent displayed pictures of flowers, while others were just designs that, to Jack, looked a lot like tie-dye. Jack found the pictures inviting and was tempted to approach the tent and look in.

At that moment a mass of children ran out of the tent and dashed around to the back, engaged in a game.

Jack paused, captivated to see other children his age for the first time in this strange world. "Wow."

"What? You want to go over there?" Lucky asked, feeling a bit hesitant about dodging two dozen scampering feet that carried a dozen squealing heads.

"Yeah."

"Now?"

Jack turned to Lucky. "Well, we don't really have anything going for us right now. It's daytime now, but what happens here at night? And I *am* getting hungry. And we *have been* walking forever. And we *need to* find out where we are. And we *have to* figure out how to get home—and did I mention—I'm tired of walking? Yes, we go now."

"Whoa, whoa, whoa," said Lucky. "So, what you're saying is you want to stop for a while and hang out?"

Jack paused with an aggravated huff and eyed his favorite feline friend, and Lucky eyed him right back, obviously pleased with his remark. At home, his cat had always seemed able to read his mood spot on. Now that he was able to speak and be understood, it really tested the boy's patience.

Jack took a deep breath, speaking slowly. "Look, Lucky, we need a plan. We need a place to stay. Unless you have a better way, right now our best option is to talk with somebody. Maybe we can figure out where we are and the easiest way to get back home."

Lucky brushed up against Jack's hand and started purring. "Okay, you win—but if they try to eat me, I'm blaming you."

Jack grinned, shaking his head. Then they walked toward the tent.

The children came running around from the other side of the tent, laughing wildly in their frenzy, looking to be aged from three to thirteen years. Some of them spotted Jack and Lucky, and abruptly stopped running. Others soon followed. Before Jack knew it, all the kids stood in front of the two newcomers, some of them with gaping

mouths. A few of the younger ones looked a little scared and hid behind the older kids. One of the boys turned and ran into the tent, yelling, "Caveman! Caveman!"

Jack began to worry that choosing to stop here was a mistake. "Hello," he called out to them.

The kids did not answer. They just stood staring apprehensively. It was then that Jack realized that they weren't looking at him, they stared at Lucky. Lucky looked conflicted about all of the attention his presence was getting. Granted, they were just kids, but he remained close by Jack's side with his tail wrapped around Jack's leg, just in case someone might, in fact, want to have him for dinner.

Just then, a man came out of the tent. He had long hair with a long beard to match; Jack at once understood why the one kid was yelling "Caveman." Caveman looked at Jack, nodded, and then noticed Lucky. The man approached them and then went down on one knee before the little cat and said, "Greetings, Feline. We are honored by your presence. I am Caveman and these little ones are in my charge." He held out his hand, palm-side down, for Lucky to sniff.

Jack could feel his cat's tail loosen from around his leg as Lucky began sniffing the man's hand. To Jack, the man smelled of earth and sage, which he found comforting.

Lucky, as if reading Jack's thoughts, looked up at the man called Caveman and said, "Hmm, earth and sage. I like it! Hello!"

"Well, hello yourself." Caveman smiled. "May I ask your names?"

"Okay," Lucky replied. "Ask."

Caveman's smile broadened. "What are your names?"

"I'm Lucky and he's Jack."

"Where are you from?" Caveman asked.

Lucky answered, "We are from our bedroom."

Jack, becoming slightly agitated at being excluded from the conversation, spoke up. "Where are we?"

Caveman looked at Jack and then back at Lucky. "This village is called Loring."

"Never heard of it," replied Jack. "How far is it from Seattle?"

Caveman looked a bit perplexed. "I am not sure I quite understand. What is a 'Seattle?'"

"It's a city." Jack was matter-of-fact. "In America."

Caveman stared blankly at them, blinking, and was quiet for a moment. Then to Lucky he said, "If you and your charge would stay for mealtime, we could exchange stories."

"My charge?" asked Lucky.

"Yes," the man called Caveman said, "this boy who travels with you." He gestured to Jack.

"'You mean Jack?" Lucky bragged, "Why, he's only my bestest buddy in the entire world."

"Yeah," said Jack, "and Lucky is *my* cat, who happens to be the coolest cat this side of Seattle."

"Hmm," pondered Caveman. "Well, how about we all sit a spell and share bread? Then we can tell stories, and I am certainly intrigued by what your story will be. Caleb, will you take young Jack here to the wash basin so that he can get cleaned up?" Then Caveman stood and reentered the tent.

One of the older boys stepped forward from the other children and said, "Hi, Lucky and Jack, if you will follow me."

After washing up, Jack and Lucky found themselves inside the tent sitting with Caveman and the children. Jack feasted on steamed vegetables and the best bread he had ever tasted. Lucky was brought a small roasted bird that he enjoyed very much.

After dining, Caveman, the two dozen children, and Jack and Lucky all proceeded to a fire pit that lay behind the colorful tent. The fire pit was dug into the earth with several stones framing it. A fire was started as the sun was beginning to set, and the group sat in a clustered circle around the fire, where Jack volunteered to tell the first story.

A warm smile crossed Caveman's face, for, as Jack would soon discover, Caveman loved a good story. With all eyes on him, Jack could see that the children seemed eager to hear his story and how he came into the company of the cat named Lucky.

Jack began his tale the way he heard most tales begin, with *Once upon a time*. He then narrated about playing pirates with his friend Timmy. He talked at length about his parents, and it was clear to all how much he missed them. His audience asked many questions as his tale progressed. *What's a TV? What's a remote? What's a car?*

Jack then spoke of Mrs. Krauss—being very mindful not to call her Old Lady Krauss a.k.a. the Crazy Lady—and told them about the urn that she gave his father to give to him. He described the pictures on the urn with utmost clarity, and everyone's mouths dropped from the vivid descriptions that rolled from Jack's tongue, because the boy and cat in the pictures did seem to resemble Jack and Lucky.

Jack spoke next of his bedroom, describing his many toys, which sparked wonder, and just a little bit of desire, in the children who sat in the circle. He described waking up to the tapping that came from within the urn, and then the green smoke. As these words came out of Jack's mouth, he quietly wished they were home again. His hands reached instinctively for Lucky, and he stroked his soft fur for reassurance as he continued his tale of arriving in a strange land next to the winged-horse statue, and of his journey through the wood and to the village. He beamed as he described seeing a green wagon by a colorful tent, filled with children and a man who called himself Caveman. He ended his tale by describing the wonderful meal that they all shared and how he volunteered to tell the first story.

The audience cheered and applauded Jack at the close of his tale. "Well done!" Caveman laughed enthusiastically. Everyone seemed ecstatic to have a child from another world in their company.

"Well, I do not believe it," an older boy said abruptly. It was Caleb, the boy who took Jack to wash up before dining. He was slightly bigger than Jack and spoke as if he were in charge. "A world where cats and humans live *together*? Unheard of."

"No, no, no. Totally heard of. Come to my neighborhood. Everybody has cats." Jack was emphatic. "It's all true."

"Of course, it is true," Caveman cut in. "We can plainly see that here is a boy dressed in bizarre clothing, sitting right in front of us, and that there is indeed a cat sitting remarkably close to him."

"I just need to figure out how to get home," Jack said.

"Do you have any ideas?" asked Caveman.

"Well, I have one. If I can figure out exactly how I got here, then that might help me figure out how to get home."

Caveman smiled. "How you came to us obviously involved great magic that we may not be able to understand."

"Magic?" Jack's face lit up, unable to hide a look of surprise. "Really?"

"Yes," answered Caveman. "Magic brought you here, and as we know in our land, magic does not just happen. You were brought here not by happenstance, but by intervention. Perhaps now would be a good time for me to tell my story."

Jack could think of nothing to say to this. He sat down and Lucky leaned his body against his, and both boy and cat listened with great interest as Caveman began his tale.

Chapter 3

》◦《

"'Welcome, Jack, to the land of Sturgus. You must find this world strange, compared to how you described your world. Sturgus is a vast place, filled with many kingdoms and peoples. From what I gather, in your world only humans are able to talk. As you can see, this world is different. Your cat can talk here. Not only that, but in Sturgus, all cats can talk, and other animals as well. Dogs can talk. So can monkeys and songbirds. Of course, there are many animals that cannot speak at all, but that is the nature of how things are here. There are also certain creatures that I suspect do not even exist in your world, like cyclopes and Aquaticans, and some of those can speak as well.

"As for me, I was born in the village of Closan. It was a humble village, much like the village we are in now. I was to follow in the footsteps of my father and become a farmer. Life is strange because nothing is ever as you think it will be. When I was just a little younger than you, Jack, our village was raided by the Muskans, an evil horde consisting of mostly humans, but they had recruited many giants, cyclopes, and harpies. Their leader was an evil wizard named Pale. Under his control, the Muskans destroyed my village, killing the adults and enslaving the children. I was lucky. I was the only survivor of Closan to escape.

"I fled to the north, where I unknowingly wandered into wolf territory and found myself confronted with the Pack of Other

Mountain. It was by sheer fortune that the pack did not eat me. They had just dined on a stag, and their bellies were quite satisfied, so they did not have much of an appetite for me. The pack leader was named Varg, and he made the decision to keep me around for his amusement. However, his amusement soon turned into admiration because I would not cower whenever the other wolves showed me their teeth and the deepness of their growls. I would stand defiant, and this impressed Varg. So, I was allowed to stay with the wolves for a time. I hunted with them, slept with them, and, for the most part, they treated me as one of their own. There were those within the pack that wanted very much to kill me, but as long as I held favor with Varg, they let me be.

"I spent two years with the Pack of Other Mountain, and they taught me many things, but of all my experiences, one stands out among the others. It was on the night of the Great Ancestral Gathering, a night of clear sky and full moon. I was running with the pack up the side of Other Mountain. The air was electric as we made our way higher, to a plateau overlooking the pack's entire territory. With a purple night sky, the pack circled the plateau until, one by one, each wolf found its place to sit, close to each other, but alone." Caveman fell forward, bending his knees so that his arms and legs planted firmly on the ground. He moved about on all fours and loped around a couple of the children with surprising quickness, making a couple of the children giggle.

Caveman slowed and sat back on his heels. "I found my spot like the others, but made sure I was close to Varg. Whatever was about to happen, I wanted to always stay near him, as my protector. There we quietly sat, unmoving. It seemed a very long moment in time. I could feel my hair whipping about my shoulders as the wind glided in between the wolves, gathered itself, and then splintered off in new directions. We continued to wait, the moon rising until it was just above us, and then it began. Varg raised his head, and, with a true leader's strength, he howled at the moon. His howl was deep and loud. It sliced into the night with a warrior's song, sending a message into the night, demanding to be heard. To this day, it is the strongest sound I have ever heard. At first, the pack was quiet, and then, one by one, they joined their leader in song. I listened as each wolf contributed its own unique bay to the chorus, and then it was my time."

Caveman threw back his head and spoke to the children, but also to the sky. "I raised my head to the full moon and, from deep inside my throat, I bayed at the night with all the conviction of my canine brethren. *Aooooooooo! Aoooooo!* It was magic!

"I do not know how long we sat there in song. As we howled, an immense cloud began to move from behind the peak of Other Mountain. It was unlike any cloud I have seen before, and it moved with deliberation and purpose. Like a giant mythical griffin, it descended upon us, blotting out the moon. Blue light shot forth from just below the plateau we were on, into the cloud, and then back out of the cloud like daggers pummeled into earth, vibrations shuddering deep beneath me.

"What happened next was even more spectacular. Pouring out of the cloud came wolves but not wolves. They emanated from within them the same bluish glow, with a scent of history about them that reconnected the wolves to the lives of previous generations. These were all the spirit ancestors of the Pack of Other Mountain, each one noble with a fierceness that can only be seen in wolves. They came down among us and whipped about us like the wind. I sat, amazed with a feeling of ecstasy, as the spirit-wolves raced by me.

"There was one spirit-wolf which was bigger than the others. I watched as he stopped in front of Varg, and I knew then who he was. Varg had told me stories of the Great Pack Leader named Pax. All the other wolves, both alive and in spirit form, began the Grand Wolf Dance, but not the Great Pack Leader and not Varg. They sat, muzzle to muzzle, in a silent communication. Pax, the Great Pack Leader, turned then, and looked at me. It was as if his eyes pierced right through me, and for the quickest moment, I was afraid. Suddenly, with a swiftness that I had never seen before, he leaped at me and landed in an instant within inches of where I sat. He bared his teeth, fangs mere inches from my face. I could not move. And then, as quickly as he had come upon me, he moved through me and came out the other side. I was stunned.

"The spirit-wolf Pax had jumped *through* me. In that brief moment, I learned all of the great stories of the Pack of Other Mountain. I could see old memories as if I had lived them myself. I could see vividly the time when Pax was a young wolf and he killed the Sasquatch of Other Mountain, cementing his pack's hold on the territory and ensuring himself the role of pack leader. It remains one of the greatest honors of my life, to have been chosen as an honorary member of the pack and to participate in their rituals.

"I looked at Varg. The look he gave me seemed to say, *Time to run.* And so we ran, all of us, spirit-wolf, wolf . . . and me. I do not remember anything after that. I awoke the next morning with the pack. The spirits were gone, the celebration was over. Most things returned to the way they were before, but not everything. One thing was different. From that moment on, no wolf ever thought me unworthy to run with them. I was truly a member of the pack. I would never leave, or so I thought.

"Months later, Varg called me to his side. He told me that it was time for me to leave. I protested, of course, but Varg explained that while I would always be a member of the Pack of Other Mountain, in the end I was still human. He spoke of the troubles that were occurring in the human villages, how Pale was especially cruel to the people of Jalambria and all of its provinces. Varg explained that,

since Jalambria's territory butted up against Other Mountain, if Pale received word that a human was living among the Pack of Other Mountain, he might feel inclined to attack. Although Varg would welcome a chance to battle against Pale, he knew that the bony wizard would also bring his Muskan horde, that their strength would be too great, and that the Pack of Other Mountain would likely exist no more.

"I left my brothers and sisters of the pack, my second family, and traveled south for about ten days. I was only ten years old, but the wolves had taught me everything I needed to know to survive on my own. I traveled mostly at night.

"I finally reached a village called Lacklin. It lay nestled in a valley ripe with apples. It was in Lacklin that I came upon the Johannes family. Emiril Johannes and his wife, Sylvinna Johannes, were master craftsmen who made wagons of the finest quality. They had twin daughters, Avril and Zooey, who were a mere six in age. When Emiril and Sylvinna came across me, they immediately took a liking. Emiril had always wanted a son. After spending a few days in their home, I was becoming quite fond of them. Eventually, I became the adopted son of the Johannes family. I spent the rest of my childhood with them."

Caveman wiped his brow. "I learned much throughout the next ten years. The Johannes family taught me their exceptional skills in wagon-making. I also learned about farming, more than my own parents had time to teach me."

As Caveman described farming, he pantomimed driving a plow into the ground and then scattering seeds into the furrows. "At harvest time, in addition to harvesting the few crops that the family grew, I also partook in the annual picking of the apples." He pretended to hold a basket, reached up, and plucked the air as if picking apples from the trees. "Lacklin is famous for its annual Apple Fest, and all sorts of people from all sorts of places come and join in the celebration.

"I saw, for the first time, brownies and faeries, croakees, and scarecrows. We were even graced by the appearance of a faerie queen. These were good and wondrous times. Unfortunately, Lacklin lies within the borders of the kingdom of Jalambria, and it was only a matter of time before Pale again sent his Muskans to invade Lacklin, this time to claim the wealth of others as tax due to him. However, whenever the Muskans entered any village, it was always with the sword."

The storyteller stroked his beard as he positioned himself to look wider and taller in size than his compact-yet-strong stature let on. He waved an invisible weapon about, face now twisted up, snorting, and scowling with his lower jaw jutted outward. "They killed many people in Lacklin, including my adoptive parents, which reminded me of when I was young, and when Pale and the Muskans raided Closan and killed my family. But this time, they did not kill everybody. Instead, they let roughly half of the villagers live, so work would continue and taxes could still be collected.

"Many children were left homeless, and I was, once again, left without a family. My adoptive twin sisters went missing. It was assumed that they were taken as prisoners of the Muskans. This time, however, I was an adult, and I gathered as many orphaned children as I could, and we fled. We moved from village to village, bartering our services in exchange for food and supplies. Every village needed help because every village was raided by the Muskans. We helped others rebuild by replanting crops, building a barn, aiding injured people as they recovered from wounds inflicted by the Muskan tyranny. Every village had losses, and every village had orphans. I gathered those that I could. Occasionally, some that I saved from one village would decide to stay in another, having found a new home and a new family that may have lost someone, as well.

"We have been traveling for the last twelve years. The Muskans do not raid villages as much anymore because most villagers now pay the higher unfair taxes so that they will be left alone. But I have not seen my sisters since that horrible day we lost our parents, and I can only hope that they are safe somewhere and escaped the Muskans' wrath somehow. I ask about them at every village we pass through, looking for some ray of hope. No sign yet."

"Wow," Jack breathed. "That's one great story."

"Yeah." Lucky nodded. "You're better than the TV."

"But I have a question," Jack began. "This Pale guy, he doesn't live around here, does he? I mean, I really wouldn't want to run into him."

"Pale is normally in Jalambria. It is about nine days to the east by foot."

"Good," replied Jack.

Caveman smiled. He looked at Jack and Lucky for a time. "Now that my story is finished, there is something we should discuss before you venture further into this land."

"What's that?" asked Jack.

"It is of concern, being seen with a cat. In your world, it may be normal that humans and cats live together. In Sturgus, they do not. Cats have their own land, far to the south in Sahaland."

"Sahaland?" The word tumbled out of Lucky's mouth as if he had waited his whole life to speak it.

"Yes, Lucky, Sahaland," Caveman continued. "It lies to the south, past the port village of Valmar. I have never been there myself, but I understand that it is a valley filled with many trees. Very seldom does a cat travel this far north, and even more seldom is one seen with a human. Cats are considered mysterious. Even though they are small, many people are frightened by them and consider them demons. They are nervous about you, Lucky."

"Wait." Lucky's voice was shaky. "People think I'm a demon? I'm not a demon."

Jack scratched Lucky behind the ears. "No, little buddy, you're not a demon, but we're gonna have to work on keeping you hidden, especially whenever we're around people."

"You have had a busy day," said Caveman. "Caleb, will you help Jack get some bedding from the wagon and find him a nice spot where he and Lucky might sleep?"

As Jack walked with the older boy to the wagon he asked, "So, is *your* family dead?"

Caleb stopped walking for a moment and glanced at Jack. "Yes."

"I'm sorry," Jack said.

"Yes, me too," Caleb whispered as a sad expression crossed his face. Jack could see that his question pained Caleb and he regretted asking him. He thought of how fortunate he was to have parents that were still alive, still fully engaged in his life. He missed them terribly at that moment and vowed silently to himself that he would somehow find a way to get back home.

Once they retrieved bedding from the wagon, Caleb found Jack a spot inside the tent right next to him. Jack wanted to talk with Caleb a bit more before sleeping and learn more about how long he had been with Caveman's group, but exhaustion overtook him and soon both Jack and Lucky fell into a deep sleep.

Chapter 4

Jack awoke the next day to find Lucky gone. Most of the tent was now empty and the tent flaps were tied back to allow for fresh air. Rays of sun poured through the opening. Jack rubbed his eyes, plodded out of the tent, and looked at the sky. It seemed to be late morning, if days worked similarly here in Sturgus as they did at home. The sun shone brightly, but the air was still cool. He smelled eggs cooking and spied several children sitting by the fire pit, eating breakfast. Over the fire, two girls fried eggs on a cast iron skillet. Next to them sat a basket in which Jack could see loaves of bread poking out of the top.

No sign of Lucky.

One of the girls spotted Jack and motioned him over. "Are you hungry?"

Jolted from his thoughts, Jack realized he was indeed hungry and nodded. He walked over to them and was handed a tin plate with two eggs and a piece of bread. "Thanks," he said. They nodded and smiled warmly, though a bit shyly, at him as he sat on a stump and vigorously devoured his meal with a large wooden spoon.

With his belly full, Jack took in his surroundings. By now, he was the only one left sitting at the fire. The others who had been eating had finished their meals and were now scattered about, doing various things. The younger children were playing, amusing themselves with a game he couldn't quite make out. Was it leapfrog or hide-and-seek? Three other kids, slightly older than he, stood to the side watching the smaller kids play.

He thought about approaching them and maybe asking a few questions to learn more about them, when it dawned on him that they weren't just standing there watching the little ones, they were watching *over* the little ones. They were working, so he let them be. Jack looked around and, apart from the youngest children, all the other kids were working. The two girls who made him breakfast were now gathering the dirty dishes to be cleaned. Beyond them, Jack could see kids carrying twigs and broken branches. *Firewood.*

Jack felt slightly uncomfortable being the only one not working, and he wanted to find Lucky, so he got to his feet and walked around the tent to where the green wagon was parked. He noticed that another wagon had arrived and was parked next to the green wagon. This one was smaller and red with little pictures painted all over it. Jack thought it was perfectly funky-looking. Who owned it? He walked up to the red wagon, enjoying the artwork displayed on it. Unlike the green wagon, this one had a wooden canopy instead of a canvas one.

Jack stood by the front of the wagon. The painting pictured above the wheel showed a black cat riding a dragon as fire spewed forth from the dragon's mouth. Next to that one was a picture of what Jack thought to be two faeries flying above a patch of flowers. Between them they carried a large ring, obviously belonging to a normal-sized person. In the abutting picture, two individuals faced each other as fire danced around them. One was a tall, gaunt man with long, bony fingers and a crown on his head. He appeared to be offering a sword to a young, dark-complexioned girl who looked to be Jack's age. Jack walked slowly to the back of the wagon. The next picture revealed a child running through the woods with a pack of wolves. The person had wild hair. *Caveman. It must be.* Jack laughed. Perhaps these pictures were images of things that had really happened!

As Jack circled around the back of the red wagon, taking in each picture with increasing interest, he stopped short. Sitting in a circle between the two wagons, he finally found Lucky, as well as Caveman and two others, a woman and a young girl roughly Jack's age. They were in mid-conversation when they noticed him.

"Jack!" Lucky immediately hopped toward him and rubbed himself against Jack's leg.

The woman rose to face Jack. Her long brown hair interlaced with beads hung down to her lower back. Her green dress was tied at the waist with what appeared to be braided hair that had been cut and was now being worn as a belt. She was slightly shorter than the average adult and . . . Jack blinked . . . Was her hair now flowing around her, as if it were under water? Yes, Jack determined, it was.

She smiled warmly at Jack. Caveman stood next to her. "Jack," he said. "I would like you to meet Malia. She is a halfling from the Northlands and my dearest companion."

"Halfling?" Jack wasn't sure what that was.

"I am half-elf, half-human." Malia said. She brushed her hair aside with her fingers, revealing a pointed ear.

"Cool," he smiled back at her. "How does your hair do that?"

She gave Jack a mischievous look, and for his entertainment she shook her head back and forth. Her hair floated above her head like seaweed in the ocean before gently settling down on her shoulders. "It is the price I must pay for putting a curse on someone."

"A curse! I thought only witches could do that," Jack said, still captivated by her hair.

"Witches are not the only beings that can produce magic." Malia offered a small smile. She patted the space beside her. "Please, sit with us."

As Jack sat in the circle, Caveman said, "Jack, I would like you to meet Malia's student, Abigail." He gestured to a girl with freckles and skin that reminded Jack of copper. The girl was seated on the opposite side of Malia, across from Jack.

"Hi," said Jack.

"Hello," said the girl. "Is it true that you are from a different world?"

"Yeah, I think so," said Jack as Lucky climbed onto his lap and proceeded to groom himself. "That, or I'm having the craziest dream of my life."

"Wow, I have never met anybody from another world before." Abigail stared at Jack in wonder. Her fire-red hair covered her shoulders in a combination of loose curls and coils, and there was a silent determination on her freckled face and in her golden-brown eyes. Jack took an immediate liking to her.

Caveman stood and said, "I am sorry, but the day will not wait for me and there is much to do." He kissed Malia and then left to continue his daily work.

"So, Jack," Malia said, "Lucky has been telling us your story. I find it very fascinating, especially the part about the urn. Tell me, how well do you know the lady who gave the urn to you?"

"I've never even met her. She lives down the street from me. Her name is Mrs. Krauss, but us kids call her Old Lady Krauss or the Crazy Lady."

Malia scowled. "Well, that is not very nice. What else can you tell me about her?"

There was a pause as Jack noted the slightly parental tone. Was it really that bad, how he spoke about Mrs. Krauss? "Well," Jack finally answered, "there isn't anything that I've seen, but my dad went into her house. He said she had a lot of things there that most people wouldn't keep."

"Oh?" Malia's interest rose. She reached into a colorful bag next to her and pulled out a smaller bag. From the smaller bag she poured out several white stones, scattering them on the ground. Each stone had blue designs painted on it. "What kind of things?" she asked.

"Oh, all kinds of stuff. Let's see, swords, spyglasses. Um, I think Dad said something about a carousel horse . . . Hey, what are you doing with those rocks?" Jack watched as Malia began placing the stones purposely in a circular and then cross-pattern design.

"These stones help me see things," she said.

"Is it magic?"

"It is a type of magic, yes."

"What are you trying to see?" Jack asked as he leaned forward to get a better view of the designs. "Can you tell me why Lucky and I are here?"

Malia nodded. "Lucky said that the two of you arrived near a statue of a winged horse."

"Yeah, it was by a pond which had the best water that I have ever drunk. Do you know the place?" Jack asked.

"I have never been there myself, no, but I know *of* it," answered Malia. "It is called the Meadow of Tears, and it is never in the same place twice because a Spell of Wandering has been placed on it. The statue is of Ebon, a leader of this world in what we know as the Early

Age. Legend has it that Ebon was able to fly high enough to cross worlds. Stories tell of Ebon fighting a great dragon from another world and winning with the aid of the wood faeries from the Circle Forest, who come from the north. Another story describes how Ebon flew high into the clouds and brought down rains to help farmers during a long and tiresome drought.

"Ebon's end, it is taught, came when he went up against an evil sorcerer who invaded our world. Some say Pale the sorcerer killed Ebon with poison; others say the sorcerer rode Ebon to the edge of the world and threw him into the Abyss. The truth we believe, however, is that the sorcerer tricked Ebon and turned him into stone, and he is trapped in that very statue that you saw, and the pond is the accumulation of the tears he cries every night. They say that those who have goodness in their hearts who drink from that pond will have the strength and courage to face any danger."

Jack mused that Malia's story seemed to explain why he had felt so safe when they were at the Meadow of Tears. Part of his brain was terrified in these strange circumstances, but Jack was sure the best thing he could do was to appear calm, even though he wasn't calm on the inside. It was the closest that Jack could come to making sense of everything he'd experienced so far in this new land.

"You know," said Lucky, "The people from this world say the coolest things." Lucky looked at Abigail then and tilted his head, whiskers twitching. The two shared a brief moment of eye contact and Lucky slow-blinked at her. Abigail slow-blinked back at him. Lucky purred.

Malia looked at the stones, and then she looked at Jack. She looked at the stones again. She looked at Jack again, then at Lucky. "Hmm. There is something missing, something you are not telling me."

"I'm not sure what it is that you're looking for," said Jack.

Malia gazed at the stones for a moment longer and then she reached into her bag and pulled out a small stick. With the stick, she drew lines in the dirt that intersected the stones. She whispered then: "Shensa Loa."

Abigail repeated the words. "Shensa Loa."

Malia looked deep into Jack's eyes. "Jack, please hold my hand and touch Lucky at the same time. Lucky, will you please reach out a paw and touch Abigail?" Both boy and cat did as they were asked, and then Malia reached out and held Abigail's other hand, thus completing a circle. "Now, everybody, close your eyes."

Closing his eyes made Jack think of home. The last time he had been told to close his eyes was to make a wish for his eleventh birthday, just before he blew out the candles of a Kentucky butter cake with a rum-butter glaze drizzled over the top that his mother had made. The memory made him miss his parents terribly and wonder when he would ever see them again. His thoughts were cut short when Jack felt himself lift off the ground. He opened his eyes. "Whoa!" he cried as he glanced down.

"All is safe." Abigail offered him a gentle smile. "Just do not let go."

Jack looked at the others. All four of them were levitating above the ground, slowly rising higher. "Whoa!" He wasn't sure he liked this—whatever it was that was going on. It felt like he had been encouraged to go on a carnival ride that promised fun, only to end up being anything *but* fun.

Lucky, who sat in his lap with one paw still touching Abigail, seemed less surprised. Maybe the water from the Meadow of Tears had a more calming effect on cats. "Hey, we're floating. Will you look at that."

"Whoa!" said Jack a third time.

Soon they rose higher than the wagons. Malia opened her eyes and gave Jack's hand a reassuring squeeze. "Do not worry. We will not go much higher."

"What's going on?" Jack asked as he looked around at the trees and the tops of the wagons.

"Sometimes, to see other worlds, one must rise above one's own world. Sometimes."

"Oh," replied Jack, as if he really understood what Malia was talking about. He did not. "So . . . what do you see?"

Malia held Jack's hand tight as she told him. "Your mother has yellow hair, and she is very pretty."

Jack was taken aback.

"It's true," Lucky mewed. "And she smells the best."

"Your father is a man of great skill," continued Malia. She appeared to be staring intently at something, but it was nothing Jack could see. "He can make the most common person's home become a place of royalty."

"Yeah!" Jack beamed. "He retiled our bathroom and put in a new toilet and everything. It's pretty cool. It doesn't even look like the same bathroom."

"Mrs. Krauss, she lives near you?" Malia asked.

"Yeah," replied Jack, "at the end of our street."

Malia closed her eyes again. "Oh, I see it. Blessed light, there is a lot of magic emanating from within. This Mrs. Krauss of yours is deep in the energy. Hmm."

"What is it?" asked Jack.

Malia opened her eyes once more. "I am unable to see inside the house. She must have a protection spell on it."

"Hey," said Lucky. "We're lowering." Slowly the four descended, landing in the exact spots as before.

"Wow," said Jack. "That was so cool."

"You keep mentioning that it is cool," began Abigail. "It is no wonder. Look at what you are wearing." She indicated the pajamas Jack still wore.

"No, not cold. 'Cool' is an expression," said Jack. "It means I liked it."

"Oh," replied Abigail, "how utterly odd."

Jack looked at Malia. "So, do you know why Lucky and I are here?"

Malia gathered up the white stones with the blue designs on them and returned them to the small bag before putting the small bag in the larger, more colorful bag. "I still do not know the purpose of your journey here. A piece of the puzzle is still missing, but I think I may know why Mrs. Krauss gave your father the urn. She chose you to take this journey."

Jack blinked and tilted his head, puzzled at all this information and worried about what he was supposed to do with all of it. "Chose? Mrs. Krauss *chose* me?"

"In a manner of speaking, yes."

"But—why?"

"Because, Jack, I believe that there is a strong probability that one of your parents is from Sturgus."

For a moment, Jack was speechless. Then, very slowly, the words came. "Which one?"

"It is awfully hard to say. Who knows, maybe both of them."

"How do you know this?" asked Jack.

"I mentioned that there was magic emanating from Mrs. Krauss's house. I will have you know I also sensed magic emanating from *your* house. Not as strongly, but it is definitely there, and since it does not seem to have a spell of protection, I can see that its source comes *from* Sturgus."

"Unbelievable," Jack muttered. "Does this mean that I could have cousins here?"

"Maybe, although it could mean that a great-grandmother, or great-great-grandmother, is still a child living in Jalambria, or that she lived thousands and thousands of years ago. You see, Jack, when you travel between worlds, sometimes you travel between time, as well. Just a short amount of time can pass in one world, but it could be a very long time in the other."

"Whoa," Jack breathed.

"Does this mean that I'm also from here?" Lucky asked, ears twitching with curiosity.

"It is, indeed, possible." Malia smiled as she reached over and scratched under his chin, causing him to purr in appreciation. "I do not think so, though. I think you just happened to be in the room with him at the time the urn was opened. But just because you might not be from here does not mean that you were not meant to be here."

"So, what happens now?" asked Jack.

"Now," Malia said with a laugh as she stood up, "I think we should find you something more suitable to wear. It would be a good idea to not stand out."

Standing, Jack said, "I *am* kind of sick of wearing pajamas all the time. And I am cold."

"Caleb may have something you could wear. It looks like you are just about his size," said Abigail as she took Malia's bag and put it in the red wagon.

"I love all the pictures on your wagon," Jack said as he found himself looking at the painted images with intrigue once again.

"Thank you," said Malia. "They are special pictures of what has happened and what is still to come. Rosebud is a special wagon."

"Rosebud? You named your wagon?" Lucky asked as he sniffed at one of the wheels.

"Of course," replied Malia. "Caveman has a name for his wagon also."

"What does he call it?" asked the cat, sarcastically. "The Green Machine?"

"You will have to ask him," Malia said.

Jack yelled out, "Hey, look at this!" He was looking at one of the pictures on the red wagon, located near the front wheel.

"What is it?" asked Abigail.

"This is one of the same pictures on the urn," said Jack, full of excitement.

"Pictures?" Malia had stopped moving and was staring at Jack. "Nobody said anything about pictures on the urn."

Jack glared at Lucky. "You forgot to tell her about the pictures when you told her about the urn?"

"Oh, yeah," said Lucky. "No offense, but as a cat I'm not really that keen on human pictures of any kind. Now, a spot on the wall, on the other hand, I can look at *that* for hours."

"What pictures?" asked Malia again. She walked over to Jack and studied the picture on the wagon intently. "Blessed light," she gasped. "You are him. You are the Boy." She turned to Lucky. "And you are the Cat."

Chapter 5

〉〉∘〈〈

"Yes," Jack repeated, a bit perplexed. "I'm a boy."

Malia was both stunned and ecstatic. She ran her fingers through Jack's hair as tears trickled down her cheeks. "No, *the* Boy. Oh, sweet Jack, we have been waiting for you."

"I don't understand."

Malia pointed at the picture that Jack was standing in front of. It was the same as the second picture from the urn, the one with the boy and the cat standing in a boat, looking at a sea serpent. "That *is* you," she gushed, "and the cat . . . well, you can guess who that is. Jack, I am sorry I did not realize this when Caveman told me about you. A boy and a cat traveling together, I should have realized sooner. Of course, silly me."

Jack didn't understand. "I'm still confused."

"How many pictures were on the urn?" asked Malia.

"Three," Jack answered.

Malia pointed to another picture on the wagon. "Was this one of them?"

Jack looked at the picture. It was the picture of the boy, wearing pirate garb, fighting a man with long white hair. "Yes."

"How about this one?" asked Malia, pointing at another picture; it was of the boy and the girl riding a winged horse.

"Yes," Jack muttered. "What does it mean?"

Malia looked to Abigail. "I need you to find Caveman and bring him to the tent."

Abigail's eyes lit up. "What should I tell him?" she asked, sensing the urgency from her mentor and teacher.

"Tell him nothing, lest there be eavesdroppers nearby who could send word to Pale and his horde. He has spies everywhere. Now go, and hurry!"

Abigail nodded once to her teacher and got to her feet. She paused, looking at Jack curiously before dashing away.

"Now, Jack, let us go into the tent. I promise everything will be explained when we are sitting with Caveman," Malia said reassuringly.

Jack picked Lucky up and held him over one shoulder. "Okay," he said, following Malia to the tent. His arrival here was no mistake, at least. But the questions of why he was here and how to get back home were still mysteries to Jack. And Malia's serious tone made him wonder what it meant that he and Lucky were painted on the urn and wagon.

"I'm the Cat," Lucky meowed proudly.

Not long after, Jack and Lucky found themselves once again sitting in the tent, though this time it was only with Malia, Caveman, and Abigail, plus Caleb at Malia's request. Caleb had found Jack some clothes to wear. The clothes were slightly big on Jack and much shabbier than what he was used to wearing, but he kept this to himself.

"Well, Jack," Caveman began, "it seems that I get to tell you another story."

"Fantastic," Lucky purred.

"Yeah," agreed Jack, "you tell the best stories."

"Once, a long, long time ago, there lived a flying horse named Ebon—"

"Hey," interrupted Jack, "Malia already told us this story."

"I only told you the essence of it," Malia replied. "To understand why you are here, you need to hear the story in its entirety."

"Once, a long, long time ago," Caveman began again, "there lived a flying horse named Ebon. He was no ordinary flying horse, however. For, you see, Ebon was king of all the winged horses. In those days, there were many winged horses, and they were as revered as unicorns. Ebon was perhaps the greatest king of the Early Age, and many of the other races and kingdoms later ruled by his fine example. It was Ebon who discovered the existence of other worlds, for only he could fly high enough and far enough to cross the Great Divide, the enormous space that exists between worlds.

"Unfortunately, on one of his excursions, he discovered a very dark and foreboding world called Palima. It was a world where butchery, hatefulness, and deception were common even among the nicest of its inhabitants who, it turns out, were not very nice after all. When Ebon discovered how horrible that world was, he left at once to return here. However, unbeknownst to Ebon, an evil and powerful sorcerer, who had been stealthily watching his every move through a scrying pond, wanted very much to take over Sturgus. He cast a very powerful Bridge Spell and used Ebon as a bridge that allowed him to follow the great leader and have access to our world. This sorcerer's name was Pale."

"Pale, the evil wizard!" exclaimed Lucky.

"The same," answered Caveman. "For this is a story of good versus evil, and words alone cannot describe the great duel that raged between the black winged horse and the ashen wizard. The wizard unleashed several centuries of learned spells at the equine, but Ebon was too powerful for Pale's magic to have any effect. Likewise, Ebon fought by kicking Pale or beating his wings with a fierceness that could conjure winds as strong as a hurricane. However, Pale had used a spell of protection on himself. While each hit weakened the spell slightly, Ebon could not break through. During these battles, even though neither of them was backing down, Pale's very presence caused dark, foreboding clouds to envelop the entire world of Sturgus.

"After many days of battle, Pale realized that he could not defeat Ebon with sorcery alone, so he devised a crafty plan. Pale returned to his dark and miserable world and fashioned three stones of containment. He returned to Sturgus with not only the stones, but with three giant and hideous ogres as well.

"Landing in a wood, Pale, with his dark magic, destroyed enough trees to form a meadow, and hid his ogres in the trees that surrounded it. He called upon Ebon to meet him there, to announce his surrender. Ebon agreed. When the winged horse arrived, Pale feigned fatigue, appearing limp and broken, with no strength to continue their rivalry. Ebon's pure goodness made him let down his guard, and the moment he did, Pale's ogres attacked.

"Even though the ogres were no match for Ebon, they were able to keep him distracted long enough for Pale to chant his evil spell, a spell so devious that not even Ebon could have predicted it. With the energy of a lightning rod, magic shot from Pale's hands into Ebon and with that magic, Pale pulled out his heart. All the love and passion that Ebon held for life was ripped out of him. Pale put that heart into a red stone. Ebon's resilience faltered. He did not desire to fight anymore, but for the safety of his people, he remained standing. The muscles of the dark horse tensed as he prepared to attack the bony wizard. However, he was too slow, too stunned.

While the ogres attacked, the sorcerer Pale shot another bolt of magic into the mighty stallion. With the scream of a banshee, he pulled out Ebon's mind, his very thoughts, and sealed them within a blue stone. Left only with his instincts, Ebon still recognized the immediate danger he was in and kept fighting. And yet, Pale was not finished. From his hands, one final blast of magic pierced Ebon's body, this time pulling out Ebon's soul, which held everything that made Ebon unique. Pale chanted a third and final time as he sealed it inside a purple stone.

"All that was left standing was the shell of Ebon's body. Pale sneered and snarled as he raised his arms high over his head and swung them rapidly downward toward the earth. Ebon's body was frozen in mid-action as he reared defiantly at his attackers. He turned into solid stone. It was at that moment that Pale became the most powerful being in this world and assumed authority over everything. Pale fiendishly clutched the three stones in his hands. He threw the red stone high in the air and called upon the Western Wind to take it far into the west, to the edge of the world, and there leave it. Pale then threw the blue stone high into the air, calling the Northern Wind to carry the stone to the north and drop it on a mountaintop. Last, Pale threw the purple stone high into the air. He called upon the Southern Wind to take the stone far into the south and drop it deep in the wood where no one would see it.

"After such a horrible act, there was nothing left for the ashen wizard to do but hide the body. Pale conjured up the Spell of Wandering on the meadow, imprisoning Ebon's stone figure in it. From that moment forth, the meadow would never remain in the same place. One could come across it far to the west on one day, then maybe just outside Jalambria on the next day."

"The Meadow of Tears," Lucky said solemnly.

"Yes, Cat." Caveman nodded. "The Meadow of Tears. If you and Jack were to go back to where you last saw the meadow, it would not be there."

"So, whatever happened to Pale?" asked Jack cautiously.

"With his victory over Ebon, Pale waged war against the entire kingdom of winged horses and destroyed their entire population. No one is entirely sure what happened after this victory," replied Caveman. "Most believe Pale is still here somewhere in Sturgus, biding his time, stoking all the evil until he is ready to take over the land entirely, and the Muskan horde is his tool to wield that power. Others say that after infecting this world with his heinous corruption, he moved on in search of another world. It all happened three millennia ago, so we may never find out.

"But we do know this: before Pale came to our world there was no such thing as hate, spitefulness, and other such truly negative vibrations. There was not always so much hurt in our world. It is Pale's legacy that bred such division among us, some more than others. But it is the spirit in which the hurt is done, for greed, which is infecting and killing our world, and us."

"I don't understand." Jack's eyebrows furrowed. "What does that have to do with us? With me?"

Caveman's eyes widened. "Because a thousand years after Pale turned Ebon's body to stone, a talented craftsman and a wild and wonderful Conch Dancer created the Wagon of Prophecy."

"What's a Conch Dancer?" asked Jack and Lucky in unison.

"A Conch Dancer is one who uses the magic that exists on the beaches of Isiclees. She is one who weaves magic found in ice and sand with the power of the ocean held within conch shells."

"So, she is a sorceress from a very specific place," affirmed Jack. He drew a deep breath, then let it out in a heavy sigh. "Sorry, but this is a lot of information."

"I can understand that. But, yes, Jack, that is exactly right," confirmed Caveman. "Two thousand years ago there lived a craftsman from the eastern village of Marwood. He had a vision, it seems, that he was to use his superior skills to build a most unique wagon. Well, at first the craftsman resisted the vision and chose not to build the wagon. But the vision returned, and then one more time after that, until the craftsman realized that perhaps he should listen to it. So it was that the craftsman set about his task of building the wagon he saw in his vision. He used timber from the rare and exotic fungay tree and tools fashioned from the bones of monsters long dead. Next, using berries from the highly poisonous blaybluh bush, he stained the wagon red. The Marwoodian thought the wagon was, by far, the best thing he had ever built.

"He loaded the wagon up with all his possessions and hitched two horses to it. Then, having said goodbye to all his friends and neighbors, the craftsman headed north, farther north than Other Mountain, to Isiclees, the kingdom of the Winter People. It was there that the Marwoodian met the Conch Dancer with pale-blonde hair.

"Whether she had enchanted the craftsman or not was of no concern to the Marwoodian; his love for the Conch Dancer was immediate and would be forever true, as she was nothing less than a vision of true beauty. She explained to him that she had sent him the visions to build the wagon and to bring it to her. The Conch Dancer said that she had had a dream that she was to create, with the help of a noble craftsman, a movable device that foretold events to come. The dancer, using her conch shell, then enchanted the wagon with the Spell of Revelation. It was an incredibly powerful spell, the most powerful she had ever done, and it produced many illustrations on the wagon."

"Rosebud," Jack breathed in amazement, staring at Malia. She smiled back and gave him a wink.

"Yes," affirmed Caveman. "Rosebud."

Jack's eyes grew big and round. "You mean . . . your wagon is two thousand years old?"

"Near enough," Malia answered.

"Yes, Jack," Caveman continued. "The wagon is full of magic. Each picture on it represents something that has happened since the wagon was built or is yet to happen."

"Why was the Wagon of Prophecy built?" asked Jack.

"Good question. Truth is, nobody knows for sure. Certainly, for people to learn from it, that we know for sure. I can tell you that one of the pictures on the wagon is of the wagon itself. It is up in the clouds and being pulled by a black winged horse."

"Ebon," Lucky whispered.

Jack looked at Caveman then. "Okay. There's one thing I don't understand. Last night, when I told my story, why didn't you know then who I was, especially when I told you about the statue and pond?"

"I suspected," answered Caveman, "but I had to be sure, first. That is why I asked Malia to speak with you. I knew that if you were who I thought you were, then she would reach the same conclusion, and she did. I also did not want to say anything in front of all the children. The fewer people there are who know that you are here, the safer you will be. If Pale were to find out, he might send his horde after you."

"Well, that would suck," said Jack.

"Suck?" Caveman's lips puckered. "Like this?"

"No. It's just an expression," said Jack.

"Oh, like *cool!*" Abigail beamed.

"Well, yeah. But they mean the complete opposite. Cool is good, and suck . . . well, suck is not."

There was a moment's pause as Jack sorted through all this new information and the amazing stories. "So, let me get this straight," he said carefully. "You think that the boy and cat in those three pictures are Lucky and me, right?"

"Yes, Jack," Caveman answered.

"That means I'm gonna fight a guy with long white hair. I'll come face-to-face with a big scary sea serpent, and I get to ride a winged horse?" Jack was troubled. He did not want to fight anybody, especially an adult with a sword. This was a far cry from playing Pirates with Timmy in the backyard. He was just a kid, after all.

"Jack, the pictures are just interpretations of what is going to happen. They are not full explanations. Nothing is guaranteed. Many wise scholars have studied the pictures on the Wagon of Prophecy, and there are disagreements on the meaning of every single picture. With your pictures, no one is certain how you go about doing what you need to do. The end result may be the same, however. If you look at the pictures, Jack, light is emanating from your hand in each painting. Blue light in one, red in another, and purple in the third. Most seers and scholars agree that these lights represent the three stones that hold Ebon. The winged horse in one of the pictures is believed to be Ebon himself."

"Um . . . okay," said Jack, still unsure of what Caveman was alluding to.

Caveman knelt in front of the boy and looked into his eyes. "Jack, I do not know what magic brought you here, but I do know why you are here. You were brought here to find the Three Stones of Ebon and bring him back among the living so he can lead his own army to end the tyranny of Pale and bring forth a new age of enlightenment to Sturgus."

Jack felt his stomach drop. "I . . . what?"

"It is true, Jack," said Malia.

"Uh, you do know that I'm just a boy."

"Yes," nodded Caveman.

Jack stammered, "No, I'm just a kid. I don't want to fight anybody. I've never hit anybody, ever. Well, maybe my dad a few times, but I was young and upset. Why can't you guys get together and fight this Pale guy yourselves? I . . ." Jack swallowed hard, trying his hardest to keep his outward calm. "I just want to go home. Okay?"

Caveman laid his hand on Jack's shoulder. "If you have ever seen Pale's Muskan horde's handiwork, then you would realize that we would never stand a chance. They live to kill. That is what they do. Jack, no one can make you do this. I understand your point of view. I do. It does sound scary, and at times I am sure it really *is* going to be terrifying for both you and Lucky. You have been carried from your world to ours without your permission, and I will stand by your decision if you decide to decline this . . . this honor, for surely that is what it is.

"Jack, I want you to consider this. Do you think Mrs. Krauss is the type to give a child a magic urn that takes him on a great quest if she did not have full faith that he could pull it off?"

Jack thought of all the times he called her the Crazy Lady. *Maybe*, he thought but remained silent.

"Jack," pleaded Malia, "I am sorry. I realize you did not choose this, but if the prophecy is to be believed, you are our only hope for the people of Sturgus to be free of Pale's tyranny."

Jack looked at Malia. "You really think I can do this?"

"Of course. It is foretold on the Wagon of Prophecy."

"When do we leave?" growled Lucky, proudly.

"You know," said Jack, "I don't know if I'm brave enough to face a giant sea serpent. Or . . . or to do any of this stuff."

"Jack," Malia said, "the picture of the serpent is as Caveman said, an interpretation. It could be that the serpent is really a man who is very snake-like, cunning and clever. It could be a real serpent. But either way, you can do it, Jack. You drank from the pond at the Meadow of Tears, and both you and Lucky have the strength now. Both you and Lucky have the courage to succeed."

Jack looked at Caveman. "If I do this—" He swallowed. "If I do this, will I be able to get back home?"

Caveman paused and stroked his beard, then glanced at the floor with a sigh. "Honestly, I do not know, Jack," he finally replied. "But if you choose not to do this, then you still have that problem."

"Okay," Jack said, resigned. "What next?"

Caveman answered. "Now, I think you should stay here for a few days. Let Malia and me teach you what we can. Then, Jack, you will need to set off on your journey."

"Just me and Lucky?" Jack became alarmed.

"No, Jack," Caveman's look was reassuring. "Caleb and Abigail will be your guides."

Jack looked at Caleb and Abigail. Caleb had long legs, and ash-blond hair hung around his eyes. He looked just a couple of years older than Jack, perhaps thirteen, and Abigail seemed to be his age. He couldn't contain his doubt about traveling with two other children in this strange world. Jack's eyebrows bunched up, and he dropped his gaze to the ground. "Why can't you two come with me, instead?"

"I am responsible for all the orphaned children here," explained Caveman. "I cannot leave them. Malia is the Keeper of the Wagon of

Prophecy. There are places you are going that the wagon will not be able to go, and she must protect the wagon at all costs."

"But how will I know which way to go?"

"Do not worry, Jack. You'll figure it out. Just remember, with magic there are no coincidences."

Jack looked at Caveman and then Malia, worried and a little afraid of what lay ahead. Then Lucky brushed up against his leg. "Don't worry, Jack," he purred. "We can do this."

Jack drew a deep breath and smiled down at his feline friend, and somehow felt better. He walked over to the tent's entrance and looked out onto the landscape of this strange world. Somewhere out there were three stones that he had to find, but there was also an old and evil wizard who, if he knew Jack was on his world, would mostly likely try to kill him or have him killed. The very thought made Jack shudder.

In Jalambria there was an impressive castle, a light shade of blue with many towers. One tower in the castle rose higher than all the others, and in it slept an old sorcerer . . . an incredibly old sorcerer. Pale's sleep was fretful on this particular day. He tossed and turned about, then woke with a scream, sitting upright in his bed. Sweat beaded on his bony brow as he hauled his tired body out of the bed and hobbled slowly to the window. Looking out at the landscape, he knew that a cat and his boy had arrived from another world to undo his three-thousand-year reign of tyranny.

This, Pale could not allow.

Chapter 6

>>∘<<

Jack dreamed that he *was back at the Meadow of Tears. He was in his pajamas, standing barefoot by the pond. The tall grass had an orange hue as the sun hung low in the sky. The statue of the winged horse glowed in the light, and its shadow stretched gently down the slope and touched the pond. Jack peered down into the pond and was pleasantly surprised to see not himself, but his own house in its reflection. He was overcome with joy as he watched Timmy, his best friend, running toward his front door and rapping on it briskly as he was known to do. Jack's face lit up as his mother answered the door. Jack could only watch as his mother gave Timmy Jack's toy pirate sword and eyepatch, and then sent his friend on his way.*

Jack knelt by the water, reached out with one trembling hand, and touched it. The ripple changed the water's reflection, and he now found himself still looking at his house, but everything was in flames. The roof and half the walls had collapsed. And not only was his own house on fire, but also the entire neighborhood had become an inferno. Standing where the front door of his home used to be stood a tall, gaunt, ash-colored figure wearing a dusty robe and sandals that revealed blackened toenails. He was looking into the house, then paused, and turned around.

Through the void the figure's coal-black, lifeless eyes found Jack and locked onto his gaze. A terrible sneer stretched across his ruined face, and Jack's insides felt like ice, bit by bit!

Jack staggered backward. His foot slipped and tapped the surface of the water. The ripple effects caused the image to disappear. Taking heaving breaths, Jack stepped cautiously from the pond. Is that Pale? Can he see me? Running a hand nervously through his tousled brown hair, he looked up toward the statue to discover that it was no longer perched at the top of the slope. Bewildered, Jack looked around and found the great black steed, very much alive, standing right behind him. He jumped.

Ebon spoke in a deep, quiet voice that filled the meadow. "As Pale cast me in different directions, so too shall I send you, Jack Russo, in the same order. First to the farthest reaches of the west, then to the north, and last to the south."

"Not to the east?" Jack asked, bewildered by the vision he'd just had, but now overjoyed and awed by the presence of the winged steed.

"No. That is where Pale is. Find me, Jack," he continued. "Find me and free me. For the sake of this world." And with that, Ebon snorted with great emphasis, shook his great mane, and stomped the ground with one of his front hooves. The steam that curled from his flared nostrils grew into a great cloud that encompassed Jack until he couldn't see anything.

Jack awoke with a start, a strong sense of urgency radiating from the pit of his stomach. His forehead throbbed, like he'd just eaten a pint of ice cream too fast, so it wasn't something that he could ignore. It was a feeling of being pulled, similar to the sensation he'd had at the Meadow of Tears, except this time there was a tense undertone to it. Jack didn't like it, especially after the disturbing dream he'd just had.

He rose from his mat and walked to the tent's entrance. The sun wasn't up yet, but Jack could see hints of its arrival on the horizon. He walked out of the tent and then around it to the other side. From there he looked past the trees to the rolling hills to the west. The pulling sensation in his head intensified.

"So," Jack said aloud to himself. "'Looks like I'm going west." After a few days of being in this new world, it at least felt good to finally know what he was supposed to do next. Or, at least, where he was supposed to go.

Later, at breakfast, Jack shared with Caveman and Malia the dream he had and the pulling feeling in his head. "Ebon told me go to the farthest reaches of the west, but not where, exactly, or what to do when I get there. Does he want me to figure out that part?"

"Very possibly. You did, after all, drink from the Meadow of Tears," answered Malia. "Ebon's time holds very old magic. Who knows what you are capable of now. Or what other insights you may have. You may surprise yourself, Jack."

"All your bags are ready," said Caveman. "You should plan on leaving this morning. To go far west might mean to go by sea. So, now that you know which direction to go—"

Their conversation was cut short at that moment as they heard someone yelling in the echoey stillness of the morning. The sound came from down the road.

"Horde!" a woman cried. "Horde is coming! Horde! Hoooorde!" Jack heard her yelling over and over as she ran down the road and throughout the village.

"Jack," instructed Caveman, his tone abruptly stern, "gather Lucky and hurry back. Go, son. Now. Go!"

Jack nodded and sprinted from the tent toward the wagons, where he knew he would find Lucky. He knew Lucky had taken a liking to hanging out in the Wagon of Prophecy with Abigail while she read from an assortment of magic books that Malia kept in her possession. Lucky had told Jack that he found it relaxing to listen to her read. That, and she also sometimes had a small piece of cheese for him, which he enjoyed.

As Jack reached the wagons, other children darted and dashed in all directions around him, and he almost ran full tilt into Abigail, who was running in the opposite direction with Lucky by her side.

"Caveman wants us in the tent." He spoke breathlessly.

Abigail nodded. "Yes, I just heard. A horde will be here soon. Let us go."

Moments later, Jack, Lucky, and Abigail burst into the tent. Caleb was already there with his bag slung over his shoulder. He hugged Caveman tightly. Malia handed both Jack and Abigail their respective bags, then threw her arms around Abigail, whispering in her ear.

Caveman draped his arms over Jack's shoulders. "Well, Jack, Boy from Another World, looks like the time is now. Malia believes in you. And I believe in you. You were chosen to do this because you *can* do this." Caveman hugged Jack and crouched down to hug Lucky. Then it was Malia's turn. She hugged them and whispered blessings to them both.

"But what about you guys?" asked Jack. "What will you do?"

"Do not worry, this tent and everything here will be packed up very quickly, and we will be out of this village before the horde arrives. We are nomads, accustomed to being on the move."

Abigail stopped short. She looked at Malia, eyes filled with worry. "But how will I find you, after this is all done?"

Malia gave Abigail a reassuring smile. "We will both have to look for each other. Do not fret, Abigail. I have trained you well. It should not be too hard to find the right spell to return you to me. Now hurry, dear! Go!"

The three children and the cat rushed from the tent even as other children were in the middle of dismantling it. Caleb led the trio out of the village, away from villagers and from the horde that would arrive very soon.

Jack's feet hurt. The three children and the cat traveled for days. They stayed away from the main roads, sticking to the hills instead. Whenever they passed by people, Lucky hid in the underbrush. When there was no underbrush, he hid in the shoulder bag that Caveman had given Jack. In this bag, Jack also kept some provisions, a blanket, and his pajamas. Malia had given each child an Amulet of Protection, which they wore around their necks. It was no guarantee to keep them entirely safe, but it would help. Abigail, Jack had learned during his all-too-short stay at the encampment, was a sorceress-in-training. She told Jack that she had dreams of one day becoming the Keeper of the Wagon of Prophecy after Malia retired but was now wondering when she would see Malia again. Caleb was the strongest of the three. He carried a bow with a quiver of arrows and was quite adept at hunting and living off the land. Along with Caleb's arrows, each of them carried a small knife.

"We will be in Valmar soon," said Caleb. "What will we do then, Jack?"

"Well." Jack shrugged. "I could go for a cheeseburger. Maybe we could hit a drive-thru or something." Noting Caleb and Abigail's bewildered expressions, he realized he was trying to find humor in what was about to be the most frightening thing he'd ever done.

"Sorry," Jack said, "that's just 'my world' humor. Anyway, in the dream I had, Ebon told me to go to 'the farthest reaches of the west.' So, that means first we need to find a ship that goes to the edge of the world."

"No ship will go that far," Abigail put in. "Everyone knows their boat would go over the edge."

"Hey, I was kidding." Jack said. "It's just a saying where I'm from. The world is round, so it can't have edges."

"Jack," Abigail said, "your world may be round, but ours is not. It is flat—well, except for the mountains and valleys. Here, the edge of the world is real."

"Impossible," returned Jack.

"Why? From what you have told me, there is no magic on your world. If you can accept that there is magic here, can you not accept that our world is flat? I trust you when you say your world is round, but believe me, a round world is a difficult thing to accept."

Jack considered Abigail carefully. "You're right. I'm sorry. Your world is flat, so having an edge of the world makes sense."

"I mean, I would think the people who lived on the bottom would just fall off." Abigail caught Jack's eye and gave him a smile.

They walked in silence for a bit. Caleb, having the longer stride, occasionally walked ahead of the others.

"He sure can walk fast," Jack told Abigail.

"Caleb? Agreed, but he is older than us. Do not worry. I think he likes to go ahead, sometimes. He is scouting. He may not show it, but Caleb is very honored that Caveman chose him to be your guide. He does not take this responsibility lightly."

"I see. What about his parents? I know they're dead, but . . ."

64

"Caleb's mother died giving birth to him. He was raised solely by his father, until their home was invaded by members of the Muskan horde. They killed his father. He managed to escape and found his way to Caveman. He has had a hard time adjusting, as he misses his father desperately."

"Oh," replied Jack quietly. "What about you then? How did you become Malia's apprentice?"

"I was too young to remember losing my family. I have been with Caveman's group since I was two. Malia took a liking to me when she first met me, and when I turned five, I became her apprentice. She said it was because she saw a spark in me."

"A spark?" asked Jack.

"Yes," Abigail replied. "Malia told me that it was a spark that could only be found within those deep in the magic. She said I had possibilities, and that she became a sorceress's apprentice in the same manner when she was young."

"So, do you live in the Wagon of Prophecy?"

"Well, when I am not helping a boy and cat from another world, I spend most of my time with Malia and her wagon. However, there are times when she must travel away for a bit, whether for business or to hide the wagon from those no-good Muskans. On those occasions I stay with Caveman."

Looking forward, Jack noticed that Caleb had stopped and was waiting for them.

"Look," said Caleb, nodding ahead of them. "Centaurs."

Everyone looked. Both Jack and Lucky were speechless. There were seven of the creatures walking along the very same road they traveled, only in the opposite direction. Being half-human and half-horse, the centaurs looked very formidable.

"Wow," Jack whispered, "that's so cool."

"'Cool' being a good expression," Abigail confirmed.

"Very good, yes." Jack was pleased. "I'd love to talk to them."

"We cannot do that," said Caleb. "We do not know if they serve Pale or not. We should take care who we decide to talk to. Do not worry, though—when we get to Valmar you will see all sorts of people that do not exist in your world. Come, let us keep walking."

It was roughly an hour later when they crested a hill and found themselves looking down on the port village of Valmar. Jack had never witnessed a town quite like this one. The village wrapped around the bay, hugging every alcove. Sea grass tucked into craggy rocks. Most of the buildings were made of wood, with some reaching as high as three stories, all huddled very close together, many with no space for an alley.

The roofs were flat, the streets narrow. What held Jack's attention most was the large lighthouse that sat far out in the bay. It was larger than any lighthouse that Jack had ever seen, even on television. It stood nearly as tall as the Space Needle, jutting straight out of the water and defying the might of the sea. The glass windows that housed the beacon at its top were taller than most of the houses in his neighborhood back home. Below that, pipes and staircases spiraled down the side of the lighthouse to water level, where a dock moored six small boats. The lighthouse was golden-red with metallic bronze outlining the glass. Even though it was daylight, the lighthouse was on. A beam of intense orange light shone out across the sea.

"Wow," said Jack, "that's some lighthouse. It's so *big*."

"That is the Ahmega Lighthouse," Caleb informed him.

"The light coming from it looks different from normal light. It almost looks solid."

"It is magic light," said Caleb. "The beam of light will pierce any fog or thunderstorm and it travels to the end of the world."

"Why does it need to travel that far?" asked Jack.

"So ships know which way is land, and which way is the Falls."

"The Falls?"

"At the end of the world—well, at least on the known side of it—the sea cascades into the Abyss. We call it the Falls."

"Why can't ships just use a compass?" asked Jack.

"A Com Pass?" chimed in Abigail. "What is that?"

"It's a tool that you hold in your hand, and it tells you which way is north," said Jack. "When you know which way is north, then you can determine which way to steer the ship."

"Hmm." Caleb smirked. "Maybe there is magic in your world, after all."

"So has anybody survived falling into the Abyss?" asked Lucky.

"We do not know. Those who fall never come back."

"Oh." Both Jack and Lucky fell silent.

"Well, Jack." Caleb smiled, putting his hand on Jack's shoulder. "I think it would be a good idea if we found a tavern and had a meal before deciding how next to proceed. Surely you must be tired of eating rabbit and berries all week?"

"I could use a change," Jack agreed. He looked at Abigail. "You must be tired of eating just berries."

Abigail smiled at Jack and spoke firmly. "No, I am fine with it. I do not eat living creatures."

Jack smiled back. During the last week, both he and Lucky had developed a real friendship with Abigail and Caleb. They were both nice and patient with him as he learned about their customs and the strange land all around.

Jack called, "C'mon, Lucky, it's time to climb into the bag."

Lucky looked at Jack in defiance for a moment and then, in resignation, jumped into Jack's shoulder bag. "Okay," he said, "but when we get to the tavern, you'd better order some chicken so I can have some."

"Fair enough, little buddy," Jack replied. A small hole had been fashioned into the side of the bag so Lucky could peer out without being seen.

"Jack, when we get to the village, will you try not to look too surprised and gawk at all the new types of people that are about? You need to try to blend in."

"Okay, Caleb, I'll try not to."

With the cat safely hidden in the shoulder bag, they headed down the hill toward the village.

Jack tried his absolute best to appear nonchalant, but it was one thing to see a giant cyclops in a movie and an entirely different thing to see a real one, not to mention one walking uphill from the village and toward them at an incredible pace. From the great strides it took, Jack thought that it would pass them in a matter of minutes. Jack couldn't help himself and froze in his footsteps in awe. He let out a series of sounds that could only be described as *ahbaba gumpy* or perhaps *ebuhbuh gha see*.

He stumbled backward a few steps before tripping and landing on his butt. Abigail and Caleb looked back at Jack, but he did not see them. All he saw was the cyclops, his gaze transfixed. Standing taller than two basketball players, the cyclops reached them in less than half a minute but never bothered with so much as a glance their way with his single, enormous eye. He strode past them as if they weren't even there. Before they knew it, the cyclops was over the hill and out of sight.

For a moment, no one spoke, then Caleb and Abigail burst into laughter. Caleb fell to the ground next to Jack, and he could not stop laughing. Abigail clutched her side as tears streaked down her freckled face. Finally, Lucky stuck his head out of the bag and declared, "Ahbaba gumpy? What's that, baby talk?" which, of course, brought forth even more laughter.

"That was a cyclops!" Jack stammered. "He . . . he was gigantic! I thought he was going to eat us."

Caleb, still laughing, pushed back his ash-blond hair and said, "If we were in a wood and came across him and he was hungry, then, yes, he might have made soup of us. In Valmar, however, there is an agreement. If you wish to do business here, there must be no violence. Valmar is the biggest port on the west coast. Not even a cyclops would risk being banned from here, no matter how hungry he was."

"Oh," said Jack, feeling a little silly. Caleb reached out a hand to help Jack up, and the group continued on their way. Jack followed closely behind Caleb and Abigail, this time minding that he did not draw attention to himself. As they walked through the narrow streets, Jack saw many creatures; some he identified easily from fantasy lore from his own world, but he had no idea what some others could be. One creature that Jack saw looked an awful lot like a rabbit, but it stood five feet tall and, instead of fur, it had grey scales and a club tail. It was walking in the street, conversing with a thousand or so tiny flying creatures who had flown together to form the shape of another five-foot rabbit. Later, Caleb would tell him that the "rabbit" was called a flpepntack, which Jack was never able to pronounce correctly. The tiny flying creatures were called sparkles. They were known for imitating whomever they were with.

They rounded a corner and Jack saw, for the first time in his life, real pirates. He had read about real pirates in history, and he had seen pirates in his world, but those were actors portraying historic buccaneers of the seas or adults playing games for the amusement of children. He remembered playing Pirates with Timmy the very day that his father brought the urn home, but here he was seeing honest-to-goodness real pirates. Boy, if Timmy could see this! Six of them hung around an open doorway to what appeared to be a pub. Four of them were humans. The other two looked like walking fish-people. All of them were dressed in what Jack considered to be traditional pirate garb. There was one woman in the band, tall, with long, dark, flowing curls. As they walked past the pirates, the woman's eye caught Jack's and she winked at him. Jack averted his eyes, not sure what to make of the woman's gesture.

Right then Jack saw the most astounding thing yet. It walked alone, white coat shimmering reflectively in the sun, hooves making an almost musical clip-clopping sound on the cobblestone road. From its bobbing head rose a single horn that cast gold highlights onto the beast itself. It was majestic. *It* was a unicorn. Jack couldn't help himself, and once again stopped walking to gawk as the unicorn walked by. More graceful than any mere horse, it was the most beautiful thing that Jack had ever seen.

A gentle tug from Abigail, and Jack's feet were moving once again through the streets. He was happy that Lucky sat in the shoulder bag, watching everything from the safety of his little peephole. Caleb led the group to a tavern with many tables and chairs out front. Most of the tables and chairs were sized for people like them, but Jack noticed a few at the end that were gigantic. *For giant people,* he thought, *like that cyclops we saw.* Caleb took them around the side, to the back of the tavern, where the walkway came out onto a terrace, overlooking the buildings one street over. They were fortunate to find a vacant table, for the tavern was brimming with customers, at the far end of the terrace.

"Ooh," Abigail breathed. "It feels so good to sit. My toes are happy."

"I agree," said Caleb. "We will eat, And then take stock of supplies, then discuss our next step."

The terrace was full, and, looking into the back entrance, Jack could see that the inside was packed as well. He could see and hear a group at the bar singing along to festive music. The waitress came by, and they ordered their meals. Jack remembered Lucky's request and ordered chicken. During the meal Jack periodically dropped pieces of chicken into the bag, enough to satisfy the cat's hunger.

After eating, the three children sat for a bit, taking in the view. In addition to the several hundred little boats in the bay, Jack noticed three large ships anchored out beyond the lighthouse. Two of the ships looked similar, three masts on each with an overall brown look to them. The third ship had two masts. Its hull was painted red and had a colorful mermaid figurehead sculpted into the bow. Although its sails were not extended, Jack could see that they were black compared to the white ones on the other two ships.

"Now," said Caleb after a time, "let us see exactly what we have to barter with."

"I have three Potions of Healing, one Spell of Transport, and an Enhancement Potion," Abigail said, rummaging in her bag.

"What's an Enhancement Potion?" asked Jack.

"It makes whoever drinks the potion extremely good at whatever it is that they are trying to do or accomplish," she replied.

"Oh. So, like, if I'm walking, it will allow me to be really good at walking." Jack snickered.

"Yes, I suppose it would," Abigail said, rolling her eyes. "But better yet, say you have never ridden a horse before and then drink the potion, then you will know how to ride a horse—quite exceptionally, I might add."

"Well then," Caleb put in, "the only other things we have are the bow and arrows, the three knives, three blankets, and the Amulets of Protection that we are each wearing.

"Oh," Jack added, "and I still have my pajamas, and I have a cat."

"We may need the potions," Caleb continued, ignoring Jack's latest attempt at humor. "We will also need the bow and arrows, the knives, and blankets. Basically, we have nothing to barter with."

"But we need a ship today," offered Jack, "so I think we should ask around to get passage aboard one of those ship and offer to work in exchange."

"Not a bad idea," Caleb mused. "But we had best decide soon. The less time we spend here, the better. There is no telling who is in alliance with Pale here. But thanks to all the village raids, orphans are everywhere. The positive thing is, at least we do not stand out too much traveling by ourselves."

While Jack, Abigail, and Caleb were deep in their conversation, Lucky sat in the shoulder bag at the foot of Jack's chair. Having finished dining on chicken, Lucky took to peering out of the hole in the bag. Jack had positioned the bag so he could watch the other diners and see into the back door of the tavern.

What happened next was entirely Lucky's fault, but, in his defense, he was a cat. It didn't matter that Jack had given him enough chicken to eat. When he spotted the mouse inside the tavern, he went into hunter mode. The mouse had skittered under the chairs by the bar, nibbling on bits of food that had fallen from the table above.

During the time that Lucky had been in Sturgus, Caleb and Abigail tried to teach both him and Jack the subtle differences between talking animals and non-talking animals. This mouse, from what Lucky had learned, was a non-talking mouse. For one, it didn't walk on its hind legs the way talking mice did. Also, it didn't engage in conversation with any of the patrons.

So, to Lucky's mind, this mouse was fair game as a snack. Lucky watched as the mouse scurried out of his vision. Before he himself could decide to pounce, he found himself already doing it. On one TV program he'd watched in his home world, a documentary about cats had a word for it: instinct. He leaped silently out of the shoulder bag and into the tavern. Lucky moved with the skill and grace of, well, a cat. He saw the mouse sitting between someone's feet, under a table. Unfortunately, the mouse was facing him and had time to react. It ran fast, weaving in and out and around the multitude of legs in its path. Lucky naturally followed in hot pursuit.

He was about to make the killing leap when a human leg suddenly collided with him. Lucky fell over sideways but quickly found his footing. Then he looked up to see a woman looking down at him. The woman's eyes widened as her face twisted in horror. Lucky's pupils dilated and his ears went flat as the woman towered over him.

She shrieked, "A cat, a cat!"

A hush fell over the tavern. All eyes zeroed in on Lucky.

"Oh, no." His voice came out in a whimper.

Then somebody yelled, "Kill him!"

The entire tavern burst into an uproar with everybody yelling. Lucky darted between swinging feet and hands that grabbed at him. A glass stein, filled with brew, shattered at Lucky's feet, drenching him with its contents.

"Jack!" Lucky was frantic. He tried to run back to his sack, but because of the chaos, he couldn't figure out which way he came in. People were screaming at him, kicking at him, and throwing things at him. Lucky, for the first time in his short life, was truly scared. He was even more frightened than the day he entered this land. People were trying to kill him, people who didn't even know him. Despite his wet coat, his orange fur stood on end from head to toe.

Lucky sped up, launched himself up and over a low wall, and landed on a rather long table filled with an impressive array of food and drink. Lucky bounded across the table as fists and swords pounded against the dishes directly behind him. A man with a fork suddenly appeared in front of him. He had the fork raised, ready to come down on Lucky as he approached. Lucky crouched and leaped a great and impressive leap and landed . . . directly on top of the man's head! Lucky dug his claws in, and the man screamed as he staggered around. He brought the fork up to jab at Lucky, but the cat released his grip and dropped to the floor in a flash, and the man stabbed himself in the head, letting out a loud and painful howl.

Lucky once again found himself running under tables as glasses showered down all around him. He darted in and out of the jumble of too many legs. As he neared the edge of a flapping table cover, he finally saw the exit. *Freedom!* But the thought came too quickly because something snatched him roughly by the scruff of the neck and he was hoisted into the air, his surroundings a blur of colors and noise, then suddenly muted when Lucky was tossed into a coarse bag. The drawstring closed over his head, shutting out the light and leaving him in pitch blackness.

Outside on the terrace, Jack and his companions were in deep discussion about their plans when all the commotion from inside the tavern caught their attention.

"I wonder what's going on?" Jack said, craning his head to take a look behind him.

"I do not know," Abigail replied. "It sounds like a party of sorts, or a dance about to begin."

Caleb shrugged, looking as lost as his companions.

Then they heard the screams. "Kill the cat. Kill it!"

Jack's insides lurched in panic. He darted to his shoulder bag to investigate. It was empty. "Oh no! Lucky!"

The assassin entered the throne room with determination and purpose. His boots squeaked as he walked across the marble floor, leaving wet footprints in his wake. Water dripped from his clothes, body, and hair as if he'd just been caught in a rain shower, though it hadn't rained in three days. It was an unfortunate curse put on him by a sorceress; he would always look like someone who'd just stepped out of the bath, always wet and dripping.

On either side of him, armed lizard-people stood at attention as his guards, their armor gleaming red. Before him, made of solid gold with sapphires and diamonds inlaid throughout, was a great throne. Seated on the throne was a tall, very bony and ashen man who was not a man. His nose was hooked, and his chin was heavy. He had the lurid look of someone used to having his way, with no regard for its effect on other, less important people. The crown on his head did not hinder this effect. There was only one word that truly described the

sorcerer accurately, one word that both defined the physical charac-
teristics and mental outlook of the man: creepy.

Pale sat on his stolen throne, slouched low in the seat with his
head only slightly higher than the arm rests. The crown dug hard
into his brow, as if it had been sitting that way for hundreds of years.
But it had, in fact, been *thousands* of years.

Entering the boy's dream a few days ago, finding a workaround in
Ebon's magic to see where the boy had come from, and instilling fear
in the boy's heart had drained him more than he'd thought it would.
Ever since his great battle with that naïve fool of a horse several millennia ago, his powers weren't quite as potent. And forcing darkness,
spite, and hatred upon this world—it wasn't easy to keep crushing the
morale and will of once-proud, mostly happy, and prosperous people for so long a time. They were more resilient than he'd given them
credit for. But he was ancient. He could continue to wait, to wear
them down with more raids by his ranks of Muskan hordes while he
regained strength. In another century or so, he'd be strong again.

Pale looked over the ever-soaked assassin with a mixture of bore-
dom and disdain. A moment passed as Pale waited for his unde-
served bow from the assassin. The dripping man, waiting for Pale
to tell him why he was summoned, grabbed his long white hair and
wrung the water out. The throne room echoed as the water slapped
the floor with authority. Both men glared at each other in silence.
Upon realizing that the assassin had no clue or care of proper proce-
dure, Pale spoke first.

"Dayvid the Damp," he announced with an authoritarian yet
raspy voice. "The assassin."

"Huh" was the only reply as the assassin eyed the guards on either
side of him. He was always wary, always on guard.

"I have an assignment for you."

"You have summoned me, and I have come." The assassin looked at Pale, ever more suspicious. "Speak your business."

Pale said, "Somewhere, out there, there is a boy traveling with a cat. They are searching for the Three Stones of Ebon. I want them dead."

The Damp, who did not surprise easily, shifted uncomfortably and eyed Pale. "You . . . you want me to *kill* a little boy and a tiny cat because of some old folktale?"

"Did you not hear me?" Pale snarled. "They are after the Three Stones of Ebon."

"I heard you fine," the Damp replied frankly. "But if I recall, the last time I worked for you, you said that you would remove this Curse of Perpetual Dampness. But as you can see, I'm still sopping wet. All. The. Time. It is very difficult to do my job. I cannot sneak up on people in this condition."

"And I told *you* that you needed to find the sorceress who did this to you and bring her to me. I need to destroy her, and then your curse can easily be lifted. Until then, I believe that it is my responsibility to eradicate any and all threats to my kingdom, no matter how benign they seem. I nearly destroyed myself containing Ebon to gain control of this world. No one, and I mean no one, is allowed to . . . undo that work."

"Even a boy and a cat?"

"Yes, Dayvid, *especially* a boy and a cat."

"Do you know where they are now?"

"They're currently heading west, but you will not catch them in time to stop them from obtaining the first stone," croaked Pale. "No, you will have to stop them either at Other Mountain or at Sahaland."

"Sahaland?" Dayvid's face clouded. "That is cat country. One cat is bad luck. Hundreds of cats are lots of bad luck."

Pale couldn't be bothered by the assassin's superstitions and complaints. "Yes, Sahaland," he continued. "I will be sending a horde to both places. You can travel with them if you like. Just find the boy and the cat and kill them." Pale waited for the assassin to bow in acknowledgment and take his leave, but when Dayvid did not, a sliver of rage ran though Pale and he fought to contain it.

"You may go," Pale said through clenched teeth.

Dayvid the Damp remained still a moment longer as Pale watched on, incredulous at the impertinent killer. Finally, the Damp moved. Dayvid took his once-again-drenched hair in his hands and wrung it out with meticulous care before finally turning and walking out in a chorus of squelching strides, leaving enough water on the floor to fill a bucket.

Wearily and irritably, Pale rose from his throne, then left the room.

Chapter 7

≫ ◦ ≪

Jack was frantic. "I have to go in there to get Lucky!"

Caleb grabbed Jack around the shoulders and body, attempting to restrain him.

Abigail pleaded with Jack under her breath. "Do you know what would likely happen to us if it were found out that humans were traveling with a cat? You cannot just rush in there all wild-eyed. And we cannot all go in there at once, or else we could be taken for allies of a cat. I will go check myself. Try to not despair, yes?" Abigail ducked into the tavern alone to search for the tiny feline. About ten minutes later, she came back empty-handed.

Caleb, seeing how upset Jack was over losing Lucky, rose from the table. "Abigail, will you stay with Jack while I check around a bit outside—"

But Jack stopped him, climbing to his feet.

"Look, I really think I need to do this, Caleb. I'm calmer now. I can do this. I mean, Lucky really likes both of you and all, but with everything going on right now . . . if he is hiding in there, he needs to see that I'm there."

Abigail and Caleb exchanged quick glances, and they both grimly nodded. "You have reason," the elder boy finally said. "Just be careful. We will remain here."

Jack decided to bring his bag along as he went to scout the inside of the tavern. If he and Lucky did spot each other, he could quickly scoop him up and out of sight, and retreat quickly before anyone noticed. His eyes scanned the room. Only moments before, with all of the screaming and carrying on, everybody had seemed intent on trying to kill Lucky. Now things had already quieted down inside, and people had resumed their meals, drink, and socializing. And Lucky was still nowhere to be found. A tiny mouse scurried past Jack on its four legs and darted into its hole in a nearby wall.

Jack returned to his friends and sat down with a frustrated huff. Caleb and Abigail looked down, not knowing what to say, so they just sat there a moment.

As they sat, Jack gazed out toward the water. The three ships bobbed gently in the harbor while the lighthouse remained rigid and true. As Jack watched the red ship, he suddenly *knew* that it was where they needed to go next. That odd *pulling* sensation started up again, just like it had when he was back at the encampment with Caveman and Malia, right before the horde arrived.

Before, the pull had been more subtle. Now, the pull was much stronger, and Jack knew he had to trust it. It gave him a sense of direction, at least, which Jack found comforting. However, the pull told Jack that he belonged on that particular ship, but it didn't tell him why. He also knew now that Lucky needed to be with him, because Malia had told him that it was no accident that both he and his cat were brought to this land. He also knew that—regardless of any prophecy— he was not leaving Valmar without his beloved cat.

"Jack," Caleb started, "how about we three split up and try looking—" when a garbled voice interrupted him.

"Ye . . . be Jack." The voice sounded as if it came from underwater. Standing in front of them was one of the pirates that Jack had seen earlier, its gills flapping slowly as it breathed the warm summer air.

Jack, Abigail, and Caleb sat stunned, gazing at the humanoid fish. Finally, Jack found his voice, stood up, and said, "Who wants to know?" It was the only comment he could think of on the spot.

The fish pirate leaned forward, planting his fin hands on the table. "If ye wants to see the cat alive, ye would do best to come with me." Then he paused, considering the other two, and added with a sneer, "*All* of ye."

"What have you done with my cat? If you've hurt him—"

The humanoid fish waved him off. "He will be a'right, so long as you come along quietly. We best be a-going."

He knows where Lucky is, thought Jack excitedly. He grabbed his shoulder bag and followed the fish pirate, but not before catching the look of quiet urgency and concern that Abigail and Caleb shared as they each grabbed their bags and reluctantly followed Jack. As they walked, Caleb caught up to his determined friend. "Jack," he said under his breath, "what are we *doing*, following this creep? I do not like this."

"They've got Lucky. And I can't explain how I know, but I know this is the right thing to do."

Caleb slowed to fall to the back of the group, looking frustrated and worried.

As Jack followed the fish pirate, he was better able to get a look at him. The body was very human in shape, but the hands were fins and he seemed to move various parts of his fins as Jack would his own fingers. He was blue with a *very* fishy head. His clothes were decidedly "pirate," complete with a cutlass and a bandanna. He was tall, about a foot taller than most people.

Caleb boldly called, "Hey, where are you taking us?"

The fish pirate turned suddenly and came upon Caleb. With his free fin-hand the fish pirate pressed Caleb down against the cobblestone street and held his cutlass close to the boy's face. "Ye best to keep silent, or ye may feel the sharp end of me friend here. I trust we be seein' . . . eye to eye."

"No!" Jack interrupted. "Leave him alone, or we're not going with you." The next thing he knew, he kicked the creature's leg in an attempt to defend his friend, then instantly regretted his decision.

The fish pirate's body stiffened, and he slowly turned his head to look at Jack. For a moment, the fish pirate just held Caleb there, staring at Jack with his odd, unblinking fish eyes, his gills slowly flapping. Then he slowly released the older boy, turned, and resumed walking without a word. Jack and Abigail helped Caleb up, and the three children followed in step behind the fish pirate.

The fish pirate led them to a dock where, at its end, was moored a red dinghy. "Get in," he ordered. The children hesitantly obliged, and the fish pirate followed suit and sat facing them as he grabbed both oars. He began rowing. As he rowed, the fish pirate glared at the children menacingly. Both Abigail and Caleb were frightened, especially after the way he had threatened Caleb. Jack's toes were throbbing from kicking the pirate. He was scared, too, but also angry, determined to get his cat back. The fish pirate, Jack reasoned, could have ended them all right there and then, but for some reason, he didn't. Abigail and Caleb sat looking down at their hands, occasionally glancing out onto the water. Jack, however, sat with a glint in his eye. Soon he would be with his cat again. If Lucky were hurt in any way, someone would answer to him!

As the fish pirate rowed past the Ahmega Lighthouse, Jack realized that they were going to the red ship with the black sails. His pulse quickened, and he got that ice-cream-headache feeling again, which—despite the discomfort—was a good sign. The ship was smaller than the other two ships moored in the harbor, but no less impressive. The red wood of its hull shone richly throughout, and Jack could see two cannons peering out of the starboard side of the vessel. He could also see some damage to the ship, and the crew was hard at work to repair it. *This ship has seen battle,* he thought.

A rope ladder hung down the side of the ship and they were told to climb it. As they climbed onto the deck of the ship, they were met with silent stares from the crew. The fish pirate led them toward the stern of the ship, past the helm, to the captain's quarters.

"If one word comes from ye lips, it is a tongue ye be losing," he said, his words coming in gurgles as he herded them through the door. Once the children were inside, the fish pirate entered the room himself, closed the door, and stood guard.

Jack looked around. The room was nice, and might have felt inviting too, if they hadn't been brought there by force. To one side was a dining table with two pirates sitting at it. The two pirates looked like twins, with identical scraggly beards, hip-length tunics, and pants that stopped just below the knee. Both were barefooted and drinking from ceramic mugs. On the other side of the room was a little alcove leading into a stateroom. Straight ahead, however, sitting in an upholstered chair, was the pirate that Jack had seen in the street when they'd first arrived at the village, the one who had winked at him. She wasn't looking up at the children at all. Instead, her attention was on her lap, where her hands were rubbing through the fur of the orange-and-white tabby cat on her lap. It purred emphatically with eyes closed.

"Lucky!" Jack was ecstatic despite the threat that the fish pirate had made just a moment earlier.

Lucky's eyes flew open, then he was off the woman's lap and on Jack's shoulder with one sure-footed leap. "Jack! Did you miss me?"

Jack held Lucky close to his head, taking in the familiar purr of his best friend. "Aw, you know it, buddy. I'm so glad you are safe."

The pirate rose from the chair and stood tall in front of them. She was broad-shouldered with long legs. Raven-colored hair fell around her shoulders in curls with several beautiful braids lined throughout. Her clothes, while very piratical, were made of deep red leather. Across her shoulders she wore a type of metal armor that was made up of what looked like hundreds of tiny, overlapping scales. To Jack, she looked like a medieval superhero.

"Children"—she spread her arms wide—"welcome aboard the *Minnow Sowta*." The twin pirates both raised their mugs in the air and took deep drinks from them, while the fish pirate stood solid as he guarded the door from any attempt at escape that the children might have.

Jack stared at her, unsure of what to say, if anything at all. This pirate had stolen Lucky. Her fish pirate held a cutlass to his friend Caleb's throat. And then he'd forced them into the rowboat only for Jack to find Lucky safe and sound in her lap. While Jack was glad to have his cat back, he wasn't sure what to make of this woman, or if she was friend or foe.

The woman walked up to Jack, with Lucky now in his arms, and scratched Lucky lovingly behind his ear.

"This cat speaks very warmly of you, Jack from Another World." She looked at the other two and continued. "You two are Abigail and Caleb from the Midlands. I am Fay, captain of this little ship."

The children remained silent. Captain Fay stepped in front of Caleb, who looked down when she approached. She grabbed his chin and brought it up so she could see his face. "What is the matter? Cat got your tongue?" Caleb scowled and cast his eyes at the floor in defiance.

It was Abigail who replied. "Begging your pardon, Captain, but it is not the cat that we are worried about when it comes to losing our tongues."

Just then, laughter erupted from behind them. The children did not have to turn around to know who the boisterous laughter through brackish water could be coming from. There was only one among them who sounded like that. Fay peered past the children to the blue fish pirate leaning against the door, doubled over in merriment.

"What is so funny, Carponius?" She looked at him quizzically.

The fish pirate slid down the door to the floor, his laughter intensifying.

"Well," Fay began after some time, eyebrows furrowed in a bit of frustration. "I do wish you would let us in on whatever joke you heard so that we, too, can join in on your rude interruption."

"I am sorry, Captain," said the fish pirate, between fits of laughter. "You told me to convince them to come aboard, so I had a bit of fun. My words were, 'Ye best come with me if ye wants to see the cat alive,' and then I said . . . I said, 'If one word comes from yer lips, it is a tongue ye be losing!'"

"Carponius! You did not!" exclaimed the captain, wearing a half-smile as she shook her head. "Well! I trust you at least didn't rough them up." Fay turned to the children, then said with some concern, "He did not rough you up, did he?"

Carponius blinked through laughter-induced tears. He finally took a deep breath, cleared his throat, and answered his captain. "Well, ma'am, I did hold my cutlass to the big lad, there, but he is no worse for wear." The fish pirate still sat on the floor, catching his breath, gently dabbing at one of his eyes.

Fay looked at the three children again and gave a snort. "Well! I am sorry if my first mate caused you distress. Apparently, with so much time on the move, my crew has developed some very odd ways of entertaining themselves. Aquaticans in particular." With that, she glared briefly at Carponius.

Caleb finally spoke. "So, we are not prisoners?"

To this, Fay and the two pirates that looked alike joined the fish pirate in uproarious laughter (and yes, the two other pirates who looked alike also laughed alike).

"Heavens, no," retorted Fay, containing herself at last. "You are our guests!"

"So does that mean we can leave?" asked Abigail.

The laughter had finally subsided. "Young lady, you can leave right now if you wish."

Abigail grabbed Jack by the sleeve. "Good. Come on then, Jack, let's go."

Jack surprised her by saying only one word. "No." Lucky dropped to his feet as Jack looked over at Fay. "So, how much has Lucky told you?"

Fay beamed at Jack. "Well, this little guy told me that an urn brought you to this world. He told me there are paintings of you two on something called the . . . Wagon of Prophecy, was it? And I know that you are searching for the legendary stones of Ebon. Did I leave anything out? Ah, yes. Abigail is a sorceress-in-training . . . and yoooouuu"—she beamed at Lucky—"are the cutest little thing. Oh, yes you are!" Lucky purred and drooled shamelessly.

Jack thought for a moment. "So, you're the one who saved Lucky at the tavern, aren't you?"

"I threw a bag over him and got him out of there as quickly as possible. They were going to kill him."

"Well, thank you, then" Jack said, "for saving him."

"No need." There was a genuine softness to her voice. "I would have done it for any cat, but because of the superstitions of people, having anything to do with cats is a crime in and of itself, and not something my crew can know about. So, tell me, Jack, how do you plan to find these stones, if you do not mind my asking?"

"I'm not sure how to describe it, but ever since I was at the encampment with Malia, Caveman, and all those kids, I've been feeling some kind of tug, a kind of pulling. It happened on the morning just before a horde arrived at the village. And now . . . well, it brought me here."

"So, you think one of the stones is here, in Valmar?"

"No," said Jack, "I think one of the stones is out *there*." He pointed westward, toward the sea.

"What, on an island?" Fay was curious.

"I don't know, but it has something to do with a serpent."

"Oh, that is right. Lucky mentioned one of the paintings having a serpent. Why do you think that that picture represents this particular stone?"

"Because on the urn I was given before I left home, the picture that had the serpent had a red stone right there with it. The red stone, according to stories, is in the west. So now that you know, I just thought I'd let you know about the possible danger before I ask you for passage." Jack surprised himself by being so blunt and matter-of-fact as he spoke.

The room was quiet for the moment. Fay sat back in her chair, mulling over the boy's information, looking at Lucky and then at the two twin pirates. "Jack, this is a pirate ship. By taking you on this journey, my actions could be misconstrued by some as wrongdoing because there is an unspoken rule among pirates about having children onboard. Whenever we set sail, some peril is certain. It is no place for children. Not to mention, the crew would lose their senses if they found out about a cat onboard. Why not try one of those cruise ships out there? If you don't have enough money, I will gladly purchase your fares."

"If it's all the same to you, this is the ship that we need to be on," Jack said resolutely.

"Why?" asked Fay.

"Because it's red," Jack answered.

"Huh?" said Fay. Everyone in the room looked at Jack with collective confusion.

"Yeah," continued Jack, "the stone in the west is red, and this ship is red. This is the ship we need to be on."

"Jack, hold on," Caleb interjected, a trifle frustrated. "One of them *did* just hold a sword to my throat. And just because they are both red doesn't mean that this is the ship we need to take.

"Yes, it does. Caveman told me that in magic there are no coincidences. This is the ship we need to be on. I can feel it."

"Jack." Fay spoke softly and clearly so he would understand the seriousness of his request. "Do you know what this ship engaged in before we came to Valmar? We were out in the Kester Islands, where the rich and well-to-do—which in our world are only made up of those who profit from the Muskan dictatorship—have their summer homes. We were storming their retreats and robbing them of any item of wealth that we could find. Well, bad fortune was with us that day. Another pirate ship in the area, the *Scalawag*, was being chased down by a Muskan warship. Now, the *Minnow Sowta* may be small, but she is by far the fastest ship in the seas. No other ship comes close. So, we went to the *Scalawag*'s rescue and took a hit near our starboard bow, and another ball went right through one of the sails. I lost many of my crew in the battle, and the *Scalawag*, well . . . she went down. We rescued a good number of her crew and got out while the getting was good. Many of them disembarked in Valmar, but some are staying on for our next voyage."

"You have reason," Caleb cut in. "I hate to admit but it is good of you to stand up to the Muskans like that. But why are you not worried? Would not the Muskan warship come here and find you?"

"Oh, not to worry about that," Fay replied with a casual wave of her hand. "We pirates have developed a watchdog system at all the major ports. If that warship comes within thirty leagues, we will be getting ample warning. That is a guarantee. Anyway, the ship is almost repaired. Tomorrow, we set sail on our next excursion to steal from the Muskans and contribute further to our ultimate cause."

"Your ultimate cause?" Jack repeated.

"Yes, Jack. My cause is to do everything in my power to hinder the effects of the reign of terror caused by Pale, his Muskan hordes, and frankly, anyone who supports him. I think they are horrible and should be stopped. They are disrupting the flow of harmony that this world would otherwise have, without question. Not that any of us have lived knowing anything different than this, but still. We know it is here. Somewhere, it is here."

"Okay, but hear me out," reasoned Jack. "You want Pale stopped. We have our own reasons, but we also want to stop Pale. Why wouldn't you want to help?"

"Look, Jack, I do not think I believe in the legend of Ebon and all this prophecy stuff."

"Do you believe in magic?" asked Jack, looking at her fish pirate and his talking cat. In this world, magic was everywhere.

"Sure, I do," Fay scoffed, "but I believe in real things. Things that are here and now, things that I can see and witness with my own eyes, yes? But you are talking about three-thousand-year-old stories. Do you want me to believe that the boy and cat from some paintings on the legendary Wagon of Prophecy—you and Lucky—are standing before me right now?"

"Okay." Jack tried remembering when he did not believe the stories himself. "But, just suppose there was a small chance that what I say is true. Isn't it worth the chance to rid your world of these people who are benefiting from the Muskan horde's raids?"

Again, Fay found herself quiet, as she pondered the words that Jack spoke.

"Please," Jack pleaded. "I didn't choose this adventure, but here it is, in front of me."

Fay was silent as she considered Jack. She glanced at her first mate, Carponius, for a moment, who instantly knew what that look meant and uttered a groan. "Oh, Captain," he garbled nervously. "I do not know about this."

Fay began to pace the floor of the captain's quarters. "Jack," she began, "when I say that there is not any ship faster than the *Minnow Sowta*, I mean it. The reason that is true is because there are five propellers attached to the hull. A very sweet and endearing sorceress put a Spinning Spell on them. There is a lever by the wheel, and my Aquatican helmsman and first mate, Carponius, needs only to pull on it to activate the spell. This ship is fast, very fast. It is the only ship in existence that can get within fifty feet of the falls and not be pulled over the edge from the current."

"Wow," Jack said.

"Hmm. Jack, I think this boat's propulsion system might be why you need to be on this ship in particular. Why no other ship will do."

"What do you mean?"

"Well, maybe the reason no one has ever found the Red Stone of Ebon is because it is near the edge of the Abyss, where no one except flying creatures is able to go. Even so, few of them would dare to venture that far because there are few places to land and rest. There are some places where the land at the bottom of the sea comes up at the edge to help contain it, but much of the edge of the world is uncharted."

"What about the Aquaticans? Can't they swim close to it?"

"No, the current is too strong. There are very few sea creatures of any kind that can survive near the edge, except a select few of the most giant of sea serpents."

"Kind of like the serpent in one of the pictures of me?" Jack asked.

"Based on Lucky's description, maybe." Fay lowered her voice to nearly a whisper. "Jack, a good lot of my crew is new to me. I have not known them long enough yet to know if I can trust them. Half of those I do know would surely mutiny if they knew that I allowed a cat on board. You have seen what most humans in this world think of cats." She stood, drawing a deep breath. "Right, then, this is the deal. We will travel to the Falls and take you to find your stone. But absolutely no word of this yet to the crew. I will decide when to give the command. Also, absolutely no word about Lucky. He stays in my cabin, and he is to never leave it. Ever. Abigail, you can sleep here, as well. You two boys can sleep below with the crew."

"But, Captain," protested Carponius, "what do we tell the crew about why the children are here?"

"Tell them that our guests are my kin. Two brothers and their sister have lost their parents to the Muskans and have come to stay with sweet Aunt Fay. They are my concern. Not the crew's."

"Aye, Captain," replied Carponius, and with a nod and slight bow, he spun on his heel and exited the room to deliver the orders.

Jack grinned broadly and watched as Lucky rubbed his flanks along Fay's legs and wrapped his tail around one of them. "Thank you, Captain," said Jack. "Thank you so much."

Chapter 8

》○《

As the *Minnow Sowta* sailed west toward the Abyss, the days that followed were exciting ones for the children and for Lucky, as well. None of them had ever been on a ship before, so they all struggled with feeling ill while they gained their sea legs. Abigail spent a lot of her time in the captain's cabin with Lucky, trying to work on her spell conjuring—in particular, a Spell of Communication to let Malia know of their progress. She was unsuccessful because she needed rotflower root and roc feathers on hand for the spell to work. Malia had planned to provide Abigail with more tools of the trade, but their time was cut short when word came of the Muskan horde.

Caleb took to life on a ship as though he were born to it. Carponius taught him how to work the lines. On one day, Fay allowed him to man the wheel himself, under Carponius's tutelage, of course. It was on that day that Caleb fell hopelessly in love with Fay, even though she was more than twice his age. As for Jack, he was absolutely thrilled to be on a bona fide pirate ship, even though he struggled more than his friends with seasickness. After that phase finally passed, Jack divided his time between learning from the pirates, helping Fay adjust course whenever he felt them straying from their intended target, and staying in the captain's cabin to spend time with his feline friend. Lucky, although he had to stay quiet in the captain's cabin, remained ecstatic. He loved the smell of the sea, and there was much in the cabin to keep him occupied, including a walk-in hanging locker where he would hide and nestle into various jacket sleeves.

The sea, for its part, supplied waves eager to carry the ship forward, and above them were clear skies and a healthy wind to fill the sails. At night, Jack and Caleb would lie on the deck and look at the stars, although roughly every ten seconds a beam of orange light from the Ahmega Lighthouse would travel across the sky. The stars were different in Sturgus than they were in his world, and its moon, although similar, was a bit smaller than the moon that Jack was accustomed to seeing outside his bedroom window. Jack learned, in fact, that Sturgus was much smaller than Earth. From Caleb's description, Jack surmised that Sturgus was roughly the size of a large country in his world, or maybe the continent of Europe. He also learned that the world of Sturgus was surrounded by sea, except in the south. "You can actually walk to the edge of the world there," Caleb explained to him at one point, "except humans do not go there because that is Sahaland, Land of the Cats."

The pirates were an interesting-enough bunch. The children found it easy to tell Fay's original crew apart from the new recruits from the *Scalawag*. The original crew was very faithful to their captain, and they trusted her judgment unquestioningly. Well, almost unquestioningly. Any grievances they had always went through the proper channels: first, they reported to the quartermaster, who in turn reported to the first mate, Carponius, who in turn told the captain. The *Scalawag*'s crew, on the other hand, was both suspicious and sullen. They complained regularly about conditions, even though they were better than what they had received on their now-sunken former ship. They barked regularly at the children. In one instance, a new crew member snapped directly at the captain. To show them all that she was to be respected, Fay moved faster than anybody the children had ever seen and was on that pirate in moments, sword drawn, and she pummeled him swiftly on the forehead with the flat edge of her blade. He slumped to the deck, unconscious. When he came to, he found himself bound tightly and hanging upside down from the bow with only the mermaid figurehead to keep him company. This just made Fay even more fascinating to Caleb.

There were two Aquaticans on board, Carponius and Gill. While Carponius was blue, Gill was orange, and a pretty orange at that. He wasn't as tall as Carponius, and unlike Carponius, he had a dorsal fin jutting from his back. One time, Jack referred to them as fish pirates and Carponius corrected him, saying that they were called Aquaticans, and they came from an underwater city in the Eastern Sea. For this, Jack apologized. It reminded him of the thoughtless name-calling he used on his neighbor, Mrs. Krauss, and the baseless rumors he had started about her.

Jack observed that, once a day, Carponius and Gill would jump into the sea for a good swim and to hydrate their bodies. They were exceptional swimmers. On one day they were joined by a pod of mermen. The lot of them would dart under and around the *Minnow Sowta*, each showing off their swimming talents.

While Caleb had taken to Carponius despite their rocky start, Jack found himself forging a friendship with Gill. Gill wasn't as boisterous as Carponius and Jack liked that. Gill always spoke softly through his garbled Aquatican voice. Whenever he did anything, his movements seemed more calculated, as if he were weighing the pros and cons of even the simplest task. Because of this, Jack thought that perhaps Gill was a strategic person, and likely the smartest person on the ship. But out of respect for the captain, he kept this to himself.

One evening, while Jack sat on top of the captain's cabin, enjoying the view of the deck and the sea, Gill came from below deck, climbed up the cabin, and sat down next to Jack.

"How is my favorite human boy from another world doing this evening?"

"Hi, Gill," Jack greeted his new friend. "Your favorite boy from another world is doing just fine. How is my favorite orange Aquatican doing this fine evening?"

"I am 'peachy keen,'" he replied, using a term that Jack had used on him just a day earlier.

"Gill, I have a question."

"You need only but to ask," the Aquatican answered, his voice low, his gills fluttering ever so lightly.

"Who is a faster swimmer, you or Carponius?"

"Huh." Gill looked out at the waves. "Well, that all depends."

"On what?" pressed Jack.

"On where we are swimming."

"I don't understand."

"Say Carponius and I were to have a race back to the mainland. In that instance Carponius would win. It would be no contest because we would be swimming at or just under surface level. If the race took me four days to complete, he would complete it in just three. However, let us imagine that the race had to be held at the bottom of the sea instead. With the many obstacles down there, the water turbulence, pressure of the deep, and all that factored in, then you would do best to lay odds on me to win the race."

"Hmm." Jack thought about this. "Is that because you have a dorsal fin and Carponius does not?"

Gill made a gurgling, split-toned laugh as he looked at Jack, his slightly bulbous eyes blinking slowly. "Very observant. That is *exactly* why, my friend. My dorsal fin protects me from rolling as I maneuver and assists when I make sudden turns and stops. However, that does come at the expense of having a slight drag effect as I maneuver through the water, which is why Carponius is faster than me when swimming in one direction. I hope that answers your question, young Jack."

"It does, but why do you have a dorsal fin and Carponius does not?"

"That just depends on who your parents are. My mother had a dorsal fin. My father did not. It is a maternal trait, so I took after my mother."

"So, why are you on this ship, instead of with your people?"

"Why do most people travel? For a little adventure in their lives, right? To see more of the world in order to better understand one's own. Well, that would be the answer for me."

"And Carponius?" asked Jack.

Gill reflected a moment before saying, "Carponius is running away."

"I don't understand."

"Our city is called Algas Marinas, and one day hammer whales attacked."

"Hammer whales?"

"Yes. They are very big. Fifteen feet long and very strong. They were enlisted by the Muskan horde to attack our city. It was a very sad day because although we ultimately fended off the hammer whales, we Aquaticans lost many of our people. Among them was

Carponius's only son. After that, Carponius could no longer stay in Algas Marinas. Everything reminded him of his son, Marlino."

Jack let out a low whistle. "Oh, wow. I'm sorry to hear that." Both sat quietly for a moment, before Jack asked, "So, what's it like down there?"

"In the sea, you mean?" asked Gill, to which Jack nodded, so the Aquatican continued. "Well, for me it is perfect. It is so vast and deep, and you never know what you might see. When I swim in the deep, it is unlike anything I can do out of the water, or even on the water's surface. Everything feels so . . . perfect."

"Wow, I can only imagine what that must be like."

Gill's face lit up. "Why, Jack, you do not have to imagine. There is a way for you to experience this with me."

"But how?" the boy asked. "I would have to stay near the top so I could breathe. I mean, I'm a pretty good swimmer, but only in calm water. Nothing like this." He spread his arms wide and gestured at the vast depths.

"There is something about being an Aquatican that I have not told you yet." Gill laughed, obviously delighted in his conversation with Jack. "We Aquaticans have a special ability that, I must say, we are quite proud of. We can mind-connect with individuals."

"Mind-connect," Jack repeated. "What's that, like telepathy or something?"

"In a sense, yes. You see, Jack, when I mind-connect with another being, they can see everything that I see and hear everything that I hear, even feel what I feel. You will still be able to see and hear from your own body at the same time. I should warn you, though, the experience can be a bit unsettling for some people. It can also make them very dizzy because traveling underwater includes many sudden changes in direction. Because most non-Aquaticans don't have the equilibrium to deal with it, you can fall or become ill. That is why I always recommend that beginners find a nice safe place to sit down and close their eyes."

"Wow. Does Fay know about this?"

"Definitely. In fact, she connects with both Carponius and me all the time. It is usually Carponius when she is off-ship and is trying to get information, and me when she needs to know if she has a problem with any of her crew. She will sit in her cabin while I am below deck, allowing her to learn things other ship captains cannot, like who to trust." Gill stood up and stretched his arms high. "It is time that I head below. I will take you with me the next time I go swimming, and who knows, maybe I will even race Carponius." He jumped from the cabin top and found the stairs leading him below deck.

Jack sat alone, thinking about his Aquatican friend. Thoughts of his best friend back home invaded his mind, and Jack wondered how Timmy would react to seeing an Aquatican for the first time. An Aquatican pirate, no less!

Just then, Jack heard footsteps as Captain Fay walked up to him and sat exactly where Gill had sat just a moment before. "May I join you?"

Jack nodded silently and scooted over for the captain, even though there was plenty of room. Jack noticed some of the pirates were carrying various musical instruments topside and others were preparing grog and grub for a feast. "What are they doing?" he asked the captain.

Fay rubbed her hands together. "Well, we are nearing the Abyss. The crew is getting jittery about it, and they need some distraction.

What better way than to throw a party? Putting them in a better mood will make it easier to get them to rally behind the plan."

"I'm a little confused about this Abyss," Jack admitted. "How it works, I mean. If the sea plunges down the Falls, wouldn't the sea level drop and eventually dry up?"

"You would think so, but no, it does not seem to work that way. There are some who believe that the sea goes over the Falls and then somehow, through magic maybe, comes back up from underneath Sturgus by way of many deep-sea caves, but this has never been proven. Aquaticans and mermen have never reported finding any such passageways."

They both sat in silence for a moment as the smell of roasted fish began to waft up from the galley below. Fay had a black bag at her side and moved it closer to Jack. "Here, this is for you."

"What is it?"

"Well, reach in and find out, silly."

Jack reached into the bag and pulled out a small, single-edged, bladed weapon with a slight curve to it. "Cool, a cutlass," he breathed in quiet awe, eyes traveling along the blade to the wire-wrapped hilt.

"Indeed, one that is not so heavy, a little more your size. Go on, though," she urged, nodding at the bag. "There is more."

Jack reached in a second time and pulled out various fabrics. Clothes? "Pirate garb!" Jack exclaimed as recognition crossed his face. "Hey, these look like the clothes that I'm wearing in those pictures on the urn and on the Wagon of Prophecy."

Fay's eyes widened at Jack's words. "Really? Well . . . perhaps then I was wrong. The prophecy must be true." She gave him a sheepish grin.

"Thank you," Jack said, beaming at his new garb.

Fay waved him off. "Think nothing of it. These belonged to one of my crew I lost when we tried to aid the *Scalawag*. He was about your size. He would be honored that I gave them to you. I gave more appropriate garb for Caleb and Abigail to wear, as well."

"Was he a kid?" asked Jack. "The one who died, I mean?"

"No, he was a gnome, a nice one."

At that moment, Caleb came bursting out of the captain's cabin. "Jack, look at me," he cried gleefully from below. He had donned his pirate garb and had his own cutlass in hand and a smile dominating his face. He held out his arms and turned in a slow circle to model the look.

"Hey, nice! Me too," said Jack, holding up some of his new clothes.

"Put 'em on, Jack," Caleb insisted. "Wear your stuff for the party."

Caleb looked up at Fay then. "Thank you, Auntie Fay," he said and bowed dramatically low before her, ending in a flourish of one hand.

"You are most welcome, Caleb, and you are right. Jack should wear his new clothes tonight. Abigail, too. Tonight, we feast and dance, for tomorrow, adventure awaits us."

From the galley below, the food was brought up. Fish and scallops, steaming vegetables and fruit ripened to perfection. There was grog to drink as well as cider, and juice from a fruit Jack had never heard of. It was all delicious.

They feasted then, making toasts to their captain and for fallen comrades. No pirate was excluded. Even the pirate on watch in the crow's nest was given a hearty meal. At one point, Jack snuck away for a bit with a generous portion of fish that he gave to Lucky, still hiding in the captain's cabin.

With their bellies full and spirits high, Captain Fay stood atop her cabin and raised a mug of grog high above her head. "Alright, you crazy pirates, listen up. That goes for every *Scalawag* and *Minnow Sowtan* onboard. Listen up, and I will tell you a story.

"You have all heard of the legend of Ebon. We all have, about a flying horse, dark as the night, fearsome as a stronsay. Most of us have never believed the tales about the Great Ebon, Traveler of Worlds, Water-Giver of the Water-Starved, and Dragon Destroyer, but we know well the tale of how Ebon was turned to stone, and the stones scattered. Know this, mates. The red rock, the heart of Ebon, was cast into the west. Where it landed, none of us know, but find the red rock and join it with the other two, and a legend can be reborn. Bring back the legend, my friends, and we bring about the end to our most hated mutual foe, Pale.

"I tell you this now because I wish to put a challenge upon each of you. I have discovered the secret to the whereabouts of the red stone. For years, I have been searching for a map that might help us find the Red Stone of Ebon. At Valmar, we found out it is near the Falls."

Murmurs spread throughout the ship; disbelief read on most faces of the crew.

"Yes, my fellow barnacles," she continued, pulling from her belt a rolled-up piece of paper, and holding it high above her head. "I speak truth. I have acquired information that could lead to the very downfall of these wretched Muskan hordes that have been plaguing our lands!"

Jack was impressed with the captain's persuasive story. Later, he would learn that the rolled-up piece of paper was indeed a map, but one leading to a very different treasure that Fay and her crew had already seized a few years earlier.

Some of the crew thought that perhaps the captain was pulling a fast one on them, a grand joke on such a festive night. The pirates all started talking at once, the murmurs turning into shouts.

"What is in it for us?"

"That is only one stone."

"How much loot can be shared from a single stone?"

"How did you discover this?"

Fay gazed across the deck at her crew with fire scorching in her eyes; her tongue was swift and silver as she went on. "How I came across this information is my business. But I can tell you this: as I speak, fellow rebels-in-arms are gathering the blue rock in the north, while others still have gone to the south to claim the purple rock." Jack knew that Fay was changing the story a bit to protect him. If the crew were to know that Jack was part of the prophecy, they might feel deceived and tricked by their captain, and his life could be in danger.

"I know many of you do not believe in legends and such, and I do not blame you for that. There are so many tales and fables to be heard that it can be difficult to separate what is truth and what is a coarse lie. I expect many of you to have severe doubts about my words, so I propose an accord that I am sure will please you all. Follow me as close to the Falls as we can go without going over—and yes, we all will be scared as little children—and help us seek the red stone there. Once the stone is retrieved, I promise you that we will head back to the Kester Islands, and relieve the Islands Master himself of all his grand treasures that he took from honest men. The entirety of the loot can be shared amongst yourselves. No loot for the captain, and none for this ship."

There were a few moments of silence as the crew weighed this news before the cheers swelled and erupted into such a clamor that the noise rocked the ship.

Fay thrust her mug of grog toward the night sky and yelled, "Yes! LET THE NIGHT FEEL OUR MIGHT, FOR WE ARE PIRATES AND OUR CAUSE IS RIGHT!" And with that, she emptied her vessel of its contents, and the others did likewise. She unleashed a roar then, like a banshee or a roc before it swoops in for a kill, leaped dramatically from the top of the cabin and landed firmly on the deck.

Drums were brought forth, along with some odd horns and stringed instruments that Jack had never seen before. Then it started, slowly at first, drums beating in rhythm. The pirates stood near the edges of the deck to give her room. Fay, still grinning almost maniacally, started moving with the beat. She shimmied across the deck with more grace than a pirate ship's captain should ever have. With arms arced over her head, she leaned back at the waist until she faced the stars. Jack was memorized as she spun in one spot with all the beauty and litheness of—well, a cat. *No wonder she gets along with Lucky so well,* Jack thought. *She is something of a cat herself.*

Fay danced across the deck as the strings joined in just as the beat picked up. Her hands danced an intricate pattern separate from the rest of her body, as if she were weaving a spell, both tranquil and transient. Her legs left the deck to freely move in space before landing low on the wooden planks, only to do it again. The horns finally joined in, the pace ever quickening. Fay spun across the floor to Caleb. She grabbed his hand, beckoning him to join. He obliged with a slight blush and soon found himself getting caught up in the rhythm. Fay let go of his hand then, reached out again, and next brought Abigail out into the dance. Abigail was a natural and spun in a circle, celebrating the night. Fay then invited Jack, pausing before him, holding out both hands.

"Absolutely," Jack whispered to himself, barely audible. He grabbed Fay's hands, and she swung him toward the others. He was barely aware of what he was doing, but got caught up in the music, letting it guide him. Soon, pirates were joining in the ever-growing sway. Jack looked around—he could not stop smiling—and saw the entire crew caught up in the magic. The music was nothing he had ever heard before. It was wild, untamed, and tribal. The boy from another world looked up and had to stop dancing for a moment to take it all in. He witnessed thousands of shooting stars parading across the sky, exhibiting various colors; red, blue, and purple. The ship itself rocked back and forth to the steps of the dancers, to the pulse of the drums.

As Jack danced, it reminded him of Caveman's story of dancing and communing with the wolves as blue light shot forth from the mountain itself. That, in turn, reminded Jack of how the blue stone was carried by the Northern Wind and dropped on a mountain far into the north. And it was at that moment that Jack had another epiphany. Before even acquiring the first stone, Jack knew where to find the second one . . .

Other Mountain.

Chapter 9

>> ◦ <<

"Ready, now, this is it, people," Captain Fay sternly called to her crew. "It is time."

The current was beginning to pick up. It was now early dawn and Captain Fay ordered the sails down and the ship to turn around.

Caleb stood with Carponius at the wheel. "Wait, why are we turning around?" he asked.

"We are nearing the edge of the world," Carponius explained. "The propellers can only keep us from going over if we are moving against the current."

All pirates were at the ready. Tension was high, but morale was solid. Each pirate tended to his post with vigilance mixed with silent apprehension. Lines were pulled and cargo was secured.

From the roof of the captain's cabin, Jack and Abigail could see the light from the Ahmega Lighthouse, still streaking across the sky every ten seconds, ending abruptly roughly a mile or so from where the ship was being pulled toward. It was as if the light had hit a barrier and could shine no further. Below the light, the children could see the sea end and spill over into a spray that lifted into the air, while the sky continued into the horizon. Over the edge and below, they felt the faint, rumbling roar of the Falls.

"The edge of the world," Abigail whispered.

The ship completed its turn and now headed astern toward the Falls, picking up speed. Captain Fay climbed on top of the captain's cabin and stood next to Abigail and Jack. She looked down at Carponius and Caleb and commanded, "Propellers on full! Full stop, Carponius!"

Abigail gripped Jack's hand tightly as Carponius pulled on the shaft located next to the wheel. "Aye, Captain." Water sprayed past the ship and downward toward the Abyss as the *Minnow Sowta's* propellers spun fast enough to slow the ship down until it held in place, with the tenuous aid of rudders, now a mere hundred yards from the edge.

Fay put one hand on Jack's shoulder. "Jack, we are here. Now what? We can travel north and south along the Falls if you like, but if that stone is over the edge, well, then, I am sorry. I can go a little closer, but no more."

"But it's right *here*," said Jack. The pulling that Jack was feeling had intensified. It had never felt as strong as it did at that very moment. This was where he was supposed to be, he knew it like he knew he was on a strange ship, in a strange sea, in a strange world. "I can feel it, right below us."

"Well, that sinks it, then." Captain Fay pulled the leather tricorn hat from her head and cast it to the deck in frustration. "I'm not sending any of my crew into this current. They would be swept away in a moment's breath." She bit her lip and turned to the boy from another world. It was a moment before she could meet Jack's persistent gaze. "I am sorry, Jack. Truly I am. But just *look* at that out there." She gestured at the roiling waters.

Carponius shouted up from the wheel. "Captain, I have an idea! You could send me down, tied to a line. I should be fine."

The captain thought for a moment, turned, and walked away a few paces, shaking her head. "I do not advise it. If something big was caught in that current, it could kill you."

"Captain, we are pirates. We put our lives at risk almost every day."

Fay pondered Carponius, who indeed made a fair point about their dangerous occupation. Then she glanced over at Jack for a moment, who seized the opportunity and silently mouthed, "send Gill." Fay gave Jack a quick wink, spun around again, and strode toward her crew. "No. Gill is going instead."

"But Captain—" Carponius began, but Fay halted his words by holding up her palm.

"Carponius, you are my first mate. I need you at the helm. Furthermore, Gill is better at maneuvering in the deep, and we all know it. He is going. Take us away from the edge, about fifty meters more if you will."

"Aye, Captain," Carponius answered grudgingly and pulled at the lever to increase the spin of the propellers. The ship moved slowly away from the world's edge.

As the captain explained the situation to Gill, and the crew readied a line to attach to him, Jack leaned to Abigail. "Why are we moving away from the spot where the stone is?" he asked.

"It is the current," she replied. "If we send him down directly above the stone, the current will send him away from it, but if we position ourselves upstream from the stone, then the current will carry him to the stone."

"Oh," he replied. "I knew that."

The truth was that he didn't know, which Abigail noticed. "Sarcasm?" she asked, offering him a faint smile.

Jack nodded, smiling back. They'd come to understand each other well by then. They watched the crew prepare themselves. Caleb left Carponius at the wheel and joined the other pirates in readying a line for Gill.

"Have you noticed how much Caleb has enjoyed himself on this voyage?" Abigail said.

"Yeah," replied Jack, "he's become a regular pirate. The sea life agrees with him."

"Oh, I know. Have you seen the way he stares at Fay? The boy is in love." Abigail laughed then, and Jack couldn't help but join in.

"Did you see him last night? He was giddy with love when she asked him to dance." He giggled.

"Boys are so silly," Abigail said, smirking. "Does he not realize that she is *old*?"

"Do you think I'm silly?" asked Jack.

Abigail looked at him for a moment, still laughing. "No, not yet, but you will be."

The current rocked the ship with fury, forcing both children to sit down and grab a nearby rail, lest they be sent skidding across the deck below.

"I forgot to tell you," said Jack, changing the subject. "Last night, while we were dancing, that pulling feeling came to me again. I know where the next stone is located now."

"Where?"

When Jack told her, her eyes widened. "Are you absolutely sure?" she asked.

"Yes," said Jack as he turned and began walking down the steps toward Fay, Gill, and the others "I'm sure."

Meanwhile, Fay was talking to Gill. He had stripped down to his skivvies to allow full use of his forearm and calf fins. A pouch was tied around his waist. "Remember," she was saying, "no fancy stuff down there."

"Not to worry, Captain, I like living," he replied in his garbled, watery-sounding voice.

"I mean it, Gill. You go down there, find the red rock, and return to the surface so we can pull you back in. Is that understood?"

"Captain, you forget. It is Carponius, not I, who is the dare-doer among us Aquaticans. I will stick with the plan. I promise. No fancy stuff." Gill was genuine in his speech.

"Wait," Jack said, "how is he going to know which way to go once he's down there? He's not feeling a pulling toward it, I am. Is there a way I can go?"

Fay looked at Jack. "That is a point that I do not want to entertain. The waters are too fast, and it is very, very deep. You can see my hesitation to even have one of the Aquaticans go down there. Anyone that isn't an Aquatican does not stand a chance."

"But what if we mind-connected?" Jack interjected, which caught Fay by surprise. "Gill told me about it yesterday. That way, I would still be on the boat, but could guide him."

"It is a reasonable idea. Just know that it can be a strange experience for those who have never tried it," cautioned Fay. "You will need to take a seat."

"Okay," Jack said, noting it was the same advice Gill provided last night. "What do we do next?"

"Jack, come here," said Gill, motioning him off to the side. Jack stood in front of his Aquatican friend, whose scaly skin now glistened in the morning sun like leaves on a sunny autumn day. "Now, do not worry, this will not hurt in the slightest." Gill put both of his fin hands to Jack's face. The thumbs covered his eyes while the fingers covered his ears. Jack felt a spray of liquid shoot into his eyes and ears, which made him flinch in surprise. "There, all done. Now, blink several times, Jack, and look at me."

Jack did as he was told, then opened his eyes and was taken aback at what he saw. An image appeared overlaid by what he was already looking at, except in reverse. It was jarring, to say the least.

"Shut your eyes and sit down, Jack. It will help," Gill suggested.

Jack sat on the deck as he was told and shut his eyes. What he was left looking at was nothing short of amazing. He was looking at himself sitting a few paces away from Fay with his eyes closed. The view was different from the way humans see. It was as if he were looking through a fisheye lens of a camera, with the center part of the picture appearing to be very close up, and everything else bending away at the edges.

"Wow!" whispered Jack.

"While I will not be able to hear what is going on around you, I will be able to understand what you say from the vibrations you make in your throat while you talk. That way you will be able to travel with me and guide me on which way to go once we are down there," Gill said. Then he spoke with just his mind. *Understood?*

Jack nodded. *Got it.*

The ship's line was tied around one of Gill's ankles and the crew dropped him from the ship's stern and into the water. Caleb and a small team of pirates slowly let out the line, ready to pull it back in when the captain gave the order. Jack sat on the deck, his eyes shut, while Abigail watched over him.

Assisting in the line, Caleb stood next to the twin pirates. He had just recently found out that they were named Jorge, and that they were not twins after all.

"If you don't mind my asking, I learned that you aren't twins. So, were you the victim of a sorcerer's spell?" Caleb asked.

"No," Jorge replied. "It was a birth defect. One me, two bodies."

"Ah." Caleb nodded as if he understood, though he did not really understand at all. It was no matter, really; Jorge was good people. They kept a vigilant watch on Caleb and his friends.

Under the surface, the current pushed Gill westward, the water thick with bubbles. As they swam together down into blackness, leaving the light above, Jack's eyes adjusted with Gill's to the darker surroundings. Gill had previously told Jack that Aquaticans had comparable vision with humans when outside of water, but in the brine, they could spot a clam from twenty fathoms away, which Jack found to be true. As they looked west, Jack could see the sea floor rise up at the edge. *Like a bowl,* he thought, *overflowing with too much soup.* In response to this thought, Gill chuckled a bit. They swam ever deeper, and the harsh current eventually subsided. It wasn't long before the waters were calm, nearly gentle. The bottom of the sea came into view, and Jack could see several cave openings on the sea floor.

Well, Gill said to Jack's mind, *what do you think? I am betting that we must go into one of those caves. But . . . which one?*

Sitting on the deck of the *Minnow Sowta,* Jack felt Gill was right. *Swim and let's stop a moment over each one,* he said. *It's definitely in one of them. I can feel it.*

They swam and floated over the first one.

No, said Jack as he covered his ears with his hands to block out the noise from his immediate surroundings on the ship. *Try the next one.*

They swam upon the second opening in the ground—a rather large cave. They hovered over the vast opening, peering in. The cave dropped several dozen feet, before veering off to one side, out of view.

Jack's head pounded. "This is it," Jack uttered aloud from topside, his throat tightening. Then he took a deep breath. *Yep. It's down there in that cave. I can feel it. Let's go in.*

They swam into the cave with the hope that Gill would have enough line from the *Minnow Sowta* to see past the corner. Slowly they swam down, down, down, into the black, into the dark nothingness, so dark that even Gill began having trouble making out his surroundings.

We can barely see, Jack told him.

Yes, Gill confirmed, *it has become very dark for us down here.*

The cave walls curved ahead, and as he rounded the corner, Gill and Jack were met with a curious sight: a red glow pulsed in the blackness of it all. They froze for a moment, bobbing in the stillness of the water. Could that be the Red Stone of Ebon, the heart?

Jack? he questioned.

That's it, replied Jack. *That is the red stone.*

They tried to swim closer, but the line held Gill's body fast. They had reached the end of his rope, quite literally. *We are at the end of my line. We cannot swim any closer.*

"What? No!" yelled Jack, catching Fay's attention.

"What's going on?" she asked, bewildered, striding over.

"He's at the end of the line," repeated Jack, his eyes squeezed shut as he sat cross-legged on the deck.

"Tell him to come back," Fay said. "We will see if we can tie onto the line somehow."

Jack, Gill said. *No. We should not come back empty-handed, especially after being this close.*

Jack's vision appeared to swivel downward as the Aquatican untied the bowline knot at his ankle.

We are going to swim straight for it, grab the stone, do an about-face, and hopefully come straight back to the rope. If necessary, we can use the glow from the stone as a torch to help us find the line more easily.

Gill, be careful, Jack pleaded.

They glided forward, barely moving save the slight flutter of calf fins. With arms extended in front of them, like an arrow, long and lean, they approached and could soon tell that, yes, the red glow was a stone.

Topside on the ship, Jack couldn't help but beam himself at the sight of it and speak. *That's it.*

It sat nestled amongst some much larger stones that were speckled yellow with a little bit of green. They hovered over the round rocks and then, ever so carefully, picked up the red, glowing stone. It felt warm to the touch, and it was inviting to their senses to cradle it in their hands. It was beautiful. Perfect. Gill and Jack briefly enjoyed the stillness of that moment.

The very next moment that came to them was one of horrified realization. Jack felt Gill's body jolt and then became completely rigid as his bulging eyes blinked and gawked at the other rocks. Jack's breath quickened.

The larger stones, the ones that were speckled yellow with a little bit of green, were not rocks.

They were eggs.

They hovered over the half-dozen or so eggs, nestled into that part of the cave floor next to a peculiar-looking wall. A peculiar wall indeed, which had begun to move.

Neither of them remembered turning around. They swam through the cave, toward its exit, with speed that would have made any Aquatican proud. There wasn't even time to secure the Red Stone of Ebon in the pouch. Instead, it was clutched in one hand with a vise-like grip, as if life depended on it. There wasn't time to tie the rope back on either; they swam past it without a second thought. The roar that came from behind them was sudden and deafening.

On the deck of the *Minnow Sowta*, Jack's heart thudded hard in his chest. He stood, wobbly on his legs, and began yelling and gesturing with his arms. "Gill! Gill! Swim! Swim!"

Abigail worriedly kept guard in front of Jack, trying to make sure he didn't draw too much attention.

"Why? What is going on?" asked Fay, striding over to the children.

"He's untied," gasped Jack, his eyes still tightly shut, breathing heavily, "and there is something chasing him. Something big."

Fay spun on her heel and began barking commands at the crew.

As they shot out of the mouth of the cave, the Aquatican managed to get a quick glimpse behind them. In that moment in the murky, churning waters, they saw serrated teeth and enormous, gaping jaws that widened as they neared, threatening to swallow Gill whole.

It is a stronsay! Gill screamed.

"It's a stronsay," Jack echoed aloud. He relayed this news for the captain's benefit, but also because he was terrified!

"Oh no," Fay said. She turned and signaled to Jorge, who yelled, "STROOON-SAAAY!"

The crew on deck gasped and double-timed their efforts to ready the line for Gill. Those not working the line drew swords, and two more went belowdecks to ready the canons.

Jack felt incredibly dizzy, felt like he was watching a fast, blurry videogame as they made a few quick course adjustments and they noticed the stronsay was not quite as quick, as its huge body had to take a longer, wider arc.

"It's your dorsal fin," Jack exclaimed, shaking off the carsick feeling, and forgetting that he didn't need to speak. *Its speed is no match for your dorsal fin. Come back up, come back up to the surface now, Gill!*

This quick maneuver bought Gill the briefest of moments to reorient himself and start swimming eastward, away from the edge of the world.

We cannot start our ascent, at least not yet, Gill said. *The current would still grab us and send my body over the Falls into the Abyss.*

The stone pulsed in their fin-hand, bringing more strength.

The stronsay was once again closing in at a terrifying speed, and the creature's gaping jaws came all around their peripheral view, threatening to snap its mouth shut. They edged just ahead of the beast and then pivoted, another surge and pivot again, and again, zig-zagging their way ever eastward.

Was Gill farther eastward than the *Minnow Sowta* now? Jack wasn't sure, but he could feel that Gill was beginning to tire and knew that Gill had to do something decisive, and soon, or the stronsay would most surely make a bite-sized snack out of him. Jack could feel the stone guiding them then. *Go up. Go up now,* it seemed to say. So, they pivoted once more and swam upward.

It was just after this moment that Gill released his mind-connection with Jack. *Sorry, Jack. This part will be tricky. I do not want you to see what might happen next, especially if it is bad. May I see you soon, friend.*

"No—!" Jack shouted as his view suddenly went dark.

Meanwhile, on the deck of the *Minnow Sowta,* the crew waited impatiently for any sign of their imperiled shipmate. They knew that any moment Gill would resurface, and they wanted to be ready to help in any way they could.

With the mind-connection broken by Gill, Jack's eyes flew open in a panic and he stood more quickly than he should have. He stumbled along the way, shaking off the effects of the mind-connection, and he grabbed Abigail's hand and they rushed to the bow of the ship. They were the first to see Gill. The Aquatican breached the water at a remarkable speed, just east and in front of the ship, arced higher than the ship deck itself, and, as he descended, was heading straight for them. Abigail grabbed Jack and pulled him aside as Gill torpedoed in, smashing onto the deck with a loud thud. He skidded into the pirates holding the line. His body a crumpled heap, he uttered a low moan, then lay still.

Fay sped at once to Gill's side. The Aquatican lay injured, looking at her with blurred, half-open eyes. He lifted his good arm, holding it out to her.

"My captain," he croaked in a garbled whisper and pressed something small into her hand.

Just then they heard it, the mighty bellow of the stronsay as it burst from the depths. All eyes on the ship turned forward, and the entire crew let out what could only be described as a collective gasp. They would talk about it for years. It would become the stuff of fables and legends. Well over one hundred feet in length, the stronsay rose high out of the water, higher even than Gill had, its scales glistening red in the afternoon sun, its four massive, webbed limbs pressed solidly against its body, its long neck supporting a massive head with razor teeth and cold, black eyes. The beast shot over the bow at an angle and chomped down on one of the masts, snapping it in two. The stronsay's arc of descent carried it past the stern, where it disappeared back into the sea.

The crew scattered to both sides as the mast came crashing down and punched a hole into the roof and foremost section of the captain's cabin. It barely missed Carponius, who staggered at the impact and clutched at the wheel of the helm to keep his footing. The captain yelled at her first mate. "Carponius, get us out of here!"

The blue Aquatican nodded once and pulled back on the lever, and, below the waterline, five propellers spun even faster than before, pushing the *Minnow Sowta* in sea, away from the edge of the world and away from the livid stronsay.

The stronsay resurfaced and gave pursuit, defying the current. This was her home and she bowed to nothing, not even the sea. She came upon the *Minnow Sowta* from the port side, biting into it mid-ship with a ferocity only reserved for a mother protecting her not-yet-born kin. Then, just like that, it was over. The *Minnow Sowta* was indeed fast as Captain Fay had said, and they evaded the great beast. Now that the ship was churning away from her territory, the stronsay returned to her nest, satisfied that this intruder would not return.

The damage to the *Minnow Sowta* was extensive, but the hull was intact. Jack sat on the deck and took it all in. The main mast lay across the deck and both on and in the captain's cabin. Was Lucky okay? A sizable chunk of the deck, mid-ship on the port side, was missing altogether.

Gill lay motionless on the deck.

It was clear to everyone that he was in bad shape. In the late afternoon sun, Jack noticed that his normally vibrant orange color now had a greyish tinge to it. Whether he would recover was not a question that Jack himself could answer; the brave Aquatican had crashed pretty hard. The crew's collective expression was somber and anxious.

Expecting that this adventure might not go as planned, Malia had armed Abigail with three Potions of Healing. Now, the flame-haired sorceress-in-training sprinted over to Gill's broken body, and Fay stepped aside to give her room. Jack watched with both amazement and appreciation as Abigail administered a vial to Gill's fish-lips. The potion had an almost immediate effect. The Aquatican sat up slowly, smiling weakly but with gratitude at Abigail. His normal color was returning. Slowly, he tested his left arm as the broken bones inside began to fix themselves. Then he brought a hand to his midsection where earlier he had felt intense pain inside his body. Gill winced at the sensation, all the while blinking appreciatively at Abigail. Members of the crew nodded and spoke quietly amongst themselves. Some breathed a sigh of relief.

Seeing that Gill was going to be okay, Jack now got to his feet, intent on finding Lucky in what remained of the captain's cabin, but it suddenly became a moot point.

"Caaaaat!" someone yelled.

All eyes were now focused on the opening in the wreckage of the cabin. Lucky's head looked tiny as he peered out of the gaping hole in the cabin, a little dazed, hackles raised in alarm. More of the pirates started shouting.

"Demon cat!"

"Throw it overboard!"

"It carries bad luck. Kill it! Kill it!"

"This is why the sea serpent attacked us!"

Fay ran to stand between Lucky and her quickly angering crew and swung her sword back and forth in her hand as if it were a natural extension of her arm. "No one, and I mean no one, touches this cat!" she hissed at them. "I have offered him safe passage."

The crew was not convinced, and there was a great deal of yelling back and forth. Jack darted behind Fay and scooped up Lucky, holding him close. Abigail ran into what remained of the captain's cabin for a moment and reemerged, carrying the three shoulder bags of the children. Caleb stood amongst the pirates, stunned, looking unsure of what to do. He tried to make his way to Lucky and the others but found it difficult with so many pirates in his way, as well as the fallen mast.

Through all the yelling, the pirates cautiously and deliberately took sides. Most of Captain Fay's original crew stood by her, even though many of them had clear reservations about her decision to bring a cat onboard. Caleb stayed close to Jorge. The former crew of the *Scalawag* was united in their hatred of cats. It was clear that they wanted Lucky dead. Aside from a few snarls and mumblings, the deck became eerily tense and silent. All that could be heard was the creak of the ship itself.

Kneeling silently behind where Fay and Jack stood, Abigail reached into her shoulder bag and pulled out a small pouch. She carefully but quickly emptied the pouch onto the deck. Silver powder poured out, mixed with leaves and beach sand. It smelled of magic. Abigail took a deep breath and sighed contentedly. Even surrounded by all the commotion, the smell of magic always made Abigail giddy inside.

Fighting erupted among the pirates. The sound of steel clashing against steel thundered across the deck.

Abigail grabbed Jack by the leg, and the boy whipped his head around and down. "Stay close," she called to him, and then she started chanting while waving her arms over the small pile of silver powder. Silver smoke rose from the powder at a furious rate. Abigail's chanting rose with the smoke, getting louder as the smoke thickened ever higher. She had to concentrate especially hard now to get the wording and tone right, to block out the chaos surrounding her.

Jack put Lucky down between Abigail and himself. One of the pirates ran past Fay. With sword raised, he screamed with anger as he attempted to kill Lucky. But Jack was there, and before he realized what he'd done, he brought his sword down on the pirate's foot. The pirate's screams of anger turned to screams of pain as he fell hard onto the deck, blood gushing from his foot. Jack's heart was pounding with adrenaline. They'd come so far: no one was going to harm Lucky!

Caleb, upon realizing what Abigail was up to, increased his efforts to get to them. Suddenly, one of the pirates grabbed him, jerking his body backward. "Thinking of joining your friends?" slurred the pirate with fury in his eyes. "I do not think that will be happening today."

Caleb swung his cutlass at the pirate, but the more-skilled seaman easily deflected it. Caleb then spun in place and swung low, cutting the pirate in the back of his leg. The pirate slammed to the deck, cursing as he fell. Caleb made a break for it, but still could find no clear path to his friends. He started to zig-zag his way toward the silver smoke with determination.

The smoke had thickened and as it spun and swirled, it grabbed onto the ship, causing it to pitch and yaw. Abigail stopped chanting and pulled Jack and Lucky close to her. "Where is Caleb?" she shouted as the smoke engulfed them.

Fay looked for Caleb then and saw the sea of pirates between her and him. The smoke was beginning to diminish, and she turned to Carponius and shouted, "The ship is yours! Watch over Caleb." Fay, captain of the *Minnow Sowta*, jumped right into the smoke just as the last of its billowy wisps dissipated. Eventually, the crew stopped fighting and looked about the ship in utter and complete confusion. The cat was no longer onboard the ship. For that matter, neither were Jack and Abigail, nor their captain.

Chapter 10

>>∘<<

The next thing Jack knew, he was standing ankle-deep in snow. His first reaction was surprise, before the events that had transpired began to sink into his head. Abigail had successfully activated the Spell of Transport. Now, wherever they were, it was yet another place he'd never been before, and Fay was with them.

Why was Fay with them?

"Caleb!" Abigail cried. "We left Caleb!" She was frantic. She began pleading to no one in particular, to somehow undo what had been done. What she, herself, had done.

Jack stood dumbfounded, with Lucky in his arms. The sudden shift from living on a ship to standing on land made Jack dizzy. His legs felt like rubber, his stomach a bit queasy.

They stood in the woods, on a mountainside. It was snowing lightly, and the sky was the color of iron with bluish highlights.

Abigail, eyes blurred with tears, stumbled about. "Caleb, I am sorry. I am just—so sorry."

Fay stood by Jack with quiet composure.

"Okay. I am glad you came with us," said Jack with a furrowed brow, "but why?"

"Because you forgot something," she said and strode over to Abigail.

"But we need to go back for Caleb," the girl kept saying.

"Unless you have another one of those spells, you know we cannot do that." Fay spoke low and evenly and put her arms around Abigail's shoulders as they lurched with each uncontrolled sob.

"What have I done?" Abigail could not be consoled.

"You did what you had to," Fay reassured her. "I am sorry it had to be such an adult decision, but you made the right one. Even Caleb knows it. You are on a mission to collect the Three Stones of Ebon. Sometimes you must choose between options even when you do not like either one. Also, everything was happening at once. I think you made the right choice, Abigail."

Abigail wept into Fay's shoulder a little longer, then looked up at her friend with a wail. "And the stone. We forgot the stone, the most important thing in this crazy journey!"

After a moment of silence, Jack gasped in realization. "Wait, Captain. You said you jumped in because we forgot something. *You* have the red stone, don't you?"

Fay grinned and reached into her pocket. "Smart young man. Yes, it is right here." She pulled out the glowing red stone and pressed it into Abigail's hands. Instantly, Abigail felt a calmness rush through her, and her erratic breathing slowed to near normal.

"It is beautiful," she whispered.

"Yes, I think so, too."

Jack walked over to them with Lucky still in his arms. Lucky, Jack noticed, was not too keen on the idea of walking in the snow. The young tabby was content to be cradled by his favorite human. Jack was happy about it too. He was cold himself, not dressed for the chilly climate.

Abigail eyed Jack. "Here," she said, and handed him the stone. "I am feeling better now."

Nearly as soon as he took the glowing red stone, Jack felt warm again, and his land legs returned as well. Lucky purred and rubbed his chin across the stone. Jack looked across at Fay with mild awe, as she seemed to not be very bothered by the cold.

The boy gazed down at the red stone, which glowed more softly now. "Wow. Gill did it," Jack whispered. Then he looked at Abigail with a sensation of respect and pride. "And you, you healed him. That was very cool."

The flame-haired girl beamed through her tears, now drying on her freckled face. "Thanks, Jack."

Jack then looked at Fay. "You abandoned your ship to make sure we got this?"

"If the prophecy turns out to be true, then it is worth it. Besides, I told Carponius that the ship was his. He will take care of her until I can find them again. I also told him to watch over Caleb, which I know he will do anyway, as he has taken to him like kin." Fay looked at Abigail as she spoke of their left-behind friend. "Now, from the looks of our surroundings, I would say that we are somewhere in the Zuffen Northlands."

"Yes," replied Abigail. "Other Mountain, to be exact."

Fay's tone was wary. "Other—that is wolf territory. We humans do not belong."

"Maybe not," said Jack, "but it's where the next stone is located."

"Are you sure?"

"Caveman told me the story of how he lived with the wolves of Other Mountain for two years," Jack explained to her. "He spoke of a special night, the Great Get-Together of Old Wolves or something."

"It was the Great Ancestral Gathering," corrected Abigail. "I have heard the story as well."

"Right," continued Jack without a hitch, "what she just said: the Great Ancestral Gathering. Anyway, during the event, blue light shoots out of the mountain into the sky. I believe that the blue light comes from the blue stone."

The ship's captain considered Jack's words, biting her thumbnail. "Hm. You feel that strongly about it." She said this more as a statement than a question.

"Yes. I was right about the red stone."

"Yes. Yes, you were," the pirate captain agreed thoughtfully. "Well. It is definitely colder here. I propose that we set up camp first, and then we can discuss our next step. We do not want to encounter the wolves without some sort of plan."

Jack and Abigail agreed, and Jack helped Abigail gather wood while Fay cleared some snow and built a fire pit. Lucky, not a fan of snow, jumped onto a stump while they worked. He used his paws to brush off the snow, clearing a not-too-wet spot to sit on.

With the fire built, Abigail distributed the three shoulder bags among them. Fay took Caleb's bag and was pleased to see that he had kept his mini-bow and arrows in it. Each bag still contained a blanket, which made everyone smile. Abigail, who was particularly good at botany, knew exactly where to look to find some tasty jigger root and ice berries for them to eat. Jack wasn't too keen on the jigger root, but he ate it without complaining.

During their meal the three talked extensively about the events of the day. "That was definitely the biggest animal I have ever seen," Jack continued between chews. "We have whales in my world that get pretty big, but nothing compared to that."

"Stronsays," Fay stated, "are quite rare. In all my seafaring years, that is the first one I have ever seen. I once saw a dragon that was nearly the same size, but not quite. You are right, Jack—now that we have a bit of distance from it, I would say seeing one for real was very . . . *cool,* to use your expression."

Jack smiled. It pleased him that both Fay and Abigail made efforts to use his lingo when talking to him. He was also amused that people seemed to gravitate toward learning the word "cool." Then, just as quickly, his smile faded. "Fay, is Caleb going to be okay?"

"I should think so," she replied. "Until Caleb decides differently, he is part of my crew now, and Carponius has taken more than a liking to him. This is not my story to tell, but suffice to say that Carponius had a family once. A family that was lost to war. Caleb is the same age that Carponius's son would be if he were alive today."

Jack nodded in confirmation. "Actually, Gill told me that about Carponius. Thanks for reminding me. Yes, Caleb is in good hands."

"I am just glad nobody else was hurt," commented Abigail.

"Yes," replied Fay, "that was fortunate."

"Sorry about your ship getting damaged. Again, I mean," Jack told Fay.

Fay tilted her head and wrinkled up her nose slightly. "An unfortunate setback, but well worth the risk. She is under Carponius's command right now. I know he will take care of her until I get back."

"What about the crew? Do you think he will be able to calm them in the meantime?" asked Abigail.

Fay stoked the fire with a long branch. "I hope so. Carponius has all the respect of my original crew, plus Lucky is no longer onboard. That should appease the situation a bit."

"The mast is broken. Will they be able to sail back to Valmar?" Abigail asked. Jack nodded in agreement, concerned for his friend Caleb.

"They have propellers infused with the Spinning Spell. As long as the stronsay did not damage the rudder, they should be fine. They might not necessarily go to Valmar, though. There are a couple of island ports that are closer. They will get the mast replaced, then disembark anyone who still feels some sort of way toward mutiny. Those who hold favor will sail out to the Kester Islands to claim the bounty promised to them for helping retrieve the red stone."

They fell silent then. All around them seemed quiet, too. No animals could be heard. There was no wind and—save the fire—there was no movement anywhere else, either. The trees were still and now the snow had stopped falling. The ground was a dazzling white as the sky grew ever darker.

Jack reached into his pocket and produced the red, glowing stone. The feeling of it gave him confidence. It warmed his body and banished any fears of what might lie ahead in his quest to acquire the other two stones.

"So," he said aloud, "this is the heart of Ebon."

"That is a glowing red stone that holds the heart of Ebon," corrected Abigail.

"I see," said Jack, although he didn't. Jack didn't understand nuances of magic because there was no magic like this in his world. But he tried to correct himself as he continued, "And the blue stone holds the mind of Ebon."

"Yes," Abigail said quietly. "And the purple stone holds his soul."

"What will you do after you collect all three stones?" asked Fay as she popped a handful of ice berries into her mouth.

"I think we need to bring them to the statue, which is also the body of Ebon," replied Jack.

Just then they heard a low growl. Standing a dozen or so feet away was a great wolf. Her fangs were exposed, and her stance was guarded. Blood soaked her upper flank, but if she was injured, she didn't show it. She stood firm, golden-brown eyes locked solidly on them.

Lucky sprang into Jack's arms and Fay readied herself with her sword. She made two swift strokes in the air from side to side to prove to the wolf that she knew how to use it.

Yet the wolf moved steadily closer, instantly giving away that she was wounded with a limp that she clearly attempted to mask by advancing on them diagonally. "First, you murder us, and now you think your children can move in not one day after your bloody massacre."

The children stood behind Fay. Jack had his own cutlass out and held it ready, though it was difficult with Lucky climbing behind his shoulders for safety.

Fay looked at the wolf with calm reserve and asked, "What massacre?"

The wolf glared with a deathly demeanor. "Do you think me a fool? Am I to believe that it is merely coincidence that humans would dare enter wolf territory less than one moon after the Muskan horde's attack?"

"Muskan attack?" breathed Abigail, her breath quickening from fear that the wolf was about to leap at them. "Oh, no! They have been here?"

"Listen to me," said Fay to the wolf. "This is the first time that we have heard this terrible news. I assure you, we are *not* with the Muskans."

"Liar!" The wolf snarled viciously. "This is not the first time that you have heard this news, for, without fail, you would have seen the massive numbers leaving Other Mountain as you arrived. You would have known that they were here to kill us."

"We traveled a different way," Jack interjected.

"There *is* no other way, human child."

"A few hours ago, we were far away at the western edge of the world, at sea. The girl behind me is a sorceress's apprentice, and she used a Spell of Transport to bring us here," Fay explained.

"Still, you lie," snarled the wolf.

"No," insisted Fay. "I speak truth. Look, as a gesture of good faith, I am lowering my sword."

Lucky, still on Jack's shoulders, said to him, "Hang on—why is she lowering her sword?" His fur was slightly raised, and he tried his best to fight his instincts and not dig his claws through his human friend's clothes and into his skin.

Jack whispered, "Because we need to show the wolf that we are not her enemy."

Lucky wasn't convinced. He jumped from Jack's shoulders, bolted across the snow, and, with his claws extended, latched onto and dashed up the nearest tree. "There," he said from a branch, "*now* we can all be friends."

"Lowering your weapon is not good enough," snapped the wolf. "Now tell me: why should I trust you?"

"Because," Jack interjected, "we are friends with Caveman."

If it was at all possible to startle a wolf, Jack did it. She tilted her head, ears perked forward, and her golden-amber eyes widened as she studied Jack for the first time. Then she narrowed her eyes into slits and growled with suspicion. "And how do you know Caveman?"

"It is a long story," Abigail put in. "Perhaps if you will let us tend to your wounds, we can trade stories."

"You will answer the question now! How do you know Caveman?"

Jack spoke more quickly. "He was one of the first people that my cat and I met when we first came to this world. He told me about the time when he lived with the Pack of Other Mountain."

"Came to this world? Where exactly are you from, human child, that I should believe such nonsense?" Her hair began to stand on end, her words slicing through the chilled air.

"Believe him. Please," said Abigail. "Look." She pulled out a small bottle from her shoulder bag. "This is a Potion of Healing. Please, let me help you."

The wolf stood, still growling, unsure of what to do.

"We seek to parley," said Fay to the bristling canine, "I am going to take all our weapons, including the ones in our bags, and put them under the tree over there that the cat ran up. Surely, if we tried to harm you, you would kill at least one of us before we could get to our weapons." She then gathered the items, not taking her eyes off the wolf, and moved slowly with them toward the tree. "Let my friend Abigail heal you. Let us trade stories. Both children do know Caveman; it was he who sent them on their quest."

There was a long moment with everyone unmoving, save for the warm, tense breath that steamed from nostrils and parted mouths. The wolf stared them down with darkening eyes, and her hind flanks quivered ever so slightly. Then she sat, and it was only then that it became clear to all that only defiance had sustained her until that moment, and now her pain was such that she could not stand up any longer.

Abigail slowly approached the wolf, her body trembling despite the strength that the red stone had given her, a Potion of Healing gripped firmly in her hand. She paused before putting her hand up to the wolf's mouth because it frightened her to no end. "This has a slight sour taste to it," she told the wolf. Then she shut her eyes, held her breath, and tipped the vial between the canine's great teeth.

Surprisingly, the wolf lapped up every drop of the potion. An immediate sign in the wolf's eyes showed that she already felt better. Her ears perked up as the wound in her flank began to heal, the skin resealing itself from where a sword had been driven in. Once the wound closed, her blood-soaked coat was the only sign that she had recently been in battle.

The wolf peered at Abigail, now with calm eyes. "Human child, you have the makings of a great sorceress. Thank you for healing my body. Now, if only there was a way to heal my heart. I feel I may never recover from losing my entire pack."

"I think I can help." Jack stepped forward, with extreme caution, and stood next to Abigail. He reached into his pocket and produced the glowing red stone. "Put your nose to this."

The stone began to emit a warmness before the wolf even touched it. Then, as she pressed her muzzle against it, Jack could sense a renewed vigor course through her body, her defeated attitude shedding from her like old wolf hair.

"What is this stone that it can heal such a broken heart?"

"I think," said Fay, "that now would be a good time to trade stories."

"Agreed," said the wolf. She gazed up into the tree. "You can come down. I promise not to eat you."

"If it's all the same to you, I think I'll stay here," replied Lucky.

"As is your choice," she said, licking her chops at him.

The wolf sat with the others by the fire and introduced herself as Quasita. She then fixed her gaze on Jack. "I am curious. Where do you come from and how did you come about such a marvelous stone?"

With a deep breath, Jack told the wolf his story, and at the proper moments Abigail and Fay added their unique perspectives. The wolf was especially interested to hear about Caveman; where he had been all of this time, what he was doing, and how he was doing. They told Quasita everything: about Valmar, Lucky's mishap at the tavern, the *Minnow Sowta,* their encounter with the stronsay, and leaving Caleb behind. Abigail became teary-eyed as she recalled the last part. They even told the wolf why they had come to Other Mountain.

Quasita looked at Jack incredulously. "You think that the blue light that shoots out of the mountain and allows our ancestors to commune with us comes from a blue stone that holds the mind of Ebon?"

"Yes," answered Jack truthfully.

"This is all very interesting," continued Quasita. "You come at a time when all that is left of the pack is me. Once I die, the Pack of Other Mountain will be no more. There is no reason I should not help you, especially if it will ensure the eventual defeat of my enemies. I am curious, though: what would you do if I said no? Would you fight me for the blue stone?"

"No," said Jack without hesitation. "I now consider you a friend. We wouldn't do that."

"I see," said the wolf. "Would you give up your quest, then, or would you steal it when my back was turned?"

Dead silence. Finally, it was Fay who spoke up. "Quasita, you were right not to trust us when we first met. The truth is we would steal it. I am sorry, but what the stone represents is that important to us."

"Thank you." Quasita looked at Fay with the intensity that could only come from a wolf's stare. "Honesty is very important between friends, would you agree?"

Then the wolf began her story. "If you have spoken with Caveman, then you know that Varg is . . . was . . . our pack leader."

"Yes," said Jack, "he told us."

"I was his mate. One week before the Muskan horde attacked, a blue heron visited the pack and told us the horde was headed our way."

"A blue heron," interrupted Fay. "Did he mention his name?"

"He said his name was Baron. Do you know him?"

"I do," confirmed Fay, the corners of her mouth turning up slightly at the thought of her avian friend. "But please, go on with your story."

"Well, a choice had to be made," continued Quasita. "Run or fight. The pack looked to our leader. Varg made the decision to stay. Other Mountain was our home, and we would not leave it. We hid the cubs and rallied together, then waited for the approaching horde. The Muskans outnumbered us four to one, yet—in the beginning—it seemed that we would be victorious. The land is ours and we move through the wood with deftness and brutality that precede our reputation.

"We were fierce, and the frontline of the horde fell quickly before our bite. They kept coming, though, and the battle shifted. We began to fall under the onslaught of swords and arrows. I found myself battling a centaur at the top of an embankment. I wounded the centaur terribly but, before I could deliver the finishing bite, the centaur's sword found its way into my flank. I then tumbled down the slope, landing unconscious at the bottom. By the time I woke, it was all over. The Muskans were loading my dead kin onto a wagon; their pelts to be made into clothes. It was all I could do to stay hidden in the trees when I saw my beloved Varg, unmoving, at the top of the pile."

It was Abigail who first spoke. "I am so sorry." Her eyes were watering, and she surprised Quasita by putting her arms around her and pressing her cheek to the wolf's muzzle. Her action was not denied, and the wolf allowed herself to be held briefly by the human child.

Quasita again looked at Jack. "Other Mountain is sacred wolf territory. I may be the last wolf of my pack, but I am still honor-bound to the laws of it. No, I cannot just let all of you go, even though we are friends."

Jack studied Quasita's intense face. "So, you will allow me to retrieve the stone, but only if I go alone." Before she could say anything, he continued. "Of course. Enough trespassers have trampled your hills."

"I will wait here with your people. Can you find the stone by yourself?"

"I think so. I'm feeling the same pull I felt when we were searching for the red stone."

Fay spoke up. "If we take the blue stone, you might not be able to commune with your ancestors anymore."

"There will be no more ceremonies." Quasita's voice dripped with sadness.

Jack looked at Fay. "Will you hold onto the red stone until I come back?"

Fay declined and held it out to him. "You should take it. We have the fire to keep us warm. The red stone will do the same for you."

Jack nodded and then looked up at the tree. "Hey, are you gonna be okay until I get back?"

"Yeah," called Lucky to his human. "Not to worry, I'll be right here."

"It is getting dark," said Abigail. "How will you see?"

Jack pulled the red stone back out of his pocket. It glowed brightly. "This should do."

"Good luck," said Fay.

Jack looked up at Lucky, still sitting on his branch. The two looked intently at each other but neither said a word. Jack knew that Lucky wanted to follow but would not. He would remain resolute and brave and scan the trees for Jack's return.

Chapter 11

〉〉∘〈〈

It was dark as Jack made his way up the mountain. Everything shimmered red as the stone supplied enough light to see a good fifteen feet in any direction. If he were still at home, Jack would have been tired by now, but the stone, or his own sense of determination—or perhaps a bit of both—kept him going, pushing further up the hill. It was cold enough, Jack knew, that if he did not have the red stone he would freeze to death, but he felt no chill and steadily trudged upward, toward the blue stone.

The land leveled, and Jack found himself walking through the very trees that bore witness to the battle between the Muskans and the wolves. The red stone gave off an appropriately eerie glow, and Jack pondered with dread the many slashes in the tree trunks made by axes and swords. Arrows jutted out of them too, as if to replace the branches that broke off during the battle. Large swaths of the snow-covered ground were bathed in dark stains, blood from a wolf or a Muskan.

Without notice, the ground began to shake. Jack tried to keep his footing but fell into the snow as the earthquake intensified. A hundred feet before him, the ground violently split open and a vivid blue light erupted from it, shooting in an arrow-beam upward into the clouds. Then, as quickly as it started, the rumbling ceased. A hush fell across the landscape once more, but the blue light remained.

Jack climbed carefully to his feet again, the snow sticking to his clothes like cotton candy. He stepped toward the blue light with a bit of caution, and as his eyes focused, he saw that there was something standing between him and the light. Jack stopped short when he realized it was a wolf, a big one, bathed in the glow of the blue light. He waited a moment to see what the wolf would do. Aside from a brief flick of one ear, it remained where it was, ears now trained forward in his direction.

Jack started to back away from the strange creature, but at that moment the red stone in his hands shone more brilliantly. Jack glanced down at it and realized it must be telling him to go. Go! Taking a deep breath, Jack listened to the stone and dared to take a step closer. Now he could see that the wolf wasn't just bathed in the light, *it was made of light.* The wolf was translucent, and at certain angles, Jack could see right through him.

The spirit-wolf's gaze was steady as it considered Jack, and Jack did the same.

"Uh, hi," started Jack.

No need to speak, the wolf said, not aloud but directly to Jack's mind. *I can hear you well enough without your tongue. I am called Varg.*

Oh, thought Jack to himself and in thinking it, he realized that the spirit-wolf heard it. *My name is Jack.*

I know who you are. You are Jack from Another World. You are on a quest to retrieve the Three Stones of Ebon and return him to the land of the living.

How do you know that?

Ebon told me.

You can talk to Ebon?

For three thousand years, the Pack of Other Mountain has been able to communicate with its ancestors. This would not have been possible without the stone that holds the mind of Ebon. He has acted as a conduit between the pack and its history. Without the stone, I would not be able to communicate with you.

Jack regarded the spirit-wolf with awe and just a bit of fear. Varg glowed cobalt and stood self-assured, a leader of his pack, a wise, cunning warrior of the forest. *So . . . what happens now?*

Walk with me, Jack.

The boy walked with the spirit-wolf through the wood that was home to the Pack of Other Mountain. They came upon a ridge with a fallen tree acting as a barrier to the steep hillside on its other side.

This is the spot where I died. I had an arrow in my shoulder and I was fighting three of the Muskan horde. Two of them were human and I fought them off easily enough, but the third was a minotaur and, as I turned to face him, he delivered the blow that ended my life.

Jack felt a lump rise in his throat and looked at the spirit-wolf sorrowfully. *I am sorry.*

You do not need to be. I died defending my pack. The spirit-wolf slow-blinked at Jack with conviction and a slight nod. *Life was good.*

Then the two turned and headed away from the hill and toward underbrush that, to Jack, seemed thick and impassable.

There is something you should know, Jack. There is a man, a man with great cunning and skill, who has been selected to find you and the cat that travels with you.

The spirit-wolf's news made Jack uneasy, turning knots in his stomach. He looked at Varg with pained, questioning eyes. *But—why?*

The sorcerer Pale wants you both dead. He knows that if you are successful, then everything he has done will be undone.

Pale, the evil sorcerer? And what man?

The man is known as the Damp. You will recognize him from his perpetually dripping-wet hair that is pure white in color. He was traveling with the Horde that came through here.

I guess I can understand why he would want to stop me, but why would anyone want to kill Lucky? He's just a cat.

Because Lucky is the only one who can get the purple stone.

Jack was confused. He wanted to know more, but they had stopped at an underbrush, and Varg had more to say.

Jack, there is something that you can do for the Pack of Other Mountain.

What?

There was a noise coming from within the bushes. The spirit-wolf led Jack through a path that was hidden from view. *You can save us.*

Back at the camp, and now just within Jack's earshot, he could hear Abigail in a battle of wills. "You know, Lucky," said Abigail, "it is warmer down here by the fire than it is up in that cold tree."

"That's okay," replied Lucky, now too comfortable up in his tree to consider coming back down, and still not fully comfortable being in the company of a canine. "The view from up here is fantastic. You should see it, really. Just spectacular."

"The sun is coming up," said Fay. "He should be back by now, right?" Jack knew that she, as a captain, always needed to know what to do next.

The wolf spoke, noting the pirate's anxiety. "If Jack does not return by the time the sun beams through the trees, then we will go find him," said Quasita matter-of-factly.

"I am glad the sky has cleared up," said Abigail suddenly. She looked in a considerably brighter mood than when they had first arrived in the north. "Do not worry, Fay. I think Jack is doing just fine."

"How can you be so sure?" asked Fay warily.

"Because"—Abigail grinned devilishly, pointing—"there he is, and he has brought some friends."

"Hey," Jack announced, almost as if on cue, as he trudged back down the hill. "You guys can stop worrying now. I'm fine. And so are they."

Fay and the others looked up the hill, and there was Jack, in all his *Jackness*, carrying a wolf cub in his arms while eight others bounded through the snow after him, happy as any pup could be when discovering a new friend.

Quasita gawked at them, her face a mask of near disbelief. The cubs that the pack hid with the slim hope that they would not be discovered by the Muskans, were, in fact, undiscovered. She leaped toward them, tail wagging furiously, and then she dropped and rolled in the snow as the cubs pounced on her with glee. The pack was saved. It would live on. Quasita inspected each one with love and concern to ensure that none of them was harmed. Jack then set down the one that he was carrying so she could inspect it as well.

It was clear to the others why Jack had carried him; he was the runt of the three litters that these remaining cubs represented. After a thorough inspection of him, Quasita spun toward Jack and promptly jumped on him playfully, and he tumbled backward into the snow. She then proceeded to lick his face all over in gratitude.

Initially a little afraid at the powerful take-down, Jack laughed, mostly in relief.

Lucky yelled from his tree. "Hey, watch it! That's my human. Quit licking his face."

"My word, will you look at that," Fay gushed at the tiny, giant-pawed cubs. "They are *sooo* adorable."

"Yes, they are," said Abigail as she ran through the snow, eager to pet one of the cubs. Fay followed and soon both were on their knees, playing with the wolf cubs as Quasita kept Jack pinned to the ground while she slobbered all over his face, and Lucky watched with irritation from the safety of his branch.

"So," said Abigail eventually, "can we see the blue stone?"

"I don't have it," replied Jack. Quasita let him sit up, and she, Abigail, and Fay studied Jack.

"What do you mean you *don't have* it?" asked Fay.

"Yeah, I left it there."

Fay looked incredulous. "Why?"

Jack looked at Quasita, then got to his feet. "You should go there," he said as he dusted the snow off his clothes. "He wants to see you."

Quasita cocked her head, slightly confused. "Who?" Then her ears shot forward keenly, eyes gleaming.

Jack nodded in the direction of the hill. "He's waiting. We'll watch the cubs until you get back."

Quasita leaped to her feet and bounded up the mountain and into the thicket.

"I do not understand," said Abigail. "I thought Varg died in the battle?"

"He did." Jack spoke softly as he picked up the runt and petted him on the head.

Abigail was quiet in reflection, then she understood. "Ah, so that is why you do not have the stone yet."

The three humans played with the wolf cubs while Lucky watched from his branch, unsure if he should come down and meet the cubs himself.

A little time had passed when Quasita returned. Gingerly she carried the blue stone in her mouth. She walked right up to Jack and dropped the stone into his hand. The stone holding Ebon's mind had the same warmth, the same strength as the red stone. Jack passed it around so that Fay and Abigail could be reassured by its touch.

"Thank you, Jack," said Quasita. "You have saved the Pack of Other Mountain. If you had not brought the cubs to me, they would surely have died from starvation. Thank you also for leaving the stone and allowing me to see my beloved Varg one last time."

"Now that we have the blue stone, I'm sorry that you will not be able to communicate with your ancestors anymore and Varg won't be able to appear to you again," said Jack sympathetically.

"That is a sacrifice that I am willing to make if it means the return of Ebon and the eventual fall of Pale and the Muskan horde. Besides, we will still be able to communicate with our ancestors, but we need to learn a new way—to acquire patience and faith to know that they are listening to us. It is no less than how others speak to their ancestors."

The runt that had been in Jack's arms looked up at him and then playfully snapped at the laces of his boots, tail wagging a mile a minute.

"What's his name?" Jack asked Quasita.

"He does not have a name yet," the wolf replied. "Why, you should give him a name. He is obviously drawn to you, so it would be a great honor that he will undoubtedly brag about for years to come."

Jack thought for a moment. To the runt, he said, "I think that a good name for you would be Charlie."

"Charrr-lie," repeated Quasita. "That is a fine name."

"Yeah. It's Dad's name," Jack explained. "My father's, I mean." As Jack watched the cub squirm energetically about in the snow, the boy's smile faded slightly as he thought about his father, and about home. How long would it be until he could go home? *Could* he go home? Would he be able to evade the assassin hired to kill not only him but his cat, too?

Jack shook off these thoughts as he watched the wolf pup roll onto its back, tiny paws in the air, snow half-covering its masked face. It was almost as if the pup were trying to reassure him—or maybe it was to charm him—but either way, it worked. Charlie was just too cute.

Jack's smile turned into rambunctious laughter.

Still up in his tree, Lucky watched everything unfold and he had to admit, if only to himself, that Charlie was a great name for the littlest wolf cub.

Chapter 12

>> ∘ <<

Because Abigail had used the only Spell of Transport she had to get them off the *Minnow Sowta*, they were traveling on foot.

"So, tell us again what Varg told you," said Fay as they continued their hike down the mountainside, loaded down with their gear and weapons.

"Well," said Jack, with Lucky sitting on his shoulders (once again, to avoid the snow), "he said that a man with dripping-wet hair is looking for Lucky and me, because the evil sorcerer, Pale, sent him to kill us."

"Pale?" snorted Fay. "He sent an assassin to kill you. It sounds simply crazy."

"Hey," Jack retorted, "this whole adventure is crazy. I've seen sea serpents, unicorns, cyclopes, centaurs, and some stuff that I don't know *what* they were. I've floated in the air, been to the edge of the world, and talked to a wolf-ghost. But what I haven't seen is a car, and a car would be really great right now because I'm tired of walking."

Fay ignored Jack's complaints. "So, Jack. Do you have any ideas as to where the purple stone is?"

"Yes, I do," replied Jack. "Sahaland. Varg said that only Lucky could get the purple stone. Also, Caveman said that the purple stone was in the south and deep in the wood. And, come to think of it, Ebon even said so to me in a dream, that one of the three stones was in the south. We have the red and blue stones now, so—when you think about it—it's sort of a no-brainer."

"Hm" was Fay's reply.

"A man with wet hair," Abigail cut in. "What could that possibly be about?"

"I don't know," said Jack, "and I truly don't want to find out."

"Me, neither" agreed Lucky.

"Do you think Quasita and the cubs will be okay?" Jack asked Fay, again changing the subject.

"I think so," she replied. "If they can survive until the weather warms up, I think they will be just fine."

"I hope you're right. I know it's only been a couple of days since we left them, but I really miss little Charlie."

"Me too," agreed Abigail. "Those cubs were so precious."

"Aw, they were alright," said Lucky, "but did you notice that they all had doggy breath? Eww!"

"How would you know?" teased Abigail. "You would not go near them."

"Well, that's why—doggy breath!"

As the group continued to walk further down the mountain, the snow became less and less deep. Before long, the snow had all but disappeared, so Lucky was more than eager to leap from Jack's shoulders and walk among the wild grasses and flowers that began to appear. It was a beautiful day. The sun warmed the group, and everyone agreed that it felt near perfect.

It was midday when the group decided to break for lunch. Abigail, as always, knew exactly where to find some kepple fruit and beggar nuts. Jack was just glad that they were no longer eating jigger root. He would miss the ice berries, though. He thought the kepple fruit looked and tasted a lot like apples. The beggar nuts, on the other hand, tasted like nothing he had ever tasted before. He decided right there and then they were the best nuts he had ever eaten.

After lunch, the group continued their journey away from the mountain, toward rolling hills and a river that became bigger the further they traveled.

"Hey, look," said Abigail as she pointed up into the sky. The group looked and saw a bird flying in their direction. As it neared, they could see that it was a blue heron.

"It is Baron." Fay smiled as she waved at the bird.

"Baron?" asked Lucky, who instinctually hid behind Jack's legs.

"He is a friend."

"He's the heron that Quasita mentioned," Jack said, then asked, "You have a friend, all the way up here?"

"Yes. Does that surprise you?"

Jack did not have time to answer as the bird landed in front of them. He was big, nearly five and a half feet, and was bluish grey all along his body except for his head, which was white with a crown of black, with longer crest-feathers that swooped down the back of its head. His beak and long legs were both a vivid orange, and anyone looking at him would agree that he was an impressive sight. When he spoke, it was at once clear that he was very intelligent.

"Hello, Fay, it has been a while."

"Baron, my friend, how are you?" Fay approached the heron and put her arms around him.

"I am well, child," replied the bird. "And yourself?"

"Healthy and in good company" was her reply. "I assume she knows we are coming?"

"Of course. Does anything escape her?"

"Very little," admitted Fay, tossing her hair back. "Baron, I would like to introduce my friends. This is Abigail. She is a sorceress's apprentice, but you already know that."

"Yes," Baron replied, "I do." He bowed to Abigail and then fixed his attention on Jack and Lucky. "Ahh, the Boy and the Cat from Another World. Jack and Lucky, it is a true pleasure to meet both of you." Baron bowed low, so low that his beak nearly touched the ground.

Both Jack and Lucky stood, dumbfounded. Finally, Jack said "Er, hello . . . Baron."

"Well, let us get going," said Fay. "We still have a couple of hours of walking to go before we reach our destination."

"Excuse me," Jack cut in, "but exactly where are you taking us?"

"A warm place with shelter and food while we figure out the fastest way to get to Sahaland," Fay explained, shouldering her bag.

"Not to worry," Baron assured them, "it is a safe place."

They continued their journey downhill, away from the mountain. The landscape of sloping hills and pleasant valleys soon revealed fluttering butterflies—lots of butterflies. The children grinned uncontrollably, and the cat reveled in the smells of the flowers—and in butterfly-chasing. The heron walked with them and took a liking to Lucky as the cat recounted their journey and told him much about his life with Jack back home.

Fay was right. A couple of hours after meeting the heron, they came upon a pleasant cottage, mostly made of wood, sitting near a river, with smoke swirling out of the chimney. There were non-speaking chickens outside, clucking up a storm. Placed next to the cottage was what looked like a watchtower, except that straw spilled out from the platform. As it turned out, it was Baron's nest, and it even had a small roof on it to keep rain out.

The front door of the cottage opened, and a small woman stepped out. She had a pleasant smile and tousled flaxen hair, and her vivid blue eyes squinted as she stepped into the sun.

"Hello, Fay," she said.

Fay laid down her shoulder bag and ran into the woman's arms. "Hello, Mum," she said as she buried her face into her mother's hair.

"Oh, Fay, I am so happy to see you." They hugged for a moment and then both turned to the others. "It has been too long."

"Mum, I would like you to meet Abigail, Jack, and Lucky. Everybody, this is Lady Beverly." Fay was smiling as she introduced her mother to her friends.

"It is nice to meet all of you," Lady Beverly said. She looked at Jack and Lucky. "So, you two are visitors from another world."

"Okay—I'm wearing clothes from your world now, so how does everybody seem to just . . . *know* that?" asked Jack.

"Well, *she* knows because she is a sorceress," Abigail declared with a knowing-but-not-telling smile. Jack laughed boisterously at Abigail's enthusiasm.

"And *you* are a sorceress's apprentice," Lady Beverly quipped. It did not go unnoticed by anybody that Abigail was immensely pleased to be in the presence of another sorceress.

Then they went inside Lady Beverly's cottage, which was as warm in both comfort and color as the outside had been quaint. To Jack, it was the closest he'd felt to being home since arriving in this world. There were chairs and a table, paintings hanging on the walls, and a fire in the hearth, its flames dancing orangey-yellow flickering tones across the walls. A pot sat over the flames, cooking a soup that quickly and thoroughly beckoned the senses.

"Please, everyone, make yourselves at home," Lady Beverly said as she stirred the soup.

Jack found a chair and sat in it as Lucky walked around, sniffing at everything. Jack could see an open doorway that led to Lady Beverly's bedroom. There was another door that was closed, and, along the far wall, Jack could see a ladder that went to a loft.

Lady Beverly noticed Jack looking up and said, "That is where you will be sleeping while you stay here."

No sooner had she said that than Jack found himself climbing the ladder and lying on the mattress overlooking the living room.

He watched the others from his sleeping post. Lady Beverly was talking to Lucky with Baron looking on, and Fay was showing Abigail around the kitchen. Everyone spoke in low, conversant tones. That was the last thing Jack saw before going into a deep sleep.

He dreamed of a man with long white hair, dripping with water, chasing him and Lucky with a sword. It was one of those dreams people have where they wake up right before something really bad is about to happen. In his case, he watched horrified as the Damp's sword plunged into his own midsection. He awoke with a start, gasping for air and subconsciously clutching at his abdomen where the assassin's sword had been.

"You okay, Jack?" It was Lucky, curled up next to him.

"Yeah, Lucky, I just had a bad dream." The room was dark, save a warm glow from the fireplace. "How long have I been asleep?"

"Long enough for it to be nighttime now."

Jack cupped a hand behind Lucky's head and scratched his friend lightly behind the ears.

"Ooh, that feels good," purred the cat as he shut his eyes.

"You know, Lucky," said Jack, "if what Varg said is true, then you must be the one to get the purple stone."

"Okay. Ooh, don't stop, don't stop," Lucky insisted as Jack began to move his hand away. "That really does feel so good."

"Seriously, I want you to be careful, okay? I want you to promise me that, no matter what you've got to do, you will be careful."

"Sure thing, Jack," purred the cat.

Jack stopped scratching to bring his face close to Lucky's. "Most of all, I want you to watch out for the man with white, dripping-wet hair. If you see him, I want you to run. Got it?"

"Run? Jack, look. See these?" Lucky stretched out a paw and unsheathed his claws. "These are *claws . . . of . . . justice.*"

Jack rolled his eyes and let out a deep sigh, still groggy from sleep. "Yes, Lucky, I know. Just—be careful." Looking down into the center room of the cottage by the fire, he spied Lady Beverly talking quietly with Fay. There were emptied bowls sitting on the table, and the aroma of soup still hung in the air. .

"I'm hungry. Is there any soup left?"

"Yeah," replied Lucky, "Lady Beverly said we had to save you some. Are you going down there?"

"I am. Do you want to come with me?"

"I sure do."

Jack scooped up Lucky and put him over one shoulder, and together the two descended the ladder. Lady Beverly and Fay were happy to see Jack awake, even if it was late. Lady Beverly ladled some soup into a bowl for Jack, and Jack and Lucky sat with the two women by the fire. He felt content.

"How is the soup?" asked Lady Beverly as Jack attacked his meal.

"It's really good," he managed to say between slurps. "Are there beggar nuts in this?"

"Yes." Lady Beverly looked pleased. "There are. You are learning."

"I really like beggar nuts. We do not have these kinds of nuts in my world."

"A world without beggar nuts," Lady Beverly sighed and shook her head, "just imagine. Poor child." Lady Beverly leaned back in her chair and looked at Jack with wonder. "So, tell me, Jack, what do you think of our world?"

"I really like it. I do miss my parents, though."

"Me too," put in Lucky.

"And what do *you* like about our world?" Lady Beverly asked Lucky.

"I like that Jack can actually speak normal. I like understanding him."

"Hey," put in Jack, "you're the one who couldn't speak before."

"I could speak just fine."

"I think it is great having a feline in our company again." Lady Beverly was speaking to Fay.

"Yes, I think so, too." Fay was smiling as she replied.

"It reminds me of that time when you and Sir Bootsy visited for a time," Lady Beverly suggested.

"Who is Sir Bootsy?" asked Jack.

"My mum calls him Sir Bootsy, but he is really just Bootsy," said Fay as she sipped from a cup that held something warm to drink.

"Okay, so who is Bootsy?" asked Jack.

"Sir Bootsy is a great warrior," said Lady Beverly. "He and Fay traveled together, that is until the Muskans threatened to invade his homeland. He had to return home then to take his rightful place as leader of his clowder to help stave off the attack."

"Clowder?" Jack's nose wrinkled in confusion.

"Yeah, dogs have packs. Cats have clowders. And he is a cat," said Lucky, staring at Fay.

"Yes," she confirmed, "he is a cat, who is also my dear friend. He has the greenest eyes, and his fur is like the night."

"Ah, so that's why you helped Lucky at the tavern, when everybody was trying to kill him," said Jack.

"What can I say? I like cats."

"She saved Sir Bootsy, too," said Lady Beverly. "She was traveling from the western coast, on her way to visit me, when she came upon a small group of Muskan misfits. They had poor Sir Bootsy cornered in a gully. Fay was on them faster than a heron in a hurricane."

"Faster than a—well, did you kick their butts?" Jack asked.

Fay tilted her head as she remembered. "Well, when I attacked them, Bootsy took it as an opportunity to attack as well. Together, we caused them to retreat faster than a heron in a hurricane."

"Cool," said Jack. "How many Muskans were there?"

"Ahh, I do not remember. Maybe five or six."

"Five or six?" exclaimed Jack. "You took on five or six Muskans and won?"

"Hey, you need to know how to take care of yourself if you want to be captain of a pirate ship. Besides, there were two of us against them. He may be only a cat but, believe me, Bootsy is a warrior in the truest sense of the word. He more than held his own in that skirmish, and there were times when he saved my life in tussles with other ne'er-do-wells."

"Ne'er-do-wells?" asked Lucky.

Jack jumped in, "Bad guys. They never do well by others."

"Oh."

"If you are going to Sahaland, you may meet him," said Lady Beverly.

"I'd like that," said Lucky, his tail flicking back and forth.

The group bantered back and forth about many trivial and not-so-trivial things, and Jack felt almost at home in Lady Beverly's cottage. He had just eaten a delicious, warm meal and was in the company of people he would consider friends. All that was missing was a little TV and perhaps some ice cream.

Chapter 13

〉〉∘〈〈

Since arriving in Sturgus, they'd had lots of adventure, Lady Beverly's cottage was the closest to feeling at home that they'd felt since arriving in Sturgus, and it was grounding for Jack and Lucky to stay in one place, if only for now. While Fay had been accommodating and friendly, like an older best friend, Lady Beverly was a mother, and that made Jack happy. It felt good to be a kid again. While Lady Beverly investigated ways to transport them to Sahaland as soon as possible, Jack played with Abigail, teaching her games from his world like Twenty Questions. She more than readily returned the favor, teaching him games like Princess in the Pines and Demon Square.

Lucky spent a lot of time with Baron. They became such good friends that Lucky received the rare invitation to enjoy the view from Baron's nest, which Lucky accepted with a look of pride and a feeling of importance. Lady Beverly had rotflower root on hand and even an albatross feather, so Abigail was able to conjure a spell and send news to Malia of their progress in acquiring the three stones and of losing Caleb. It was clear that Abigail took a liking to Lady Beverly. She was happy to be in the presence of a sorceress again, eager to glean what she could from Lady Beverly's vast knowledge of the magical arts.

On the evening of the fourth day of their stay at the cottage, Lady Beverly proposed a way for the adventurers to get to Sahaland. They all sat outside by the fire pit behind her cottage. The sky was clear, and their bellies were full.

"I have found a spell that will carry you to Sahaland," Lady Beverly said to Jack, her voice barely louder than the crickets in their song and the fire that crackled loudly as it burned the dry timber.

"How?" asked Jack.

"A cloud will take you."

"Huh?" said Jack.

"Huh?" echoed Lucky.

"Oh, how fantastic!" Abigail smiled, clapping her hands enthusiastically.

"I don't understand," said Jack, "how can a cloud carry people? It's impossible—"

"Jack," Lady Beverly chided, "you should have learned by now that our world is not quite the same as your world."

Jack wanted to protest further, but he thought about it and knew she was right. Although he couldn't understand the *how* of many things in this world that he had landed in, he knew that if Lady Beverly said that a cloud could carry him to the other end of this world, then it must be true. "Couldn't you just make a Spell of Transport like the one Abigail used to get us off the ship?"

"That would be the most convenient way but unfortunately I used the last of my tibber flower on a spell for someone else. I am waiting for a new shipment to come in, but it is late arriving, probably because of those cursed Muskan hordes."

"Hmm," thought Jack aloud, "I guess if that's the only way then that's what we'll do. I don't quite understand it, but if you say this will work, I will trust you."

"Excuse me, Jack," Baron put in. "I must say that Lady Beverly is the best sorceress I have ever known. When I was young, she found me by the river, dying from an arrow in my breast. She said three words—that is all—and the arrow fell away from me, and I was healed."

"Wow," said Lucky, looking at Baron in awe, and then at Lady Beverly.

"Yes," said Lady Beverly, "but you failed to mention that those three words weakened me terribly, and I was in bed for three days. One day for each word spoken."

"If you'd had a healing potion, you wouldn't have gotten sick," said Lucky.

"This is true, cat, but I did not have the ingredients to make such a powerful potion, nor was there time."

"But you could?" asked Abigail. "I mean, if you had the ingredients?"

"Yes," Lady Beverly assured her, "if I had the ingredients."

"Are you more powerful than Malia?" asked Jack.

"Who, the Keeper of the Wagon of Prophecy? I should think not. We are both students of magic, but we have each studied different aspects of the same craft and are allies of the same cause. Health. Wellness. And peace."

They were quiet then, feeling the night air brushing their skin as they enjoyed the company of each other. Jack grabbed a stick from the ground and slowly poked at the fire with it. The flames danced with the slight breeze and Jack imagined that he heard music playing.

"Look," said Lucky. The others followed Lucky's gaze as he stared past the fire toward the river. Tiny lights floated in the air, moving slowly toward them. They were of numerous colors, some blue, some yellow, others red. At first, Jack thought that they might be some sort of firefly, but they flew in formation, and, as they fluttered closer, Jack could see that they were in fact tiny, winged people.

"Faeries," whispered Abigail, her mouth hung slightly open in awe at the sight.

"Yes," Lady Beverly confirmed, "they are wood faeries from the Circle Forest." The faeries hovered around Lady Beverly, and it seemed to Jack that she was communicating with them, although she did not speak. They fluttered about her, and their lights flickered as they passed by her, close enough to tickle her skin with their wings.

The faeries quite suddenly broke away from Lady Beverly and fluttered before Jack and Lucky, doing the same thing. Their wings did tickle Jack's skin and he giggled slightly as they circled him.

"They say that they are happy to meet both of you, Boy and Cat from Another World," said Lady Beverly with a pleased expression on her face.

With the faeries as close as they were, Jack noticed they were human-like but proportioned differently. Their limbs were long for their bodies, and they moved with an elegance that Jack had not seen before, neither in this flat world or his own round planet.

"This is so cool," said Lucky, who was made almost invisible by the number of faeries that surrounded him.

The faeries then fluttered to Fay and Baron, giving them greetings as well.

When that was done, they turned their attention to Abigail.

Every faerie converged on her, brushing her with their wings, lights flickering to music that seemed to be coming from the faeries themselves.

"Oh my," Abigail said as the faeries lifted her off the ground. Lights spun around her in a rhythmic pattern as the faeries flew around her, spinning her softly in the air. Abigail giggled and glowed.

Jack was in awe, and it seemed to him that her red hair was like fire in the night. It was then that he realized something that should have been obvious from the day he'd met Abigail. She was the girl pictured on the urn. She was the one who sat with him on the winged

horse, carrying the golden wand. Malia must have recognized it immediately; that was why she had sent Abigail on this mission with Jack and Lucky.

As Abigail danced with the faeries up in the air (and surely it *was* a dance), the faeries spoke to her, and Abigail found herself understanding, even though she had never studied any faerie language. They spoke of her life, her destiny, her path; love found—and lost— the steppingstones of her life; where she would be when she was an old woman.

The faeries lowered Abigail at last. She touched the ground lightly, in rhythm to the music of the faeries. Abigail then looked at Jack as if they had been friends for a lifetime and grinned amiably at him.

Jack was dumbfounded. "What? Why are you looking at me like that?"

Abigail approached Jack, stopping inches from his face. She searched his features as if trying to memorize them.

"The faeries have revealed my destiny to me, Jack," she finally said, speaking softly. "I will forget it very soon, but I want you to know that I will always be your friend."

"Why would you forget that?" asked Jack.

"It is the way of the faerie folk," Lady Beverly explained. "If you know your destiny, you might try to change it. When I was Abigail's age, I experienced something similar."

"Oh," said Jack. He knew that this would remain another mysterious question, answered only in part.

The faeries formed a circle around the group and, in synchronized flight, flew about the group, their music carrying them with grace and thunder. They hovered lightly, some fluttering sideways, others bobbing up and down, before regrouping and then leaving in the same fashion as they arrived.

As the music died away and the colored lights faded, it was Lucky who spoke first. "You know, I really like faeries. They're tiny and colorful."

"How do they make that music?" asked Jack. "I didn't see any of them with instruments."

"The music is made with their wings when they fly," answered Lady Beverly.

"I see why you live here," said Jack. "You have really cool neighbors."

"And cool is a good thing!" Abigail grinned.

Chapter 14

》◦《

Jack ran from the trees toward the fire pit in Lady Beverly's yard with an armload of dry sticks. Fay and Abigail followed Jack, their arms full of kindling as well. Lady Beverly stood before the fire holding a staff while Baron and Lucky stood together off to the side.

"Put it all in the fire. The bigger the fire, the more smoke to work with," said Lady Beverly. She had a pouch tied to her belt and as they dropped their sticks into the glowing blaze, she would scoop out a small amount of cerulean powder and throw it into the fire. The smoke turned as blue as the powder.

Fay and Abigail stood on either side of Jack. They watched intently as Lady Beverly worked her spell.

"What's that blue stuff?" asked Jack.

"It looks like ground-up butter-lilies. A type of flower," replied Abigail.

Lady Beverly smiled and nodded once, staring into the flames. "Ground-up butter-lilies mixed with crystalized mountain snow, and the bones of a flying ferret-eagle that has been dead for at least fifteen years."

Jack wanted to ask what a flying ferret-eagle was but thought better of it, deciding to save the question for later. He watched as Lady Beverly threw in one final scoop of the blue powder. She pulled a nicely embroidered handkerchief from her pocket. She held it close to her mouth, whispering into the cloth, then released it. The handkerchief floated from her hand into the smoke above the fire. The dancing flames elevated the delicate cloth roughly five feet and as it hovered there, the handkerchief began collecting smoke beneath it. As tiny as the cloth was, the light-blue smoke was unable to rise past it. Instead, it gathered and billowed out beneath it, grew in size and shape, and formed into the cloud that Lady Beverly had spoken of.

Jack glanced at Abigail. It didn't surprise him to see the joyful look on her face, a glint in her eyes and her mouth slightly parted in wonder as she watched Lady Beverly at work.

The smoke from the fire returned to a dull, flat, smoky-grey color and stopped collecting into the handkerchief, leaving only the rich, cerulean-colored cloud. Lady Beverly then reached with her staff and stabbed at the cloud, pulled it away from the fire, and then frowned at her work. "Hm. I was hoping it would be bigger."

"It looks big enough to me," said Jack, and to him it was. It was about five feet thick and twelve feet wide.

Lady Beverly looked at Fay, jerking her head toward the cloud. "Daughter, climb on to test it out."

Fay listened to her mother, climbed onto the cloud, then carefully stood up. A moment afterward she began to sink into the puffy form until her boots stuck out of the bottom. Everyone watched in disappointment as Fay dropped to the ground below.

"What happened?" asked Jack, slightly concerned. "Does it not work?"

Lady Beverly took the pouch from her belt, held it upside down, and shook it. No powder came out. "I am out of powder until my next shipment comes in. This is as big as the cloud is going to get, and it cannot handle too much weight concentrated in one area. Jack, you give it a try."

Jack did as he was told. The cloud felt soft. It reminded him of standing on a beanbag chair, except without the noisy crunching sound. In fact, it made no sound at all as he maneuvered about on its surface. He stood up on it and looked down at the others, spreading his arms wide. "Well?"

"You are not sinking," replied Lady Beverly. "Good. It should work for Abigail, too." Then she looked at her daughter. "I am sorry, but this means you cannot go with them, Fay."

Fay looked up at Jack. Her sudden concern for the children was easily readable on her face. Jack too was sad that he would no longer be traveling with her. He had developed a real friendship with her and would miss the security she provided.

Fay told the three travelers not to worry. She had plans to find her ship and make sure that Caleb was okay, which pleased Abigail and Jack immensely. There was much crying and hugging when they left; even Lucky brushed himself hard against Baron. Baron flew alongside the cloud for a half-day before he turned around and headed home.

Riding on a cloud is nothing like riding on an airplane, Jack thought to himself. It was smoother, much smoother, and very quiet.

As Lucky napped in the center of the cloud with the provisions— mostly food and warm clothes for night, as well as basic medical supplies like bandages and several tiny vials of Potion of Healing—Jack and Abigail laid on their stomachs, looking over the edge at the land below. Jack surmised that they were a half-mile up in the sky, traveling at fifteen to twenty miles an hour. Below them, the land moved by at a steady pace. Its rolling hills and green valleys were pleasant to watch. Abigail told him they were called the Anaka Hills.

Jack had taught Abigail I Spy, and they played it often to pass the time.

"Let me see." Abigail scanned the terrain. "I spy, with my little eye, something red."

"Hmm." Jack looked around. "Is it that cluster of rocks?"

"No," Abigail said with smirk.

"Over there, that wagon has a little red on it."

"No."

"Hmm, this one is hard."

"Do you give up?" asked Abigail.

"No. Not yet. Is it that barn hiding behind those trees?"

"Very good, Jack," Abigail answered. She rolled over, eyes gazing into the sky. "Jack, if you were on your world right now, what would you be doing?"

Jack continued looking at the rolling landscape. "I don't know. If it's the same time of day there, I'd probably be at school, unless it's the weekend, then I'd either be playing outside with my friend Timmy or be out and about with my parents." Thinking about home made him a bit homesick again. The stay with Lady Beverly had reminded him about what his old normal life had been like. He missed them all. He even missed Old Lady Krau—he stopped himself mid-thought and corrected himself—*Mrs.* Krauss. Yes, she was a bit odd, but she was familiar. She was part of home, and of his neighborhood.

"The week-end," Abigail sounded out. "What is that?"

Jack stopped watching the land below and gazed at Abigail incredulously. "Oh! You don't know what the weekend is?"

"No."

"No?"

"Did I not just say that? Come on, Jack, tell me what a week-end is." Abigail leaned forward intently enough that Jack knew this was another completely foreign concept to her. He proceeded to tell Abigail about the days in the week and how on the weekend he didn't have to go to school and most adults did not work.

"Wow," exclaimed Abigail. "In this world there is always work to be done. I do not understand how people in your world can survive if there is no one tending the crops?"

"Oh, I'm sure there's someone tending the crops. That's why I said most people."

"Hmm. Here we have a few spiritual holidays where we do not work, but that is all," said Abigail.

Something dark and massive below them caught the corner of Jack's eye. "Hey, look at that."

Abigail rolled over again, leaned over the edge of the cloud, and looked down. "Muskan troops," she groaned. "Hundreds of them, maybe thousands." Her voice was low. "I do not say this word lightly, but I hate them so."

Jack and Abigail watched in awe at the horde that marched below them. From the cloud's vantage point, it was difficult for them to see much detail below, but there were all sorts of terrifying creatures that Jack couldn't identify. Abigail was only able to make out the larger creatures like the orcs, massive in size with very yellowish skin. They were tough but very stupid creatures. They and humans constituted much of the foot soldiers. Among the riders, Jack recognized centaurs because of their size. but was taken aback by human-like beings that rode what appeared to be giant bugs skittering along. "Those giant bugs, what are they?"

"I do not know what they are called, but I know from seeing them before that the ones riding them are lizard-people called hecti. It is believed that Pale brought them from his world, along with the orcs."

"They look scary from up here. I hope I never meet one face-to-face. They're headed in the same direction as us, though. You don't think that they're going to Sahaland, do you?"

"After what they just did to the wolves, my guess would be yes," Abigail whispered. "Pale must be making a move to eradicate any and all resistance."

"But cats? Really?"

"Especially cats. They may be small, but they are very smart, and although no one really knows what their numbers are, it is believed to be in the tens of thousands."

"What can we do about this? About them?" asked Jack, pointing below.

"There is nothing we can do right now," replied Abigail. "If the horde discovers that we are up here, they will get us, and we do not want that. We are, however, moving faster than they are. We should arrive in Sahaland a day or two before them. We will be at least able to warn the cats. Let us hope that it will be enough."

The two children watched silently for a while as they slowly glided over the terrifying horde. It was a fearsome sight that filled Jack with worry. Jack reached into the pouch tied to his waist, from which he pulled out the red and blue stones. Upon their touch, he immediately felt better. He handed one stone to Abigail, and the two knew, no matter what the odds, that in the end, everything would be better.

Chapter 15

〉〉◦〈〈

The cloud alighted at their destination two days ahead of the Muskan horde by Abigail's estimation, and the two children and the cat gratefully climbed off the billowy transport.

"It sure is good to be back on firm ground," said Lucky. He immediately began grooming himself, while Jack stomped in circles, reveling in the feeling of being on a firm surface again.

The air in Sahaland was more humid than it was in Other Mountain, but at least there was a breeze right then. Jack wiped the back of his hand across his forehead. "It's more jungle-y here than any of the other places we've been to." As soon as his feet had touched the ground, he had felt the throbbing in his head again, a sign of urgency that Jack was becoming all-too-accustomed to. It meant that they needed to get going.

"Jungle-y?" Abigail raised an eyebrow as she climbed back on top of the cloud to drop their bags off the sides. She then grabbed the handkerchief and climbed back down to earth. "What do you mean?"

"Yeah, well, you know . . ." Jack wasn't sure how to explain the word. "Like a . . . a . . . well, a jungle," he finished with a shrug. "Sorry, that's the best I've got."

Abigail gave him a sideways smirk. "Some words do not have a way to translate."

"Hey! Look at the cloud." Lucky motioned with his paw.

Abigail and Jack turned to see the cloud becoming thinner, first dissipating into vapor and then disappearing altogether.

"Well, there goes our ride," said Jack. He looked around. "So, is this Sahaland?"

"I think we are at the outskirts," replied Abigail as she lifted her bag and slung it over her shoulder. "Where to, oh Jack from Another World?"

Jack gathered his bag and the supplies. "I'm sensing it's this-a-way to find the cats," he said, nodding in one particular direction. "Let's get going."

"This-a-way it is," she said.

They listened to strange chirps, creaks, and croaks as they set out. For how long? They weren't sure. But in less than thirty minutes of walking, Lucky suddenly stopped. He then stalked over to the foot of a tree and sniffed for several moments with mouth open and his lips pulled back in a slight grimace. "Aha, cats!" he proclaimed. "We're here."

"Look," Jack said, pointing ahead of them.

Roughly fifty feet away, sitting unmoving in a row, were three cats. They sat stoic and glared intently at the new arrivals. One cat's ear twitched away a fly.

The air, Jack realized, had become still and heavy and now felt hot and biting. The only sounds came from a chorus of crickets. His skin felt clammy, and he wanted desperately to have an ice-cold soda, or a Popsicle like he used to have back home.

He leaned toward Abigail and whispered, "So, what should we do now?"

"Well, I think that is being decided for us," she replied, all the while staring back at the three cats. "Look."

Lucky went ahead of the group. He moved slowly and deliberately, head close to the ground, hackles raised slightly. His whiskers twitched uncontrollably as he neared the felines, and then, with just a few feet more to go, he stopped. They approached in the same manner.

The one in the center spoke first. He was taller than the others, a grey-and-white shorthair. He curled his lips and sniffed toward Lucky. "Cat, what clowder are you with?"

"Huh? Uh, well . . . none," Lucky responded nervously.

"You do not smell of any clowder I know. Your scent is unusual. You are not from Sahaland?"

"Uh, no," Lucky stammered, "I'm from Jack's house. Well, uh, it's my house, too, so I guess I'm from our house."

"Jack's House?" repeated the grey-and-white cat questioningly.

"Yeah," said Lucky. "The boy behind me, he is my human."

All three of the cats' pupils widened at this statement. "Your *human?*" the cat on the left, a sleek, long-haired breed with a mix of white and tabby markings, hissed. His vivid yellow eyes narrowed suspiciously.

Lucky didn't answer right away. He eyed the three cats cautiously. Abigail and Jack had practiced with him how to communicate with cats in this world. They would not be familiar with his friendship with Jack, as humans and cats did not normally interact in this world. He would have to be careful with his choice of words. "Yes," Lucky said as loudly and sternly as he could. "Jack is my human. Surely you must know of a cat or two who have humans, yes?"

"We have only ever known of one cat who had a human," stated the center cat, tall and leggy. "But he has long since given up that unruly practice to be with his own kind. What is your name?"

"My name is Lucky, and behind me are Jack and Abigail."

"I am Tater. This is Kyuss," he said, glancing at the white-and-tab-by mix on the left. "And this is Logan," he said, nodding to the silent cat on the right.

Logan was a long-bodied grey-and-coffee-colored tabby that could have easily been mistaken for a small raccoon. He wasn't just a long-haired cat, but a thick-haired one, as well. He watched Lucky with huge, golden-orange eyes that unnerved Lucky ever so slightly.

"Why have you come here, Lucky?" asked Tater. "Are you return-ing to your kind to stay?"

Lucky twitched his tail. "We've traveled here for two reasons. The second reason is to warn you that a Muskan horde will be here in two days, maybe less, to kill all the cats."

"What?" exclaimed Tater. "How do you know this?"

"Because Jack and Abigail saw them as we traveled down this way," Lucky said, flicking his tail violently as he spoke. This did not go unnoticed by the three cats, but they said nothing to the fact.

"You did not see them with your own eyes?" asked Tater.

"No," Lucky admitted sheepishly. "I was sleeping. I like sleeping."

Tater scoffed. "So, you bring only the word of two humans that there is a Muskan horde headed this way. That is all." It was more a statement than a question.

"Hey," Lucky hissed, his hackles rising. "I trust those two humans more than I trust any old cat. Jack would never lie to me, especially about something as serious as this."

The sternness in Tater's eyes softened a bit. "Well, it seems that you are a bit protective about your humans. You have a bit of grit in you. I like that."

During this time Jack and Abigail had been slowly moving for-ward until they ended up right behind Lucky, and the three cats now turned their attention toward them.

"You must be Jack and Abigail," said Tater.

"Yes," replied Abigail. Jack nodded.

Logan leaned forward, his orange-yellow eyes gleaming. His tail flicked once, and then he spoke up. "Tell us about this advancing horde."

"They are Muskans," the girl explained. "Hundreds if not more. Mostly humans and orcs, but we saw centaurs and hecti, too."

"But how did they not see you?" asked Tater.

Abigail responded. "We traveled from the northern region of Other Mountain on a cloud conjured by a sorceress. The cloud was camouflaged to blend in with the sky. Pale's Muskan horde decimated the wolves, and they mean to do the same to you."

"Hmm . . . and you say we have two days?"

"Roughly, yes. We were floating over the Anaka Hills when we saw them. That was two days ago," Abigail confirmed. The mere thought of it worried her, and it showed on her face.

Tater looked at Lucky. "The Anaka Hills—that is about four days from here, so yes, we have about two days. Now then, sharing news of the oncoming Muskans is the second reason that you are here. What is the first reason?"

Jack watched as his best friend paused, and then Lucky looked at Tater with firm conviction. "We are on a quest to collect the Three Stones of Ebon and unite them so Ebon will return as prophesied. We hope Ebon's return means the beginning of the end for Pale and his horde."

The three cats looked at Lucky incredulously, and Logan's gaze sharpened. Lucky was pretty sure they might pounce on him at any moment. Then Logan spoke. "What kind of catnip have *you* been rolling in, to believe such human garbage?" he asked, tilting his head.

Tater said, "Lucky of Jack's House, tell me what you know of the Three Stones of Ebon."

Lucky glanced back at his favorite human. "Jack, I think you should show them."

Jack nodded and stepped forward, knelt next to Lucky, and produced both the red stone and the blue stone. "See? We just need the purple stone now," he explained. "The soul of Ebon."

All three cats' eyes widened more, and they sniffed the stones to feel the stones' energy. When they returned their attention to the three travelers, there was no question that they now believed Lucky's story.

Tater's gaze turned to his comrade. "Kyuss, run to the Big Tree. Let them know what is going on and that I am bringing a visitor." Kyuss bolted into the jungle without a sound and disappeared. To the thick-furred cat Tater said, "Logan, you stay here with the humans. Watch them."

Then he turned to Lucky. "I will escort you myself to the Big Tree. There you can tell your tale and plead your case."

"We can't come?" asked Jack.

"This is cat country, human child. No humans or any other talking animals are allowed here without the Elders' permission."

Jack then recalled Varg's words to him on Other Mountain. Pale's hired assassin was not only after Jack, but also Lucky, knowing that the third and final stone was in Sahaland, and only a cat would be able to retrieve it. That left no doubt in the boy's mind that Mrs. Krauss had chosen both Jack *and* Lucky for this quest.

Abigail knelt before Lucky. She reached into her bag and pulled out a small, knitted harness. "Here, my little friend, time to put this on." Lady Beverly had made it for him, anticipating that he would have to go into Sahaland alone. Though it felt strange, Lucky held still while Abigail adjusted the straps. The harness held a pouch that was affixed to the front so Lucky could carry the stone back in it in a safer and easier way.

Jack scratched Lucky behind his ears. "Be careful, buddy. Okay?"

Lucky rubbed up against him, but only just a little bit, so his affection toward a human would not upset the other cats too much. "You got it," he replied. Lucky looked up at Jack for another moment, and then turned around and slinked away with Tater into the jungle.

Jack watched the point where Lucky had disappeared, half-hoping that his feline friend would come running back, but also knowing that he would not. "What do we do now?" he asked Abigail, knowing full well the answer but hoping she would say that they should follow.

Abigail began pulling out supplies from her bag. "We wait."

Jack snuck a peek at Logan, who sat several feet from them, still watching with those giant, unsettling orangey-gold eyes. "You know, if we wanted to follow, I don't think one cat could stop us."

"No, they could not," Abigail agreed, "but chances are we would not get far before we were surrounded by a dozen of them. Or more. Besides, I think it would be a wise idea to try to be their friends and be respectful on their land."

"I know, and I agree. I'm just worried about Lucky."

Abigail looked at Jack. "Try not to be. He is with cats."

"What if he decides to stay with them?"

Abigail snorted, "Yeah, right. Trust me when I tell you that Lucky will never leave you. He loves you. Hey, are you hungry?"

"Yes, I am."

"I think I saw some branna trees back the way we came. The fruit should be perfect for picking about now. It will go nicely with the beggar nuts. I will be right back." Abigail took her now empty bag and headed into the trees.

Jack began pulling stuff from his bag. He looked on occasion at Logan, and each time he found Logan glaring right back at him with a piercing intensity. It felt to Jack that Logan was looking right through him, and it made him uncomfortable. At that moment, a bug flew by Logan's face. Logan's eyes darted after it, and—in one swift movement—he leaped at the thing. Catching it between his furry, tufted front paws, he brought the bug to the ground and quickly devoured it.

Well, look at that, Jack thought. *He ate a bug.*

Logan licked his chops, then—once again—glared at him.

Chapter 16

≫∘≪

Lucky walked with Tater for what had to be close to an hour. The deeper they walked into the jungle, the denser the foliage became. Tater moved quickly, and Lucky at times had difficulty keeping up. Tater was the biggest cat that Lucky had ever seen, almost twice his own size.

The harness Lucky wore was quite comfortable, but it did take some getting used to. It brushed lightly against the insides of his front legs as he walked. The material was soft, however, and Lucky thought it had a pleasant scent to it. It reminded him of Lady Beverly's cottage and the time he'd spent there, enjoying the company of Baron and the others.

As they journeyed, Tater told Lucky a bit about life in Sahaland. There were many clowders, but not every cat belonged to one. Some were loners, by choice or by consequence. Tater himself was a leader of his own clowder, of which Kyuss was a part. Logan belonged to another clowder. When it came to border patrol, he said, the different clowders always worked together.

"How much further?" asked Lucky. They were headed to the Big Tree. There were lots of trees in Sahaland. *What makes this one so special? It's probably* really *big,* he mused.

"Just a little way more," answered Tater, who then slunk under a fallen tree. As he followed, Lucky began to feel the jungle slowly moving in on all sides. Scattered, dappled sunlight shot down in rays. Each tree's branches intertwined with those of its neighbors.

Lucky first heard the sound emerging from under the fallen tree. A deep-pitched sound that he almost more felt than heard, but louder than anything else the jungle had yet to offer. Lucky could feel the vibrations rumbling under his paws. Deep, creaking pitches belched forth from the heart of the jungle, the roar slicing through the humidity like a hot blade on melting butter.

Lucky froze, hair standing on end, ears pinning back defensively, and pupils dilating to nearly full-black. Tater turned to look at him calmly. "It is no danger," he said. "It is just the Big Tree."

"H-huh?" Lucky was ready to run back the way he came.

"It is no danger to us, truly," Tater repeated and tilted his head slightly at Lucky. "Come along now, we are almost there."

"Does the Big Tree always make so much noise?"

"Not always, but sometimes, yes." Tater turned and continued walking toward the sound.

Lucky followed, albeit hesitantly. The noise subsided, but a minute later it returned with the same intensity, the ground shuddering from the sound.

"Full stop," Tater announced. "We are here."

Almost as if on cue, the noise died away. Left in its wake was the quiet breathing of the jungle. Tater pushed through the very dense underbrush and disappeared. Lucky blinked at the spot where Tater had just been. He took a deep breath, then followed the large cat.

Emerging on the other side, he was nearly breathless. It was as if the jungle had been forced back to create a perfect circle around the tree, and the tree—the great, beautiful tree—was utterly magnificent. It was huge, maybe as tall as three trees in the yard in his home world, and the canopy would have covered their entire yard.

Its leaves were bigger than any leaves Lucky had ever seen, easily larger than himself. The branches started roughly twenty feet above the ground, and Lucky could see cats, many cats, sitting or walking all over the tree. The Big Tree was to Sahaland what the Ahmega Lighthouse was to the town of Valmar. It was simply impressive.

Along the circle, at the edge of the space where the Big Tree's land met the forest, Lucky could see many more cats, here and there, sitting, staring up at the tree. He wondered then how the cats managed to get up onto the Big Tree. The branches were much too high to scale the trunk and too far away from the jungle trees to jump from any other tree.

Lucky's thoughts were interrupted by the return of the loud, deep, and terrible sounds he had heard before. As Lucky looked up, he could barely believe that he was watching one of those massive tree limbs actually *move*. It swung down from a huge height, creaking, moaning, and belching like a giant old rocking chair, and hovered just above a group of cats waiting on the ground. Amazed, Lucky witnessed a group of cats jump from the limb to the ground. The group of waiting cats jumped easily onto the limb, and it creaked and grunted back—high, high above their heads—to its former position up in the tree.

"Whoa." Lucky remained motionless for a time until he realized that Tater was talking to him. "Huh?"

"I said that we must wait here until the Big Tree decides that we can walk its limbs."

"Until it—decides?" Lucky looked at the sprawling tree in disbelief. "Are you saying that it is alive?"

"All trees are alive, Lucky. Most of them move a lot slower, though, and this is the only tree I have ever known to acknowledge cats. Most trees go about their business as we do, and do not interact with other species."

Lucky noticed that there were indeed a lot of cats waiting for their turn to ride on a limb. "So . . . how long do we have to wait?"

"That depends on the Big Tree," answered Tater.

Just then the noise returned, and Lucky struggled to not be alarmed and awed by the immense sound. Another immense limb came down, and Lucky was surprised to see it halt just above his head, still creaking loudly.

"Come on!" Tater shouted above the noise and leaped up onto the branch. Lucky followed, and no sooner had he touched onto the Big Tree than the enormous limb ascended into the sky.

"I don't understand," Lucky told Tater as the branch came to a rest in its original position. "Why did it let us come up ahead of all those other cats?"

"I do not know," admitted Tater. "Maybe the Big Tree is interested in what you have to say."

"Oh."

"Follow me."

Walking on the Big Tree proved to be easy. The main branches were sturdy and wide. They passed by many cats. Some were huddled in groups, others sat on the outer branches taking in the view. Still others had found a nice, secluded branch and were fast asleep. Many of the cats stopped what they were doing and stared at Lucky as he passed. *That's right, check out the cool cat,* he purred to himself.

Tater continued to lead Lucky upward, jumping from branch to branch. It was when they had reached the height of the jungle trees that Tater stopped. Turning to Lucky, he spoke in a low tone. "While I do admire your grit, you are about to meet the Elders, and they expect those who seek their council to be humble. Do not speak unless they ask you to. Understood?"

"Yes, I understand." Lucky hoped he understood, anyway.

Tater walked along the branch toward the Big Tree's trunk. As they rounded a corner thick with leaves, Lucky saw an opening in the trunk. Two cats sat by the opening, one on either side. Off to the right Lucky was surprised to see two owls sitting quietly. They were a bit small, perhaps half his size, and he found their colors quite striking, mostly dark red with black banded stripes. They eyed him as he approached but said nothing.

At the entrance to the hole in the tree, one of the two guard-cats spoke to Tater. "Go on in," he said. "They are expecting you."

Tater nodded and entered the Big Tree with Lucky just one step behind him.

The room in which Lucky stood was as big as the entire house that he lived in with Jack, except this room was round, almost the whole width of the Big Tree's trunk, with a high ceiling. On the opposite end, in a semi-circle, seven stumps jutted out of the floor; they were actually part of the Big Tree. Upon each stump sat an Elder, and in the center of the room's floor sat Kyuss and a rather large owl. The owl was more than double the size of its other owl companions that sat outside, and—also unlike the others—he had yellow plumage adorning his otherwise-red feathers.

Tater walked up to the two and sat next to Kyuss. Lucky followed suit and sat next to Tater. He observed the Elders with a curious fascination—though in truth, he was enthralled with everything in Sahaland. Among the Elders, one cat in particular caught Lucky's attention. She was big and had plush-looking white fur, and she commanded attention from her mere presence. Lucky believed that she might be a queen. Because she occupied the center stump, she certainly seemed to be in charge. Lucky would learn that her name was

Persephone. The white feline gazed at Lucky for a time with piercing and beautiful eyes. Lucky began to feel uncomfortable. Then he noticed that all seven of the Elders were scrutinizing him, and he couldn't help but flick his tail nervously.

Finally, Persephone's gaze left Lucky and focused on the great grey-and-white cat. "Tater, it is good to see you this day."

"And you, Persephone," replied Tater.

"Kyuss has told us what has occurred," the white cat stated. "We know of the stones that this cat's human companions possess." Then, tilting her head slightly toward the large owl, "Sherwyn has supported the claim that an army is on its way to wage war against us. Tell us, Tater, is there any update from what we already know?"

"Only that despite the short time I have spent with this cat, I think he has honor and good intentions."

"You mean that you like him?"

"Yes, I do."

Lucky looked at Tater then and was glad for the first time that he was in Sahaland. He had a friend.

"Lucky," Persephone broke into his thoughts, "tell us how your humans and you came to acquire the stones that you are said to possess."

Lucky paused for a moment, eyeing each of the Elders. He swallowed, taking a deep breath, and told his story.

Chapter 17

>> ∘ <<

He dreamed of Baron. *Lucky was learning to fly, and the heron was his teacher. They both sat on the edge of Baron's high nest with the tufted straw sticking out the top.*

"Are you ready, Lucky?" asked Baron.

"Let's do this," the orange tabby responded. With that, he felt his legs push off from the nest and he glided out over the land. The feeling was incredible. He felt weightless riding the air currents, and for a moment he understood what it meant to be a bird. Baron appeared to the left of Lucky's vision. As Lucky glided effortlessly, the great bird nodded in approval of the cat's newborn flying ability.

As they flew away from the cottage, the landscape began to change. Lucky wondered why . . . then he realized that they were no longer flying over Sturgus. Familiar houses began to replace the open terrain and clutter the landscape, now connected by concrete and tar-paved roads. Then he saw it—his house—home. He was overjoyed at the sight and turned his head to share this with Baron . . . but Baron was no longer there.

Lucky circled the house. He wanted to land and go inside but was unable to lower himself to the ground. Baron had taught him to fly, but not how to land.

He watched as Jack's parents came out of the house and began walking down the block. Lucky grew excited and called out to them, but his words were whipped away in the wind. Jack's parents turned near the end of the street and walked up to Mrs. Krauss's home. Her house glowed yellow with energy and, as they neared the front door, it opened by itself. Jack's parents entered the house and the door shut behind them.

Lucky blinked a few times as he awakened. He yawned and breathed the air, heavy with the scent of the jungle. Sleeping on the Big Tree proved to be a lot easier than Lucky had thought. All the great limbs moving about the Big Tree were barely heard when one was actually on the tree; only a calming vibration could be felt along all the branches. Lucky was perplexed by this. Perhaps the giant leaves muffled the sound?

"So! You are awake."

Lucky spun around in his spot and eyed the branch on which he stood. The cat before him was as black as a starless sky. He sat calmly, self-assured in his golden-eyed gaze.

Lucky was unsure of what to do or say so he slow-blinked as a sign of greeting.

The black cat slow-blinked in return and tilted his head slightly. "Come." He turned and leaped to a higher branch.

Lucky scrambled to his feet and followed. The black cat leaped up the branches like the jaguars he'd seen on human television shows. Documentaries, they were called. Lucky had to work at it, but he kept pace with the ebony-colored cat. The higher they went, the fewer cats there were. So it was that Lucky found himself at the very top of the Big Tree, he and the black cat, their heads sticking out above the canopy. To the north, Lucky could see the rolling hills just past the edge of Sahaland. To the south, he could see Sahaland extend as far as it did on all the other sides, but beyond that there was only sky, and nothing else . . . no more Sturgus.

It was the southern edge of the world.

The afternoon sky was clear, and the wind strolled in at a gentle pace from the edge of the world. Lucky was puzzled that the black cat brought him up here. He turned to the feline to ask but saw that his eyes were closed. He breathed in deeply, again and again. Lucky noticed, too, that the cat wasn't exactly black. In the sunlight, the coat on his chest and shoulders shone a soft burnt umber.

The cat, his eyes still closed, spoke quietly. "So. Tell me, how is Fay?"

It was then that Lucky knew who the black cat was. "You must be Bootsy."

"Yes." The black cat looked at him, then asked again, "How is she?"

"You know my story?"

"The Elders told me."

"The last time I saw Fay, she was with her mother and Baron. She said she was going to find her ship, the *Minnow Sowta*. She was well. They all were."

The black cat, Bootsy, nodded silently with a slow half-blink, then peered up at the open sky. The light wind gently blew his fur out of place.

"You miss her, don't you?" Lucky said this as more of a statement than a question.

"As much as any cat could miss a human, yes. She was, and is, my best friend."

"Yeah," said Lucky. "From the way they talked about you, I think they miss you, too." Lucky and Bootsy were silent for a moment, thinking of their common bond of having human companions and how rare it was in this world. Then Lucky changed the subject. "So, what's the deal with those owls? Do they live with the cats?"

Bootsy answered, "Sherwyn and his family are our allies. They live in the glen just north of Sahaland."

"So, cats and owls are friends?"

"Not all owls, just Sherwyn and his family. It is a rare and special alliance." He rose, arched his back in a stretch, and honed his claws on the branch. "Well, we should go now."

"But where are we going? Are you going to take me to the purple stone?" asked Lucky.

"The Elders will discuss matters concerning you and the purple stone. Until they reach a decision, they have asked that you stay under my guard as we travel around."

"Were you asked because of your human travels with Fay?" asked Lucky.

"Yes," Bootsy answered.

"But where are we *going*?"

Bootsy looked at Lucky before bounding down the Big Tree and replying, "Why, my cousin, to the edge of the world."

Jack glared into the campfire and muttered with an edginess to his voice, "Where can he be? He should be back by now, shouldn't he?"

Abigail looked at him with the fire reflecting in her eyes. "Patience, Jack. You know, when you were up in Other Mountain by yourself, Fay behaved in the same way."

"Really?"

"Yes, really."

Jack looked at Logan. The cat had spent a good deal of the day sitting away from them. Gradually he edged closer, ending up on the other side of the campfire where he was grooming his coat. Jack thought Logan was nothing like Lucky. Logan was more wary. He didn't trust humans. The cat paused in grooming his double-layered coat and regarded Jack. His unnerving, orange-eyed stare was the one thing that Jack could have done without. Jack half-worried that Logan might attack him at any given moment. He chose instead to redirect his nervousness into conversation.

"They won't hurt him, will they, Logan?"

"I do not know. Most likely, if things do not go the way you want them to, they will just dismiss him. Of course, if he runs across Lono, then things could get complicated."

"Who is Lono?" asked Abigail.

"Lono is one of our top warriors. He is a big, short-haired grey cat who is one of the fiercest cats of all the clowders. If he meets Lucky, he might kill him for associating with humans."

"What?" Jack exclaimed. He looked at Abigail. "We have to go find him."

"You cannot," replied Logan.

Abigail put a hand on Jack's shoulder. "Jack, Lucky is going to be fine."

Jack looked at Abigail. "How can you be so sure?"

She reached for the pouch that was tied to his waist and produced the blue stone. She put it in his hands, and it warmed his senses while erasing any anxiety he was feeling. Logan sauntered around the campfire to sit close to them and gaze at the stone. Even Logan was intrigued.

"You have two stones, Jack." Abigail grinned. "And I cannot wait to see the third stone. Purple is my favorite color."

"I like blue," he said, gazing at the warm stone in his hand.

"So, what happens after we get the purple stone?"

"I'm not sure," Jack replied. "I assume we need to get these stones to the statue, or body of Ebon. I'll probably have the pulling feeling. If not, I don't know how we're going to find it, especially if the Meadow of Tears keeps moving. I just know that I want to find it before that assassin finds us."

"I was thinking about that," said Abigail. "I think you might not have to fight him."

"Why do you say that?"

"Well, remember the picture of you facing the stronsay? You did not fight it."

"Yeah, I really hope you're right, but in that picture, I wasn't wielding a sword—it was a branch."

"Maybe, but when you finally saw the stronsay, you were not holding a branch and the stronsay was not after you. And, in the picture where you are fighting the assassin, you are holding the blue stone. Well, Jack, you already have the blue stone, and you didn't meet the assassin. You met wolves. Caveman said the pictures are interpretations. I think if you do meet this man, it may not be a physical fight. Maybe all you must do is outsmart him. If that is the case, then I would not worry so much. You got us this far, Jack. I think you are pretty clever—for a boy, that is."

"Thanks," Jack said. They all fell quiet after that. Jack thought of the assassin, and, even though he held the blue stone in his hand, he shuddered.

Chapter 18

〉〉∘〈〈

It was dark, very dark. Lucky followed Bootsy through the underbrush of Sahaland, traveling at a quick pace. The jungle was alive with noise and the thickness of the air hung heavy.

Bootsy stopped suddenly. "Do you hear that?"

Lucky's ears picked up a high-pitched screeching sound. It came from up in the trees ahead of them. "What is that noise? It's awful."

"Wormbats."

"Wormbats?"

Bootsy nodded once. "Wormbats."

"What's a wormbat?" asked Lucky.

"You will see. Notice how the trees are different here at the edge of the world than anywhere else in Sahaland. These trees contain lemfruit. Wormbats crave lemfruit."

At that moment, three blurry forms sped past them. Lucky watched in amazement as three formidable cats leaped into the trees and began scaling the trunks with amazing swiftness. Twenty seconds later, Lucky could hear scuffling and screeching as the wormbats took to the air.

"We are almost there," said Bootsy. "Just moments away."

Lucky followed, and, a few minutes later, they arrived. Lucky stood at the edge of a cliff. The edge of the world; Lucky had been nervous to see it, but it was a beautiful sight. Lucky looked up. The sky was so black, and there were stars—so many stars—reaching down as if to cradle Sturgus, to hold it in its place in the universe. Then Lucky gazed down. The cliff itself extended down a couple of hundred feet before it simply ended. Beyond it, there were only stars . . . and a moon.

"That is a moon down there," Lucky muttered.

"Yes," replied Bootsy.

"But . . . that is not the same moon that you have up here."

"No," answered Bootsy.

Lucky looked puzzled, so Bootsy elaborated. "We cats believe that on the underside of Sturgus there is another world . . . a world that is upside down, but somehow nothing falls off it into space. To whoever lives there, we are the ones who are upside down. That is their moon."

Suddenly, there was loud shrieking—a lot of shrieking—coming from behind them. Lucky's head snapped up as a large group of wormbats burst from the treetops. They were slightly smaller than the cats themselves, and resembled giant earthworms with bat wings and bald, rat-like heads. They were grey, pink, and ugly, and Lucky was convinced that he really didn't want to get close to one. They flew erratically like moths did in his world; they zigzagged across the sky, awkward creatures that had no business being in the air.

Then, they heard *it*. A belching gong of a sound that reverberated in the night air.

"Now be very still in the shadows with me," Bootsy stated calmly, his voice lowering, "and watch."

It flew out from below the cliffs with its belly up, displaying its horrible and awesome claws, and its train of a tail trailing behind. Its wingspan blackened out the moon as it flew across, larger than anything that Lucky had ever seen. It was terrifying but flew gracefully and fluidly, like a dancer. It sped up the length of the cliff, eyes glowing and mouth agape, displaying razor-sharp teeth and a forked tongue. It drew a deep, sighing breath, and then a flame spewed from its mouth into the night sky, swirling around the mass of wormbats. The creatures' shrieks turned into agonized screams, their bodies trailing smoke as they tumbled into the beast's mouth.

Lucky's fur stood on end. "Holy fart!" he shrieked. He fought the urge to run to the relative safety of the jungle, and instead heeded Bootsy's instructions. He stayed still, but, oh, he wanted to run!

"Is ... is that a ... a ... ?" he grasped for words but found none.

"She is called Galadeese. And yes, she is a dragon," Bootsy whispered, correctly guessing Lucky's question.

Having consumed the swarm of wormbats quickly, the great dragon circled the night sky and dipped beyond the cats' line of vision below the cliff, as if to return to her underworld lair. However, more wormbats, farther east this time, screeched into the night air from the grove of lemfruit trees. Galadeese glided on the air currents while her breath cooked the wormbats to satisfy both her taste buds and her stomach.

She flapped her great wings as she enjoyed the roasted creatures and then shot upward again, piercing a cloud as she arced out and over the Abyss. Tilting down, she spun south, then east, then south, once more. Again, more wormbats darted out from their trees with screeches tinny and shrill, and again the dragon—with efficiency and purpose—mowed them down with a roar of thunder and a flame of lightning.

It perplexed Lucky that the wormbats kept leaving the safety of the trees, but then he remembered the cats flushing them out. He looked at Bootsy. "The cats are *feeding* the dragon?"

"Yes," Bootsy replied.

"But—why?"

"Look at the cliff. You see all the various holes all along it, yes?"

"Yes."

"Well, the wormbats live in those holes. They have to fly up to the lemfruit trees to eat. Without us cats to scare them into the sky, the wormbats would travel and feed silently, and Galadeese would have a hard time finding them. She would resort to burning the trees to

get at the creatures and destroy all the trees and vegetation in the process, including the lemfruit trees. Without food, the wormbats would either die or leave this place, and Galadeese would then turn her attention onto Sahaland and us cats as a source of food. So, we come here to flush out wormbats to feed her. What we do helps maintain harmony between the cats and Galadeese.

"The wormbats," asked Lucky, "do they speak?"

"No."

"Does Galadeese?"

"I do not know."

Lucky thought a moment. "Is Galadeese part of why you think that there's another world down there?"

"Yes. Did you notice the way Galadeese came from below? She was upside down. She emerges this way all the time. It is believed that down there, she is right side up. When she is done feeding, she will return below, and, as she turns to go, she once again turns upside down."

Lucky reflected then, taking in all that Bootsy was telling him. "Why don't your owl friends fly down there," he suggested, whiskers twitching, "and find out?"

"No one will go down there, lest Galadeese make a morsel of them."

"That's too bad," said Lucky. "If there really is a world down there, all the cats could escape from the Muskans."

"Would you risk jumping to find out?" asked Bootsy.

"Oh, no way," replied Lucky.

"That is right," said Bootsy. "No cat would. However, you have given me an idea. Come. Let us visit the only two humans living in Sahaland."

Bootsy stood and headed into the jungle. Lucky followed.

"Two humans? Here?"

"Yes," replied Bootsy as they walked. "We have a truce with them. She is a witch and he's a Thrasher."

"Witch? You mean she's a sorceress?"

"She is a type of sorceress," the black cat replied. "She once told me about the different types of sorceresses, but it was so detailed and lengthy that all I got from the conversation is that witches have cauldrons."

"What's a Thrasher?" Lucky asked, following Bootsy as they wove their way through the jungle.

"There once were forty-one human warriors who banded together to defy the rule of Pale. They attacked many of Pale's outposts with success. They were the best warriors of their kind and they called themselves Thrashers, but there was one among them who betrayed all the others. Now, there are only two left. One lives here in hiding, and the betrayer has become Pale's number-one assassin."

"I don't get it," said Lucky. "Why would anybody betray their own friends? It doesn't make sense."

"Maybe he was not friends with the other Thrashers," Bootsy replied. "Maybe he never had friends. We do not understand. Anyway, life is not without a few poetic jokes. Soon after betraying the Thrashers, the lone assassin encountered and battled a powerful sorceress who put a spell on him, making his hair sopping wet all the time."

Lucky's eyes widened as he exclaimed "A spirit-wolf told Jack that a man with wet hair was after us!"

Bootsy stopped. "That is an unwelcome omen. If he does find you, he will kill you. He is the Damp, Dayvid the Damp. Lucky, you absolutely must not let him find you."

"Well," replied Lucky, "if you cats would just paw over the purple stone, we can finish this mission and Jack and I can hopefully get back to our world."

Bootsy shook his head slowly. "I am sorry, Lucky, that decision is up to the Elders, and we have a couple more stops to make before we head back to the Big Tree. There is, after all, Pale's horde advancing on us, and I need to talk to Krystina about what can be done. She is the witch. Her husband is Greg, the Thrasher."

"Greg the Thrasher," repeated Lucky, "sounds tough. So, about this sorceress, how come she put that spell on Dayvid the Damp? Why didn't she put a spell on him that would make him be nice, instead? That's what I would have done."

"A sorceress can only conjure spells that she has taken the time to prepare ahead of time. Perhaps that was the best spell she had at the time. Anyway, that spell came at a price. For the Damp to become damp, her hair would forever float about her as if underwater. Some people are afraid of her appearance because of this."

"Hey, that's Malia," exclaimed Lucky.

"You know her?' asked Bootsy, head tilted.

"Yeah, she's the Keeper of the Wagon of Prophecy. She's one of the people who sent us on this mission."

"Hmm," said Bootsy, "small world."

"Jack says this place is smaller than our world but I don't know. It seems pretty big to me."

The two walked for a time, ducking under low-hanging foliage and leaping over a fallen branch, until they came upon a clearing with about two dozen cats and a small pond with a tree branch hanging low over it. One cat, Lucky noticed, was much smaller than the others. Her huge eyes seemed to barely fit on her diminutive face and her coat, tan with spots, reminded Lucky of a desert he had seen in a movie. She walked up to Lucky and sniffed him cautiously, then—with lightning-like quickness—gave him a whack in the head with her paw.

"Hey!" hissed Lucky, flattening his ears. "That hurt. What was that for?"

"You are the cat that everybody is talking about, right? The Cat from Another World?" she purred.

"Yeah, so?"

"So, I have never hit a cat from another world before." Her eyes twinkled. "Now I have." Then she turned from Lucky and slunk up to Bootsy.

"Alexys," he said, "you really should be nicer to our guest."

The female cat head-butted Bootsy firmly in the shoulder. He blinked slowly, but otherwise showed stoic nonchalance. "Oh, Bootsy," she purred, "that *was* nice. Where is my son?"

"Logan was put on guard detail. He is with Lucky's human friends."

"Oh," she replied, a bit disappointed, "I had a smack reserved for him, as well. Later, then."

Just then a kitten, white with grey, came bounding out from the bushes. He charged at Bootsy and tackled his ebony leader.

Bootsy allowed himself to be knocked to the ground, rolling about in mock-battle with the little one, who clutched the elder warrior cat with tiny forepaws and bunny-kicked him ferociously with his hind legs. "Hey," Bootsy said in a purr-laugh, "it's my special little guy. Akyra!"

Bootsy and Akyra rough-housed together for many moments until Bootsy pinned Akyra to the ground and began grooming the top of the little one's half-grey head. Akyra complied instantly.

Lucky looked at the scene, amazed. He had never seen a male cat groom a kitten before. "Is he your son?" he asked.

"Akyra? No, his parents perished from a falling tree. I have been raising him as my own, though, with help from the rest of the clowder, of course." Lucky then realized he was in the presence of Bootsy's own clowder.

Bootsy finished grooming Akyra and looked at Alexys. "Meeting" was all he said and then he sauntered off to the pond.

Alexys stared directly at Lucky. "Come."

Lucky followed her and all the other cats in the clowder to the pond. The cats positioned themselves around its edge as Bootsy appeared on the branch that bent low just above the pond. He sat tall on the branch and waited for all in the clowder to settle in their spots. Lucky found his own place on the edge of the pond between Alexys and Akyra and looked up attentively at Bootsy.

"Friends," he started, "I am sure you have grave concerns over the news of the approaching horde."

"Is it true?" asked one cat with grey tabby markings and just a stub of a tail, "or is it just tall tales from a strange cat who claims to be from a different world?"

"It is true, Max," replied Bootsy. "The owls confirm it, and, for the record, I believe Lucky's story of the place from which he comes. I have spent the day with him, and all I will say on the matter is that if Lucky were to decide to stay in Sahaland, I would offer him a home within this clowder."

Lucky was shocked. It had never occurred to him that he could stay. The thought bounced about in his head like a tennis ball stuffed full of catnip. *Stay?*

"What are we to do, then?" Max asked Bootsy.

"The Elders are mulling it over. I will be heading back to the Big Tree, but first I must talk to the witch. Alexys, I want you to see that all our kittens and their mothers are ready to go to the tunnels when the word is given. The rest of you, I think you should be ready. They are coming for all of us. They are much, much bigger than we are, but we cats outnumber them. I know you think that we stand no chance against the coming horde, but you are wrong. We are cats. The world has deemed us evil and untrustworthy, but those who believe so are wrong. Many, many years ago a cat was framed for the hardship that befell a village, and, because of this, all cats are now feared, hated. We have lived in Sahaland for centuries. It is our home. We have guarded it well for such a very long time, being very selective about who may live here with us. As a result, the Muskans have no idea what our numbers really are, that we number in the thousands—thousands to their hundreds—an advantage on which we can create a strategy. It will not be easy, and I will not lie to you, the odds are very much against us because of their cunning and horrible weapons, but we do have a chance. We may yet prevail."

As Bootsy continued his speech, Lucky couldn't help but feel despair for his feline friends. He thought of the wolves and knew, in the pit of his stomach, that the cats were going to be massacred. But, as he looked at the cats listening intently to Bootsy's words, he could find no fear in their eyes, only fire. They were not afraid, not even the little ones. Lucky's gaze swung in the direction of Akyra. The white-and-grey kitten looked up at Bootsy with total and complete admiration, determination, resilience, and a belief that all kittens share: that nothing could possibly go wrong.

Chapter 19

>> ∘ <<

The jungle floor felt uncomfortably hot under Lucky's paws, even at such a late hour. The humidity had increased with the night and his fur matted against him, heavy from the weight of the air. He followed Bootsy quietly as they treaded the path with its twists and turns. Given the choice, Lucky would have preferred to sleep with Jack, as he had always done. However, matters were becoming more and more urgent. He desperately wanted to obtain the purple stone and return to Jack before Pale's horde arrived.

"Are we there yet?" It was the seventh time he had asked this question, and each time, he had been met with silence.

This time, Bootsy stopped. He looked back at Lucky. His answer was simple. "Yes."

The two cats stepped forward and the jungle opened up to reveal a cabin in a small clearing, with fifteen or so cats milling about.

"Oh, look. More cats."

Bootsy couldn't help but chuckle a bit at Lucky's comment. "I take it there are not many cats in your world?"

"Sure, there are," Lucky replied, "but I don't know many of us that cluster like you do."

The cats by the cabin noticed them and three of them broke off from the group and steadily approached. Bootsy stopped and Lucky followed his lead. As they neared, Lucky recognized the very large grey-and-white cat instantly.

Tater nodded at the two as he came to a halt before them. "Bootsy."

"Tater."

"It is good to see you again," Tater said to Lucky.

"Yeah," Lucky replied.

Tater then turned his gaze back to the black cat. "So, what brings you here?"

"I need to speak with Krystina."

"She is inside," Tater replied. "Greg is with her."

At that moment, the cabin door opened, and a man stepped out, carrying several swords. He was of strong build, and his blond hair fell to his shoulders. The cats watched as he dropped the swords with a clatter on the ground next to a grinding wheel, then he proceeded to walk toward them.

"Hey, Bootsy!" he called. "It is good to see you. Is this the cat we have heard about?"

"Yes," replied Bootsy. "Greg, I would like you to meet Lucky."

The Thrasher knelt and held out his hand, palm-side down, to allow Lucky to approach and sniff. After a few moments, he rubbed Lucky briskly across his head and along his spine. Lucky's nerves went haywire, and his first instinct was to run from the strange figure that towered over him. However, he realized he liked this human, thought better of it, and allowed him to continue with what Lucky decided was one absolutely fantastic back rub.

"Lucky," he said, "it is nice to meet you. Nice little harness you are wearing there, buddy."

"Thank you," Lucky purred. "So, what are you going to do with all those swords?"

"Well, little guy, I will tell you. I have let the blades dull over time, so now I need to sharpen them for the coming battle."

Lucky's eyes widened. "You'll fight the horde that's coming?"

"Affirmative. An enemy of the cats is an enemy of mine."

"Can you stop them?" Lucky was concerned.

"Well, I am pretty handy with a sword, and my wife knows a spell or two. The cats have not come to a decision yet on what they are going to do. I do not think they can run from this one. If the Pale wants the cats destroyed, rest assured, he will send enough troops. And this is our home, too."

"You haven't answered my question." Lucky stared intently at Greg.

"Well, little guy, truthfully, no. I do not think we can stop them. There are just too many. However, you are here, and I think that should be considered."

Lucky was curious. "What do you mean?"

"Well, you and your human are on a quest to bring back Ebon, right? If you brought him back, that would most certainly turn the odds in our favor . . . assuming, of course, that Ebon would help us."

"So, you believe that we'll do well in our quest?"

Greg scratched his chin. "Lucky, I have not really given it much thought. I suppose so. My wife, however, is more—" he paused and waved his hand as if to conjure up the appropriate word, "—*in-tune* on matters like that. She is a firm believer, positive that you will succeed in your mission, and that Ebon will fight alongside us and the cats in destroying our enemies."

Lucky turned to ask Bootsy for his opinion, but the lean black cat was no longer standing next to him. Lucky looked at the cabin doorway just in time to see Bootsy slip indoors.

Bootsy entered the cabin with both caution and conviction. He was friends with both Krystina and Greg but did not want to offend them or their cats by entering unannounced. The cabin was typical of many cabins that humans tended to live in, with chairs, a table or two, a bed, and a cauldron sitting in the fireplace. The biggest difference with this particular cabin were the various smells that Bootsy picked up with his nose. The warm aroma of sage and bejorei bark filled the air. Along with other strange herb smells, these were not meant for cooking but for conjuring.

Krystina sat before the cauldron, continuing to drop in a pinch of this, a dash of that. Her clothing was made of black velvet and lace, and she wore flowers braided throughout her hair that were both beautiful and deadly. Her neck, ears, and hands were adorned with an abundance of jewelry—various stones, shells, plants, and metals. Her back was to Bootsy, so initially all he saw was her silhouette, thin, smallish, and angular.

"Hello, Bootsy," she said, her back still turned to him.

"Krystina," he replied.

"I understand that the feline of the visitors is with you."

"Yes. He is outside, speaking to Greg. I thought I would come in ahead of him so that you and I could talk first."

Krystina stopped tending to her cauldron of potion. She turned and peered at Bootsy curiously. "What is on your mind?"

"I want to hear your thoughts on a question I have that—if I am right—could turn the odds in our favor against the Muskans."

"Go on," said Krystina.

"It is about Galadeese."

"The dragon?" Krystina's eyes lit up at the name, reflecting the orange light from the fire under the cauldron.

"Yes. I want to know whether you think Galadeese would be willing to talk with us."

Krystina looked at Bootsy as if he might be mad in the head, then, slowly, understanding spread across her face. "You want to enlist Galadeese in our fight?"

Bootsy gazed at Krystina, his eyes dancing green from the light of the fire that flickered beneath the black kettle. "Is it possible?"

Krystina's lips curled into a mischievous grin. "It is my belief that the dragon would be amenable to helping us. So, yes, it is very possible. Ha-ha!" Krystina knelt before Bootsy bringing her face to mere inches to his. "The big question we now have is: how are we to communicate with her without becoming lunch, yes? Hmm."

"'You have something we could use to that end?"

"Could be, could be. It's going to be quite the spell, oh yes, quite the spell, indeed." Krystina giggled, rose, and feverishly began adding more ingredients to her cauldron.

Chapter 20

>>∘<<

One day before the horde was to converge upon Sahaland, the morning brought bright shafts of sunlight that pierced the jungle. Lucky once again sat before the Elders up in the Big Tree, inside the hollow. To his left was Tater and to his right was a cat he had never seen before, grey and very adept-looking, a warrior cat. As before, Persephone was the first to speak.

"Tater, it is good to see you, again. But where is Bootsy?"

"Apologies. Bootsy asked me to bring Lucky back in his stead. He gave no reason and left in a hurry with the witch."

"Well." Persephone's whiskers twitched erratically as she pondered over Tater's words. "That is unfortunate." She turned to the grey cat. "Lono, what words do you bring?"

The cat to Lucky's right spoke. "The horde is close. They will reach Sahaland's edge by nightfall."

"That soon?" Persephone seemed to let out a sigh. "Perhaps this news can be used to our advantage. After all, there are few animals in our land that can move unseen at night better than a cat, especially if they enter the near-total darkness of the jungle."

"That is correct," replied Lono. "But what if they choose to wait until the morning before they decide to enter Sahaland? We will have an advantage of being unseen at night *if* they enter the jungle. However, if we fight them in the meadows, the advantage will be lost, as they will easily see us by the light of the moon. The advantage is also theirs if we wait until they come into the jungle by day."

The Elders looked at one another in silence. "Tell us, then," Persephone mewed. "As one of our best warrior strategists, what is your recommendation?"

Lono, his head held high, answered with conviction. "We get every cat that is able to fight, and we line the edge of the jungle. We hide in the trees, under logs, behind rocks. We wait, then, and see what the horde plans to do. If they enter, then the advantage is ours and we attack. If they do not enter, I say we wait for them. They will grow impatient. We know Sahaland, they do not. I believe we are better off fighting in the jungle during the day than in the meadows by night."

Persephone looked at Lono for a moment. Her plush, white fur seemed to glow in the dim light of the hollow as she pondered Lono's suggestion. The other Elders all turned their gazes to her, as if to confirm what needed to be said next.

She looked at Lucky and held his gaze with eyes of piercing emerald, her wisdom and stoicism staring into the face of youthful innocence and grandeur. "I had wanted to ask Bootsy what he thought of you. Seeing, however, that he is absent from this rather urgent and important conversation," she continued, tail switching with some irritation, "I will ask you: what are your thoughts of him?"

Lucky's face brightened and he proudly replied. "Bootsy said that if I was to ever decide to stay in Sahaland I could join his clowder."

"I see! That tells me much about what Bootsy thinks of you." Persephone's eyes gleamed at Lucky's statement. "Lucky, we have come to a decision about your quest to obtain the Purple Stone of Ebon."

Persephone closed her eyes and was quiet for a moment, and Lucky thought maybe she was reconsidering, when the hollow began to shake. It started as a mild vibration, but quickly turned violent, shaking the hollow wildly. The Elders sat calmly on their stumps but Lucky, Tater, and Lono found themselves with legs splayed and their claws dug into the floor to keep from falling. In the center of the hollow, between the Elders and the three tomcats, the wood splayed and splintered before their eyes, and a live branch jutted up with many oversized leaves growing and opening. And as quickly as it had started, the quaking stopped.

The room was bathed in an intense purple glow as the last of the leaves opened to reveal the purple stone.

Lucky's eyes were wide with dilated pupils; his claws still dug into the floor of the hollow. "Holy cow!" he exclaimed. "What just happened?"

Tater and Lono had both resumed sitting calmly, but for Lono, his calm was forced as he realized what the Elders were doing. "Persephone, you cannot—?"

Persephone, her coat reflecting lavender from the glow of the purple stone, remained stoic. "Lucky," she said, "between us, sitting on this branch, is the stone that you seek. Let me tell you what it means to us cats.

"Once, long ago, we cats were forced into exile from the rest of the world through lies and treachery. We came here, to Sahaland, where we felt safe and learned to call this edge of the world home. When we discovered the Big Tree, we were frightened of its sound and the purposeful way its limbs would move, but we felt a compulsion to be close to it, to understand it. We have since learned that the true source of the Big Tree's power lies in the purple stone that sits cradled in its heart. We have heard legends of the Three Stones of Ebon and have wondered if perhaps this might be one of them. We know that it is the stone that moves this tree and has made it the size that you see today. It also created this room for us so that we may govern ourselves under its positive power. If we give you the stone, the tree will cease to move its limbs, and become just a big tree.

"We love this tree, and we love Sahaland. Regardless of whether we give you the stone or not, we Elders believe that the oncoming horde will most assuredly destroy our home as they will destroy us. They might even find the purple stone and take it to Pale. We simply cannot have that.

"Tell us, Lucky, do you truly believe in this quest on which you have been journeying?"

Lucky felt the eyes of everyone in the room focused on him.

"Well, how can I *not* believe in it? You need to understand something. Before I came here, I had never seen a centaur before, or floated on a cloud, or . . ." He paused in reflection for a moment. "Or been able to have a real conversation with Jack. How can I believe in all that I've seen since coming to your world, and not believe in the legend of Ebon? Either all of it is true, or it's not. If the legend doesn't exist, then neither do any of you."

"Reason," whispered Tater, taken aback by the young cat's statement.

Persephone eyed Lucky with shared understanding. "Know that when I give you this stone, the Big Tree will still be alive, but it will cease to move its limbs for us."

Suddenly, Lono sprang on Lucky, and held him to the ground, fangs bared no more than an inch from Lucky's face. "Understand this, kitten," he hissed viciously. "If I survive this upcoming battle and Ebon does not return, I will hunt you down and end your life."

"Enough!" howled Tater. He and Lono faced each other down for several seconds, and then the grey cat slowly backed away from their young, frightened guest, Lucky.

"Toms, let us all remember where we are," said Persephone. She hopped gracefully from her stump and stood before the stone in the branch. She picked up the stone with her mouth and dropped it into the pouch on Lucky's harness. Instantly, Lucky felt the same warmth and comfort that the other two stones provided.

Suddenly, they were surrounded by a chorus of loud creaks and groans. The Big Tree was saying goodbye to the stone that had nurtured it to its tremendous size. Outside, many of its great limbs lowered until they were only a few feet from the ground so that the cats would still be able to climb it. Then they became still, never to move again except to bend and sway with the wind, just like any other tree.

Persephone looked to Tater. "You will escort Lucky to his humans." She then looked at Lono. "It is time to gather all the clowders. Inform all mothers and kittens to head to the caves. All other cats will gather at the jungle's edge. We will observe the Muskans and what they intend to do, and hope for the sake of all of Sahaland that the way we respond will be the right one."

Chapter 21

Jack and Abigail were discussing with Logan the politics within cat society, including the power struggles displayed among its various clowders, when Lucky and Tater showed up.

"Lucky!" Jack scrambled to his feet, scooped up his furry little friend and hugged him tight.

Logan flinched and did his best to not flatten his ears at the sight. "Hmm," he huffed after a time. "If a human was to ever pick me up like that, I would have to show him how deep my claws can sink into his skin."

Tater flicked his tail in amusement at his colleague's reaction. "Logan, how goes it?"

"It goes" was his reply.

Abigail walked up and petted Lucky's head as he purred in Jack's arms. "Mission accomplished," meowed Lucky gleefully.

Jack set Lucky down and reached into his harness. The warmth of the purple stone was instantaneous; Jack and Abigail shared a look of relief. Jack pulled out the other two stones from his pouch, and with all three stones in his hands they began to glow even brighter than before.

"Well, we did it," breathed Abigail. "We finally did it."

"Not quite," replied Jack. "We still have to get these to the Meadow of Tears and the statue that is the body of Ebon."

"How will you find it?" asked Tater.

"Well," said Jack, "I felt a pulling that brought us to each stone. I think I will feel a pulling that will lead us to the statue, as well."

"Do you feel a pulling now?" asked Logan.

"Er . . . well, no."

"How long does it take?" asked Logan.

"I don't know." Jack shrugged. "It just kinda happens when it happens."

Everyone was quiet. It seemed that the jungle itself had also become very still.

"How about now?" asked Logan, breaking the silence.

"No," Jack answered.

They sat there for what felt like quite some time, Jack, Abigail, and the three cats, all waiting for a feeling of pulling that never came.

"So . . . what do we do now?" asked Lucky.

Jack let out a sigh. "I don't know."

"Well," offered Abigail, trying to be practical, "we could set off toward the west and then go north. It would take us to Valmar in about fifteen days, and we would evade the horde altogether—"

"Or," Lucky cut in, "we could stay and help the cats. They gave us the stone, but not without sacrifice. We owe them."

"What do you mean?" asked Jack.

Lucky proceeded to tell them about the Big Tree and its history with the purple stone. When he was done, it was Abigail who spoke first.

"Lucky, it is a lovely story, but we are on a quest, and it must take precedence over everything. It means making tough choices that none of us want to make. Anyway, why could the cats not just come with us?"

"You forget, we are not wanted out there, among the humans." It was now Tater who spoke. "Sahaland is our last refuge. There is nowhere else for us to go."

"Lucky's right," said Jack. "If we don't know which way to go, I say we stay and fight."

"Stay and fight?" asked Abigail. She looked at Lucky at that moment and read the desperation on his face. "Agreed. We stay and fight."

"Hey, you still have that potion of superpowers, right?"

"You mean the Enhancement Potion?" Abigail corrected.

"Yeah," Jack replied. "You could take it to make you the best sorceress possible and you can find a spell that will save the cats."

"Jack, that might be true, but even if I come up with a really great spell, there is no way I can find all the ingredients in time. Plus, a spell powerful enough to stop the horde would take a long time to conjure. You, however, could take the potion to allow you to be an expert in wielding your cutlass."

Jack looked at his friend, concerned but surprisingly calm. "Abigail," he said quietly, "I don't want to kill anybody."

"I know you do not, but it may come to that. How else are we to help the cats, except to fight too?"

Now Tater spoke up. "You could each take one of the three stones and walk among the cats so they might nuzzle them. It would provide great courage to each cat, instill a belief that we can be victorious. Then, as the sun sets, you could sneak away before the horde attacks and look for the statue. It would be foolhardy for you to jeopardize your mission."

It was agreed then and there that they would share the energy of the stones with the cats of Sahaland. As the afternoon approached,

Jack, Abigail, and Lucky found themselves walking amongst the cats at the edge of Sahaland, with Tater and Logan flanking them as escorts. In no time at all there were so many cats about them that they could hardly move. They were everywhere. Lucky, with the purple stone secured in his harness once again, found that it was easier to just sit up tall and let the felines come to him. The cats would approach, nuzzle the stone quickly and then move along. More than once, Lucky had to scramble to his feet after being pushed over by an overly anxious cat.

To Lucky's surprise, Lono approached. Lucky half-expected Lono to pin and threaten him again, but he didn't. Instead, Lono nuzzled the stone. Then, he looked Lucky right in the eyes.

"You should leave soon," he said solemnly. "They are almost here."

Lucky didn't know how to respond, so he quoted a line from the movie *Star Wars* that Jack had watched many, many times over.

"May the Force be with you."

Abigail walked among the cats, her arm hanging low so the cats could press up against the blue stone. Logan remained at her side and introduced her to Persephone when the head Elder came for her turn to touch the stone.

Persephone said, "I am pleased to meet you, human, and hope you will have success in returning Ebon."

"We are aware that you made a great sacrifice in giving us the stone. Thank you." Abigail knelt and—with permission—stroked her hands carefully through Persephone's coat. "I am happy to meet someone as royal as you."

"You do me honor," Persephone replied.

Jack held the red stone low as he waded through the sea of cats. There were so many cats, Jack mused, that they might win after all because of their sheer numbers. Jack had never seen so many cats at one time. They covered the jungle floor like a giant, moving, furry blanket, nuzzling the stone in his hand as they passed and then dashing to their clowders' designated meeting points.

"Well, hello there, little man," he heard a voice say.

Jack looked up to see a man with long blond hair standing in front of him. He held a short sword in one hand, a shield in the other, with daggers sheathed along each boot and a long sword on his back.

"Um . . . hello." Jack was flabbergasted; he wasn't expecting to see a man in the jungle.

"I am Greg," the man said. "I met your cat, Lucky, last night. He is quite the little guy."

"I didn't know humans lived in Sahaland. The cats wouldn't let me in until today," Jack said.

"They gave my wife and me permission long ago. We obey their rules and help them whenever it is necessary."

"Like now?"

"Yes, just like now. So, tell me, Boy from Another World, what does Lucky call you?"

"He calls me Jack."

"Well, Jack, under normal circumstances I would invite you to my cabin. My wife cooks an excellent stew, and I know that she would love to meet you."

Jack smiled at that. "Is she there now?"

Greg's face furrowed a bit. "Actually, I do not know where she is. She left last night with Bootsy and has not returned."

"Bootsy," Jack repeated, remembering the story of Fay and her cat friend. "Is he a black cat?"

"Why, yes. How did you know?"

"I know his human."

Jack told Greg an abbreviated tale of his travels with Fay on the *Minnow Sowta,* which led to Greg inspecting Jack's cutlass. "That is a nice blade you have there. It is the perfect size for you. How familiar are you with it?"

"Well," Jack started, "I've never used it in battle or anything like that, but I have practiced with it. Fay showed me a few moves."

"Will you demonstrate?" asked Greg.

"Sure." Jack grinned. He set the red stone on the ground so that the cats could continue to take turns rubbing their muzzles on it.

Jack drew his cutlass and did as the swordsman asked, thrusting and slicing at the air as he had trained. Greg was impressed with Jack's skill and proceeded to show Jack a few defensive measures and a maneuver that would prove to be a nice counterattack. Jack practiced the moves. He was a little clumsy with them, especially with the counterattack, but felt that with enough practice he could eventually master it.

Just then, an owl flew overhead. "Hoo! Horde! Horde! Is here!" it cried. "They are here!" it called over and over again.

Jack got goosebumps at the news, thinking back to how his time at the encampment with Caveman and Malia was cut short by cries just like these. He immediately put his cutlass into its sheath and snatched up the red stone. He scanned the area until he found Lucky and Abigail and made eye contact with both.

"Who is *that*?" Abigail asked Jack as the blond fighter strode away to the edge of the jungle to peer out into the clearing.

"That," said Lucky, "is Greg the Thrasher. His wife is Krystina, a witch. How cool is that?"

"Really, a witch, here?" Abigail couldn't help but beam at the prospect of yet another person who might teach her about magic.

"Guys, we need to talk," said Jack. "I don't want to die, but I'm not sure that I'm ready to leave yet, either."

"I know," agreed Abigail. "We may still be able to help."

"Then let's stay a little while longer. We can leave once the fighting starts." Jack looked at Lucky then and could see that his orange-and-white cat approved of his decision.

And so it was that Jack, Abigail, and Lucky found themselves at the edge of the jungle with Greg and the cats, peering through the branches out to the great horde of Muskan troops that stood just a couple hundred yards out in the fields. Some of the orcs had lit torches as the sun was setting because orcs have poor night vision. Now Jack got a much better look at the Muskans than he had from his high vantage point while riding on the cloud.

The humans were the meanest-looking humans he had ever seen. Many had scars, especially across their faces, and they donned black armor, dull and worn from their unending battles. The orcs were only a little taller than the humans, but their massive frames made them at least twice as wide, with a lumber to their gait caused by the enormous battle-axes that they had slung over their shoulders. The centaurs, too, had many scars. They wore armor as well, but theirs was much lighter in weight, extending back over their equine bodies along with a dorsal line of horrid-looking spikes that ended just above their tails. Only a fool would dare to leap onto their backs.

The hecti, although much smaller than the others, scared Jack the most. To him, they looked like tiny green dinosaurs with amazing dexterity. They wore no clothes, no armor, and carried no weapons, save their own long talons and teeth that were all fangs, sharp and deadly. The bugs on which they rode were orange and looked something like a cross between a giant cockroach and a praying mantis.

Jack's heart sank as he realized then and there that the cats were going to lose. The awful Muskan horde would destroy all the felines and Sahaland would burn to the ground, and there was nothing that Jack could do to prevent it.

"They don't look so tough."

Jack looked in the direction of the voice. Five cats away, he saw a white-and-grey kitten. It was Akyra, the kitten from Bootsy's clowder, standing next to Alexys.

"What are you doing here?" Alexys snapped at the furry little one. "You should be in the caves."

"I do not want to be in the caves," he hissed, extending his little claws. "I want to fight with Bootsy. Where is he?"

Alexys snarled at Akyra. "Impetuous kitten . . . get back. This is no place for you!"

Just then, right between Jack and Greg, a flash of light sparked fluorescent with yellow smoke and a woman in a dark gown appeared before them. Jack almost fell backward, surprised. Greg merely smiled at the woman. "Krissy."

The woman kissed her husband on the cheek. "Husband, miss me?"

"You know it."

The witch then turned and looked at Jack. "Jack. I am Krystina. I had wanted to hear all about your world, but we have a battle to win first."

Jack was about to respond when he heard a cat howl, "Look!"

The centaurs had formed a line and had their bow and arrows at the ready. The orcs then lumbered before them, their torches igniting the arrows that lay fitted in the bows.

"Oh, no," whispered Abigail, who had initially moved closer to Jack to meet the witch. "Jack, maybe it was a bad idea to stay. I think we should leave before the fighting starts."

"I don't think there's time for that," Jack replied warily as he stared, fixated on the centaurs and their burning arrows. The centaurs, in unison, raised their bows high, and then released them on command. The fireballs soared in a single, high-pitched whistling sound toward Sahaland's jungle. Jack gripped the hilt of his cutlass tightly, breath quickening.

"I do not want to die," Jack heard a cat say.

Krystina suddenly raised her arms high and wide, yelling, "Dniheb rehtona tuo dna llaw eno hguorht!"

A wide orange wall of light rocketed upward from the ground, all along the edge of Sahaland, rising as high as the trees. The arrows disappeared into the light, and the entire wall sunk back into the ground as rapidly as it had risen. Behind the Muskan troops the wall reappeared, rising as high as before, and the arrows streamed out, continuing their trajectory, except now they rained down on the horde from behind. Most of the arrows hit armor and stuck, leaving the horde scrambling to put out the various fires, but dozens found their mark and Jack gasped in joy and horror as Muskan foot soldiers fell to the ground.

"Nice work," Greg said to his wife. "I trust you have enough spells to aid us as the night goes on?"

"I have some, but not nearly enough." Krystina's arms swept downward to lower the wall of orange light as she chuckled. "I had to conjure up a high incantation for Bootsy that took much of my resources, but I think it will be worth it."

"Well, now I am curious," her husband said.

There was a great bellowing from the horde, and everyone steeled themselves. The Muskan troops had begun a rapid advance, angered by the magical trickery. Orcs with their battle-axes, centaurs and humans with swords and shields in hand, and the hecti skittering toward them astride their hideous monster bugs.

"Get ready!" yelled Greg.

Jack could see down the line at the cats—appearing no different from the everyday, garden-variety cats he knew from his world—preparing to fight the most horrific group of individuals Jack had ever seen, and they weren't running. *Neither will I*, he vowed to himself, even as his heart thudded in his chest.

As he scanned their numbers and then looked over at Greg, he noticed the Thrasher narrowing his eyes at one of the humans amongst the horde. Jack followed his gaze and landed on one who appeared to be—no, he *was*—looking directly at Jack. The boy couldn't see very well through the thinning smoke, but he noticed that the man carried a different shield from the others, like he wasn't normally part of the horde. Then he noticed the long, white, dripping hair. Jack's stomach twisted with the realization that he was being stared down by his would-be assassin, hired by Pale to end Jack and his beloved cat. Jack's temples pounded and clutched his cutlass so tight that his knuckles turned white and drew a deep breath to steady himself.

"The cats aren't running. Neither will I," he repeated, this time aloud.

Then there was a great din all around them. A shriek and bellow shook the very ground they stood on. Everyone heard it—felt it—even the Muskans heard it over their own roars and screeches.

Krystina grinned wickedly. "Bootsy was successful. She has arrived."

"It's—It's Galadeese," Lucky stammered in a small, fearful voice, recognizing the sound immediately.

Krystina looked down at Lucky. "Oh, yes." She laughed. "Galadeese, indeed."

Jack looked curiously at Krystina and then at Abigail. "What's a Galadeese?"

As if on cue, out of the sky she came, leathery wings beating against the currents with deliberate thrusts. If Jack thought that the Muskans were frightful, then Galadeese gave him a new perspective of terror. The dragon was huge and fast. Those in Sahaland watched, looking out at the Muskan troops, as the great creature swooped low over them, fire spewing forth from a gaping mouth of razor-sharp teeth, scorching scores among the Muskan horde.

Up into the sky she soared again, and the entire horde—centaurs, orcs, humans, and hecti alike—scrambled frantically to regroup and face this unexpected threat. But no sooner had the troops turned to face the flying beast than she was upon them once again. Feeble screams erupted from the horde as great flames the temperature of a thousand furnaces torched them, reducing most of their numbers to nothing but smoldering black ash. Back and forth Galadeese swept her great neck, raining what could only be described as a fiery hell on what was left of the once-mighty Muskan horde.

"Look!" shrieked Akyra to anyone within earshot. As Galadeese made an impossibly low pass over the horde, they all clearly saw a black feline crouched on her back, claws dug in and eyes aglow with determination.

Howls of delight and amazement filled the air. "Bootsy!" they called out. "Bootsy!"

It all left Jack floored and speechless. *This is absolutely fantastic*, he thought, slowly shaking his head in awe.

"That is Bootsy?" asked Abigail incredulously.

"Apparently so," Jack replied, unable to stop the corners of his mouth from turning up ever so slightly.

"Well, what are we waiting for?" yelled Akyra, again to no one in particular. "Let us go! Attaaaaack!"

Greg put his arm around Krystina. "Wife, you have done well. It is a shame, though . . . I so wanted to get a little sword clashing in tonight."

"Do not worry," she replied. "When Pale finds out this horde has been destroyed, he will surely send more."

"Then I will just have to save my weapon-thrashing until that day."

There were but a handful of Muskans left, and Galadeese was arcing around to finish them off when the unimaginable happened.

No one saw Akyra leave the safety of the jungle. No one saw him charge the Muskans at a startling sprint. Lucky was the first to eye the kitten as he leaped crazily at a centaur, snarling and hissing with ears laid flat and claws extended.

"No!" Lucky tried to cry out, but his voice was choked back to a whisper from all the smoke in the air. "No."

He watched as the centaur backhanded Akyra with astonishing force that sent the little kitten hurtling into the trunk of a tree. In the next moment, the centaur was engulfed in flames as Galadeese made her final pass over the scattered remains of the horde.

Galadeese landed just long enough for Bootsy to jump off, and then she launched her massive body aloft once more, soared high, and disappeared over the horizon to return to her side of the world.

The jungle erupted into cheerful meowing from the cat population and shouts of victory from the four humans. The threat was over. Sahaland was saved.

Jack and Abigail looked at each other, smiles of relief across their faces, and they hugged. Cats everywhere tumbled and purred with one another. The joy was exceptional. Jack looked down to see the joyful face of his favorite cat in any world, but he was nowhere to be found. *Celebrating with the cats, no doubt,* he thought, looking out at the devastation left in Galadeese's wake. He saw movement among the charred still forms of what had been a once-formidable foe, and spotted Bootsy speeding toward the foot of a nearby tree.

Bootsy's pace slowed, slinking carefully, then slumping, defeated, to the ground. His paws stretched out over the small, still form of the kitten that had been his to love and teach. Nothing remained of the leader who had just moments before ridden a dragon to victory in battle. Bootsy's eyes clouded in defeat. Akyra was gone.

Jack and Abigail watched as some of the cats in the jungle went out to join the black cat leader. They formed a circle around the still body of Akyra and lay as he did, paws outstretched toward their fallen child. Jack spotted Logan among those in the group.

"They are of one clowder now," Krystina whispered.

"Oh, Jack," said Abigail as she stifled a sob. "Look."

They watched as one more cat joined Bootsy's clowder and took his place with paws extended to touch the fallen Akyra.

It was Lucky.

Chapter 22

>> ◦ <<

"I was a little worried," Jack muttered to Lucky as he, Abigail, and the feline marched north out of Sahaland. "I thought you were going to stay with Bootsy's clowder when I saw you out there with the others, mourning."

"Part of me wanted to," Lucky admitted. "But I'm already part of a clowder. Back home."

Jack wanted to smile at that but kept it to himself. Even as Lucky carried the purple stone in his harness and was close to its strengthening and healing powers, he could tell his cat was grieving the death of Akyra. In fact, even though they each still carried their respective stones, they wandered across one rolling hill after another, unsure of where they were going. There was no sense of pulling for Jack, nothing to tell him which direction they should go. They entered a grove of trees and emerged onto yet another valley, another hill. This continued all morning, and the day grew quite warm.

"I do not know," Abigail sighed. "Maybe we should have stayed in Sahaland until a pulling came to you. I would like to have spent more time with Krystina. Besides, we are looking for the Meadow of Tears, and it moves. If we stayed in Sahaland, then maybe the meadow would come to us."

Jack didn't answer. He looked down at Lucky: his orange-and-white frame slumped as he walked and his tail hung low, almost scraping the ground. Concerned, Jack reached down and picked Lucky up. He lifted him up onto his shoulders and hugged him, tightly. They had left Sahaland for Lucky.

Lucky purred quietly into Jack's ear. "I'll be okay," he said. "I'm just sad for Bootsy's clowder."

"I know, buddy." Jack whispered back. "Abigail," he began, "each of us is carrying one of the Three Stones of Ebon. Maybe I am not feeling a pulling because we're supposed to do something with them? We know they glow and have healing properties, but what if we put the three stones together? They glowed more brightly the last time they were together. Maybe I'll feel a pulling then. Or maybe Ebon himself can come to us?"

"But he is a stone statue, Jack. How would he even know, let alone move?"

Jack shrugged. "Magic, just like the meadow?"

Abigail snorted at the idea, then reconsidered with a shrug. "Who knows?" she sighed, letting her arms flop down to her sides. "Let us try it."

They took the purple stone from Lucky's harness, then Abigail and Jack produced the red and blue from their bags. Cupping their hands in a bowl shape, they put their hands together to hold the three stones, tilting their fingers down to make the stones slide to the middle and touch.

The children jumped as the stones abruptly trembled and glowed vividly, engulfing the boy, girl, and feline companion in an ever-intensifying energy. They heard a loud whooshing sound in the trees, not far away. All three of them looked in the direction of the noise, only to find nothing. Jack barely noticed the faintest movement of tree branches, which was strange because the air was completely still.

"Jack," Abigail said cautiously. "What was that?"

"No idea." Jack swallowed hard. "But we should check it out. We need to make sure the stones keep touching. Here, hold out the edge of your tunic to use as a basket to hold them." They carefully scooped the stones into the embroidered fabric, which cradled and held them in place. Jack then drew his cutlass and turned toward the trees.

The trio entered the thicket of trees, with undergrowth shoots sprawling in all directions. "Careful where you walk," Jack cautioned as he started into the foliage with Lucky on his heels. "There are lots of brambles here."

Abigail suggested, "Maybe we should go around."

Jack shook his head. "No, they don't go that far. Besides, I see a way through up ahead."

Abigail followed Jack and Lucky closely, keeping a watchful eye on the stones as she walked to make sure they stayed touching as Jack suggested. A few dozen paces in, the brambles thinned and the three emerged in a clearing before a pond. On the other side of the water, the meadow sloped upward to reveal a large statue.

"Wow!" Jack beamed with a victorious breath of relief. "We're here. We did it."

"Yes!" shouted Lucky.

Abigail was silent at first. She gazed, wide-eyed, at the great winged-horse statue that stood in the vivid sunlight, stoic, and a bit sad.

Jack and Abigail shared an eager look. "Jack," Abigail cried, "you are a genius." The boy from another world sheepishly looked at the ground for a moment. Jack could hardly believe it himself. They were *in* the Meadow of Tears.

Jack sheathed his cutlass and impulsively walked over to the pond with Lucky. The two knelt and drank from it.

After several minutes, Jack sat at the edge of the pond, content and feeling a sense of relief that his quest was almost over. "I don't know about you, but I feel great." He looked back at Abigail. "You should try some of this water."

Abigail remained where she was, still awestruck. "That is Ebon's body," she whispered. "And this is the Meadow of Tears." She looked across at Jack and joined her friends at the edge of the pond, knelt and set the stones in the grass, then drank. "Mm, it tastes like honey," she said, wiping her mouth. For a moment, she remembered everything that the wood faeries had revealed to her that night outside Lady Beverly's cottage. She watched Jack and Lucky right then, taking them into her memory. Soon, the faeries had told her, the boy and the cat would leave this world, and she would not see them again for a long time. She would miss them so much.

The dark statue loomed over the meadow and Jack sensed that it was watching them. He suddenly felt very small before it, and a bit intimidated in its presence. Yet he was determined to complete the task. He unconsciously ran his fingers along the scruff of Lucky's neck, looked over at the red-haired girl, and breathed a heavy sigh. "Well... are you ready?"

She smiled back at him. "Yes, I believe I am. And what about you, Lucky?"

Lucky purred deeply. "Okay. Yes."

All three of them took their respective stones again—Abigail securing the purple stone in Lucky's pouch—and rose. Jack and Abigail began walking across the meadow, up toward the statue of Ebon. Lucky arched his back in a satisfied stretch and followed closely behind them.

They were close to the statue when they heard a deliberate rustling of tall grass behind them. The three turned and looked down the meadow, toward the pond.

He stood there, dressed in brown, with a burned sleeve and arm, painfully holding a half-charred shield on one forearm, now useless from the damage it had received from Galadeese's flames. In the other hand, he held his sword. His boots brushed aside the tall grass as he approached, and his long white hair dripped water profusely, his clothing saturated.

"It's Dayvid the Damp," Lucky hissed.

"You," declared Jack to the former Thrasher. "You *were* at the battle." This was the very same rogue Thrasher who had betrayed Greg and all of the warriors who had sworn to fight against Pale. Jack glanced nervously over at Abigail with an unspoken question.

She returned Jack's look. "Yes, now would be a good time." She quickly reached into her shoulder bag and produced the vial containing the Enhancement Potion. "Be sure to drink it all," she said as she pulled the stopper from the top and handed it to Jack.

"It'll make me really good at whatever I'm doing, right?"

"Trust me, Jack, this will work," she urged him on. "Quickly, though, we are running out of time."

"Okay," said Jack, and before he could give it another moment's thought, he tilted his head back and drank. He did his best to not wince at the bitter taste. Dropping his shoulder bag to the ground, he then pulled his cutlass from its sheath. "Let's do this," he said aloud, holding the red stone, the heart of Ebon, firmly in his other hand.

"Yeah," replied Lucky with a hiss.

Jack looked down. "Lucky. You stay here."

"Yeah." Lucky bared his teeth, tail whipping ferociously back and forth with determination.

Jack walked toward Dayvid the Damp cautiously. He didn't feel any different after drinking the potion. *What if it expired?* His mind raced *Is there an expiration date on the potency of a potion?* The red stone's glow amplified, as if to remind him. *No.* He shook the negative thought from his mind. *Time to focus now, Jack. Focus.*

The two stopped a few paces from each other.

"So," muttered the Damp, looking a little bored, "this is what Pale is so bothered about." He dropped his flame-charred shield to the ground, its use no longer worth its weight. He grabbed his hair and wrung out enough water to wash his face. He grumbled low, and without notice, came at Jack, sword thrusting toward Jack's head.

Effortlessly, Jack ducked around the Damp and was amazed at the deftness with which he swung his own cutlass at the Damp's midsection. The Damp blocked Jack's onslaught on a subconscious level, his sword a mere metal extension of his own arm. A swordsman all his life, he found himself increasingly puzzled that the youth was able to match his agility, skill, and planning. The Damp lunged forward with lighting speed, blade jutting a mere inch from Jack's face, yet Jack felt surprisingly calm and merely responded in kind. The cutlass felt perfectly at home in the boy's hand, while his other hand clutched the red stone, which now glowed brighter than ever with the energy of Ebon's heart. It gave Jack all the strength he needed to carry on and do whatever it was that had to be done . . . for his friends, for Sahaland, and for all of those who lived in the world of Sturgus.

While Jack fought the Thrasher-turned-assassin, both Abigail and Lucky stood at the ready. Abigail gripped her bag tightly. Lucky, glancing at her, could see that she was ready to swing it at the Damp if the fight moved toward her. The cat, however, had ideas of his own.

As Jack and the Damp slowly circled and dodged back and forth, Lucky waited until Jack was on the downside of the meadow's slope and made his move. The cat leaped at the assassin from behind, sinking his claws into the warrior's back and neck. The Damp tensed up and shrieked viciously in both pain and anger, spinning about in a circle so quickly that Lucky lost his grip and went sailing through the air. Several yards away, Lucky landed deftly on his feet.

Jack took the distraction as his cue. He ran uphill past a confused and wincing Dayvid the Damp who had dropped his sword in all the commotion. Jack raised his cutlass high into the air above his head. He felt a surge of anger at the Damp's face and all the suffering and sorrow the assassin's allegiance to Pale had inflicted on everyone Jack had met in this strange land. He brought his arm down, swinging the cutlass back at the Damp's face in a blow that could have been imminently fatal. Dayvid the Damp's eyes squeezed shut and he shrank back, preparing for the death blow. But instead of striking with the blade's edge, Jack turned his wrist at the last moment. And the cursed assassin received a blow with the flat of the child's blade instead, striking the warrior on the cheek. Having watched Fay use the very same maneuver on one of the pirates on the *Minnow Sowta,* he briefly wished she was there to witness this moment.

"HAAAA!" Jack screamed at the assassin.

Dayvid the Damp teetered backward, tumbled down the slope of the meadow, and landed in the pond with a splash. Around him, the water began bubbling and churning, and steam rose into the air. The Damp sat stunned for a moment before his face twisted up and he began to scream as if he were a soprano in an opera, thrashing his arms and legs about as he sought to reach the bank of the pond. Unable to get a footing, he fell back into the water.

Abigail giggled despite herself, in amusement and some relief, too. "He screams like a little girl."

The three watched as the Damp's cries and thrashing subsided, and he finally scrambled his way to the shore of the pond. He sat there, eyes glazed over, scared and trembling. He hugged himself tightly and began to rock back and forth, all the while muttering and staring off into space.

Jack now stood next to Abigail and Lucky, cutlass at the ready. They remained still, watching the Damp with guarded apprehension.

Abigail was the first to speak. "Well, I think he is finally no longer concerned with us. It is as if he is under a spell or something."

"Why did the water jump around like that when he fell in?" Lucky asked.

"I don't know." Jack looked at Abigail, who could only offer a wordless shrug and shake her head.

The three turned away from the Damp and headed back up to the top slope of the meadow. The statue loomed before them but seemed to beckon them closer. They came to a stop directly below it.

"There are three holes in the breast," Abigail noted.

"Yes," said Jack, "for the stones, I would imagine."

"I wonder if it matters which hole the stones go in," Abigail mused, "or which order we put them in?"

"Well, let's go with the order in which we found them," suggested Jack. "Red in the first hole, blue in the second, and purple in the third. I'll go first." Jack opened his hand and gazed down at the red stone. Its glow pulsed vividly, as if eager for what would come next. After a moment, Jack pushed the stone into the first hole. The stone fit perfectly. Then it began to sink into the statue itself and fill in where the first hole had been, completely absorbed.

"Whoa," breathed Jack.

"Did you see that?" Lucky exclaimed. "The stone got sucked up by the statue."

"Yeah." Jack looked at Abigail. "Okay, your turn."

Abigail took a deep breath, closed her eyes, and whispered something too low for Jack to hear. Then she lifted the blue stone with both hands and pushed it into the second hole. Once again, the statue took and absorbed the stone.

"Oh my," gasped Abigail.

Jack squatted next to Lucky. "Well, buddy, you have the last stone. What do you say to me picking you up and then together we can put the stone into the hole?"

"How about if all three of us do it instead?" suggested Lucky.

Jack agreed. "Good idea, buddy." He picked Lucky up in his arms and removed the purple stone from the cat's harness. Lucky pressed his paw on the stone and Abigail covered her hand over his paw. Together, the three pushed the final stone in the hole. The statue, as expected, accepted the stone. Now, on the great statue's chest, only a smooth black surface remained.

To Jack, it was as if someone had just hit a giant "pause" button on the whole land. The leaves in the trees quit rustling. The grass became still. Jack looked back at Dayvid the Damp; he too, appeared as still as everything else in the meadow.

All at once, a vivid light threw all three of them several feet back, sending them sprawling down the slope. The force was like nothing any of them had ever felt, an untamed surge with a hint of relief.

As Jack would later find out, the force of light traveled in all directions, across the mountains, plains, and woods, to the edges of Sturgus itself. Everybody—all the creatures of the world—would feel it. And in Jalambria, an ancient sorcerer in a lonely tower would shudder in the realization that it was the beginning of the end of his three-millennia rule over Sturgus.

Jack was the first to stand. Lucky was no longer in his arms, and Jack whirled about as he searched for his furry friend. As he scanned the landscape, he found Lucky several feet farther down the slope, his coat fluffed out instinctively in alarm.

"Are you okay?" Jack asked as he rushed to his cat's side.

"What—was—*that?*"

"I don't know, little guy, but I need to check on Abigail." Jack spun to find Abigail but stopped short.

The great winged horse stood waveringly. A greyish dry vapor rose from its body, its ebony-colored coat dusty from three millennia of preservation in stone. The majestic beast staggered as it became accustomed to using its muscles again.

"Holy cow," whispered Jack as the winged horse unfurled its wings, stretching them up and down and then beating them furiously to get the dust off. Its initial step was wobbly, then it struck the ground with alternating hooves, each time with more purpose and determination. Its muscles twitched and shuddered under its skin, causing a cloud of tiny rubble and dust to fall away from a coat that was as dark as a nighttime sky.

It was then that Jack noticed Abigail, standing mere feet away. She stood as motionless as Jack himself, eyes fixed on the great beast that huffed and hammered its hooves into the earth. It flapped its wings with authority and its body lifted into the air, hovering slightly higher than Jack's head. Then, sweeping its wings back into a folded position, the winged horse abruptly landed again, the impact of its hooves causing the meadow to quake. Smoke expelled from its nostrils as it snorted and shook its head with emphasis.

Jack, Abigail, and Lucky inched closer to each other until they were almost touching, almost huddled together.

"Ebon," Abigail whispered. It seemed all she could say, with eyes as big and round as saucers.

The steed heard this and stopped moving. It turned to look upon the three and they felt frightened to the point where they could barely breathe as it regarded them. The beast spoke. "Yes, I am Ebon. And I remember everything." Ebon strode toward them, elegant and powerful. "Thank you, Abigail, Jack, and Lucky. You have brought me back."

"You—you're welcome," Jack stammered, his mind a jumble of thoughts.

"What he said," said Lucky.

Ebon lowered his great head down to Lucky's tiny form. Peering at the young feline through the long, tousled forelock that fell across his eyes, he pressed his forehead into Lucky's, almost knocking him over. He then did the same to Jack and then to Abigail. Relieved, Jack and his companions were overcome with what could only be described as pure joy. Its energy was infinitely more powerful than any of the stones that they had carried, and they found themselves falling to the ground, laughing from the intoxicating power of Ebon.

Chapter 23

》∘《

The two children and the cat had spent the afternoon basking in the essence of Ebon, telling their stories and playing in the sunshine. It was an afternoon of serenity and, Jack realized, quite possibly the happiest day of their lives.

At one point, Ebon walked with the three to the pond. Dayvid the Damp still sat by the pond but so motionless was he that he seemed as still as the pond itself. Ebon motioned the three to look in the pond, and when they did, they were delighted by what they saw.

"Malia! Caveman!" Abigail shouted gleefully. There, in the reflection of the pool, were Malia and Caveman, waving back at them.

"Hey, they can see us," exclaimed Jack as he waved back ecstatically.

"Yes," Ebon replied.

Behind Caveman and Malia, they could see the children dancing and cheering, and behind them they could see the Wagon of Prophecy.

"They're celebrating," mewed Lucky.

"They are celebrating my return. They are celebrating the three of you and your success in fulfilling the prophecy.

"How do they know?" asked Jack.

"When I was freed from my imprisonment, it caused a ring of light to expand outward. The three of you felt it. That ring has journeyed so far that now the entire world of Sturgus has felt it. Those who are believers in the prophecy know exactly what has happened. Others simply know that something magical and fantastic has happened, and they would be right."

Ebon lowered his head to the pond and snorted. The resulting ripple changed the image, and they found themselves looking at Quasita and her cubs at Other Mountain. The wolves noticed them immediately and came bounding forward. The runt, Charlie, came so close that Jack wondered if he couldn't just reach in and pull him out of the pond.

Another snort by Ebon and the three found themselves waving triumphantly at Fay, Lady Beverly, and, of course, Baron.

"Hey, Baron," shouted Lucky. "I had a dream that we flew together."

"I don't think he can hear you, buddy," said Jack.

"Oh," the feline replied.

Ebon again snorted on the pond. This time they found themselves staring into Sahaland.

"Tater! Bootsy!" shouted Lucky. He could see the two cats stop talking with each other, turn, and look out at them. Behind them were the clowders of Tater and Bootsy celebrating with Krystina and Greg.

Ebon snorted on the pond one last time and once again the image changed.

"Caleb!" yelled Abigail. Her eyes welled up at that moment and she freely allowed the tears to cascade down her face. He was still on the *Minnow Sowta*, and when he noticed them, he moved in for a closer look, motioning others to come and see. A moment later both Carponius and Gill were by his side, big grins on all three of their faces. Carponius gave Caleb an affectionate side hug as the boy waved eagerly at them.

Jack turned and looked at Abigail, his chest swelling with emotion. "See, he's fine."

"Yes," she cried, with joy that her dear friend was alive and seemingly well.

Caleb looked out at them and then grasped at his Amulet of Protection to show his friends that he was still wearing it. He bowed slightly toward Ebon.

Ebon arched his neck and returned the boy's nod, briefly pawing at the air with a front hoof.

Both Jack and Abigail responded by doing the same with the ones they had about their necks. It was then that the image faded, leaving only the natural reflection of the pond.

"It is time," said Ebon gently, "for you to go home."

Jack looked at Ebon and drew a deep breath. "Okay."

"Ebon," asked Lucky, "will I still be able to understand Jack when we get back?"

Ebon looked down at the orange-and-white cat. "You have always been able to communicate with each other. You will just have to go back to doing so without the use of words. I hope this is acceptable to you."

Lucky looked at Jack, tail twitching. The cat was going to miss speaking. Jack sat next to his feline friend and scratched behind his ears. Lucky could not help but purr at this reassurance; he pressed his flank against Jack and looked back at Ebon. "Yes," he said. "It'll be okay."

"What about here?" asked Jack. "What's going to happen in Sturgus after we leave? What are you going to do?"

Ebon's enormous brown eyes locked with Jack's, and when the beast spoke in a low voice, the children and cat could only shudder upon hearing his words. "Pale must be destroyed, Jack, not just banished. He has inflicted so much pain in this world that he must not be allowed to leave and infect others. War is coming to Sturgus. Those who felt my return and believe in the prophecy are prepared to seize this moment and rid this place of Pale and his followers. When it is finally over, hopefully my world will reenter a glorious age that is free from the horrid practices of war and hatred that . . . *he* brought here."

"So, you're going to fight Pale again?" asked Jack.

Ebon drew a deep breath and looked pensively across the meadow, muscles twitching under his skin. He answered simply. "Yes."

Then he swung his great head around and looked upon the children again. "And now, it is time to go," Ebon said. He lowered his body to the ground so that the three could climb onto his back more easily.

"What about him?" asked Abigail, nodding downhill toward the pond that was Ebon's tears. Dayvid the Damp still sat by the pond, his eyes glazed over with confusion, muttering just above a whisper.

"After we leave, the Meadow of Tears will cease to be. Dayvid the Damp will find himself sitting in the middle of a bramble thicket. He will then have to make a choice—to go back to his evil ways or to travel a new path. Whatever the case, he will never be the same person again. For that matter, neither will any of you."

"I understand," said Abigail. "We can never go backward in life." She climbed astride Ebon behind Jack, with Lucky perched at the very front.

"Correct," said Ebon, then scrambled back onto his feet in a flash. "Are the three of you ready?"

"Yes," they replied in unison.

"All right then, here we go. Hang on to my mane." Ebon unfurled his wings and began flapping. With Jack winding handfuls of Ebon's thick mane securely around his hands, and everyone else holding on tight, the mighty winged horse ascended high in the air and took off toward a distant cloud.

As they soared ever higher, Jack felt both content and sad. He was eager to see his parents again but realized he would miss Sturgus. He felt Abigail's arms around his waist as she sat behind him, and he knew he would miss her most of all.

Ebon flew into the cloud in no time, as they were traveling amazingly fast. So fast, in fact, that in the cloud it became difficult to determine how fast they were going. White clouds zipped by them, at times in such a blur that the clouds began changing colors: first blues and greens, then wilder variations of pinks, purples, and colors Jack had never seen before, blended in with a sky that was full of stars. Everything sped by so swiftly that he began to feel dizzy.

Abigail pressed close to him and whispered in his ear. "Remember, Jack, I will always be your friend."

Then, without notice, everything became still.

The cloud was once again white, and it began to dissipate. Jack realized that Abigail was no longer sitting behind him. Stranger still, the great warm body of Ebon beneath him now felt cold and hard. As the cloud vanished altogether, he looked down and saw that Lucky and he were no longer astride Ebon but perched on a black wooden carousel horse, stiff and unmoving.

Ebon was gone.

Abigail was gone.

The boy and his cat looked around, bewildered. The carousel horse on which they sat was in the middle of a living room that housed many other odd and interesting things—old photographs, antique paintings and knickknacks, swords and spyglasses, statues and masks. Just like that, Mrs. Krauss stood there before him . . . and behind her were his parents.

"Mom! Dad!" yelled Jack as he and Lucky leaped from the horse, and both boy and cat plowed into his parents.

"Jack! Lucky!" his parents called back. The four of them spun in circles, hugging, delighted. Mrs. Krauss's wrinkled smile was warm and satisfied as she watched their reunion.

"Did you miss us?" Jack's words tumbled forth. "We were gone for weeks, and I saw a cyclops and I was on a sea voyage and Lucky got kidnapped and—HEY—Lucky could talk—"

"We did miss you," his father broke in, laughing, "but just so you know, you've only been gone since last night."

"Huh?" Jack was puzzled as his father picked him up and sat him on his shoulders. "Just since last night?" Then he remembered that Abigail had mentioned that time worked differently between worlds.

"It's true," his mother chimed in as she picked up Lucky and rubbed her forehead into his fur. This caused further purring on Lucky's part. It was then that Jack stopped short.

"Abigail."

"Who?" asked his father.

Jack slipped off his father's shoulders and stood on the carpet facing the carousel horse. "Abigail. I forgot to say goodbye to her."

"She is a friend of yours," his mother stated softly.

Jack gaze drifted to the back of the carousel horse where she had sat just moments before. "She was my best friend in Sturgus. I hope Ebon got her home safe."

Mrs. Krauss walked up to Jack then and said, "Do not worry, Jack. You know she cannot be in better hands than Ebon's. Now, tell us more about your adventures on Sturgus." She smiled then, and this made Jack feel better. As he listened to her speak, he couldn't believe he could have been so mean as to have called this person hurtful nicknames. This was the first time he'd met her in person, and she seemed nice. She wasn't Old Lady Krauss or the Crazy Lady. She was simply Mrs. Krauss, their neighbor who collected a lot of cool antiques and relics in her home.

The celebrating lasted awhile, with Jack spouting off his adventures in rapid succession, and Lucky with nothing but snuggles to give to Jack's parents. The adventure had been fantastic, but it was good to be home again.

"Okay, Jack," said Jack's mother, "it's time to go home."

Then Lucky did something quite unexpected. He mewed up at Mrs. Krauss and rubbed his flank against her legs before jumping up into her arms and snuggling against her neck. The old lady smiled deeply, and tears rolled slowly from her golden-brown eyes and down her freckled, copper-colored cheeks. She held the cat close to herself, as if they had been friends a long time.

Jack looked at Mrs. Krauss, slightly confused at his cat's reaction to her. "Boy, he really likes you. Um, thanks for the urn, Mrs. Krauss," he said.

"It was made for you," she replied simply, folding her hands in front of herself.

Jack, his parents, and Lucky left the old house at the end of the street and began walking home.

From her window, Mrs. Abigail Krauss watched as her childhood friends from the land of Sturgus casually sauntered home under the afternoon sky. She had kept her word and had always been their friend. After Ebon had returned her back to Malia in Sturgus, she had studied the ways of magic with her, and later she studied with Lady Beverly and Krystina as well. She had devoted her life to starting Jack and Lucky on their quest. She made the urn. She traveled between worlds and, in doing so, traveled through time.

With her life's work now complete, and her once-flame-colored hair now silver, but still thick with curls as it ever was, Abigail sighed deeply.

It was time for her, now, to return home.

As Jack headed home with his parents, he asked, "Okay, I was told that one of you is possibly from Sturgus. My question is, which one?"

"How do you know that only one of us is from there?" his father asked as he held Lucky in his arms like a rag doll. "I mean come on, who do you think built the Wagon of Prophecy?" And he spread his arms apart and drawled out, "Come oooon."

"No way," said Jack. "You?"

"Yes way, my little man," answered his mother, "and who do you think put the Spell of Revelation on the Wagon of Prophecy?"

Jack was ecstatic. "Wow, my parents are the Marwoodian and the Conch Dancer! Of course! No wonder you're always collecting seashells. Hey, that must make you guys really old."

"You already forget," his father stated, "when you travel between worlds you travel through time, as well."

"Oh yeah," Jack laughed. "Guess you're not that old, then."

Just then there was a sudden flash of light behind them, and Jack, his parents, and Lucky all spun around to look.

Mrs. Abigail Krauss' house had vanished completely.

"Whoa," whispered Jack. "What happened?"

"Mrs. Krauss's work is done," replied his mother. "I believe she's gone home."

"Tomorrow, none of the neighbors will remember that there was ever a house there. They'll recall that it's always been a vacant lot," said Jack's father. "Only we know differently."

"Oh," said Jack. "Wow."

Lucky was on the ground and rubbed up against Jack. Jack bent down, gathering his best feline friend into his arms, and together with his parents—the Conch Dancer and the Marwoodian—he made his way home.

the end

Acknowledgments

We are deeply grateful for the time and consideration that our publisher, Mary Taris, and her team at Strive Publishing invested in this book. Jermaine Taris provided initial cover concepts. Yasmin Angoe McClinton's editing expertise and guidance proved crucial in pushing us, elevating this story to a new level. LaToya Taris-James provided invaluable marketing support.

To Paul Nylander with Illustrada Book Design and Craft and colorist Anna Granholm, thank you for the added magic and flair to give this a gorgeous, fantastic cover, beaming with so much color, it sparkles!

To Kellie M. Hultgren from KMH Editing, a wrangler extraordinaire in keeping all of us on the same page and pushing forward. A truly incredible feat; no lasso required.

To Beth Wright from Wright for Writers LLC. Each time we attend your virtual Indie Author Marketing Chats we learn something new and gain more confidence in our craft. Meeting other authors has been both an exhilarating and an awestruck experience.

The Three Stones of Ebon was originally written to encourage a certain godson to read more. Many of the characters are based on some wonderful people we know, as well as animals that we've known, befriended, and loved. With that said, we would like to thank these wonderful humans for being in our lives: Jennifer, Charlie, Jack, Katie, Caveman, Greg, Kristina, and Beverly. And, of course, the animals: Lucky, Bootsy, Logan, Alexis, Persephone, Quasita, Pax, Lono, Tater, Kyuss, Logan, and Akira.

Printed in the USA
CPSIA information can be obtained
at www.ICGtesting.com
CBHW03205926I024
16331CB00083B/17